She swayed against him.

The river seemed to roar in her ears, and the thunder of her heart was only eclipsed by the sound of his. Heather felt weak and powerful all at once as emotion upon emotion ripped through her.

She thought of denial, of surrender, of love and of hate, but she was powerless to do anything but return Turner's kisses with her own awakening passion, which exploded like a powder keg at his touch.

Still, she wasn't frightened, and all her doubts seemed to float away into the twilight. She was a virgin, a girl who had never experienced the thrill of a man's passion. Yet for the first time in her life, her virginity seemed no longer a virtue, but a prison.

With Turner, she could be free....

Dear Reader,

Welcome to Silhouette **Special Edition** . . . welcome to romance. Each month Silhouette **Special Edition** publishes six novels with you in mind—stories of love and life, tales that you can identify with . . . as well as dream about.

This month has some wonderful stories for you— after all, March comes in like a lion and goes out like a lamb! And in Lisa Jackson's new series, MAVERICKS, we meet three men who just won't be tamed! This month, don't miss *He's Just a Cowboy* by Lisa Jackson.

THAT SPECIAL WOMAN!, Silhouette **Special Edition**'s new series that salutes women, has a wonderful book this month from Patricia Coughlin. *The Awakening* is the tender story of Sara Marie McAllister—and her awakening to love when she meets bounty hunter John Flynn. It takes a very special man to win That Special Woman! And handsome Flynn is up for the challenge!

Rounding out this month are books from other favorite writers: Elizabeth Bevarly, Susan Mallery, Trisha Alexander and Carole Halston!

I hope that you enjoy this book, and all the stories to come! Have a wonderful March!

Sincerely,

Tara Gavin
Senior Editor
Silhouette Books

LISA JACKSON

HE'S JUST A COWBOY

Silhouette®

SPECIAL EDITION®

Published by Silhouette Books New York

America's Publisher of Contemporary Romance

SILHOUETTE BOOKS
300 East 42nd St., New York, N.Y. 10017

HE'S JUST A COWBOY

ISBN: 0-373-09799-9

First Silhouette Books printing March 1993

All the characters in this book have no existence outside the imagination of the author and have no relation whatsoever to anyone bearing the same name or names. They are not even distantly inspired by any individual known or unknown to the author, and all incidents are pure invention.

®: Trademark used under license and registered in the United States Patent and Trademark Office and in other countries.

Printed in the U.S.A.

Books by Lisa Jackson

LISA JACKSON

was raised in Molalla, Oregon, and now lives with her husband, Mark, and her two sons in a suburb of Portland, Oregon. Lisa and her sister, Natalie Bishop, who is also a Silhouette author, live within earshot of each other.

The Legend of Whitefire Lake

It is said that when the God of the Sun creeps above the mountains and aims his flaming arrow to the sea, sparks and embers drop into the lake, causing the mists to rise like white fire on the water.

The man who drinks of this water before the mists are driven away by the sun will inherit much wealth and happiness and will be destined never to leave the hills surrounding the lake. But the man must sip the magic water and drink only until his thirst is quenched. For if he takes more of the sacred water than he needs, the God of the Sun will be angry and the man will be cursed. He will lose his wealth, and that which he loves most on earth will be stolen from him.

PROLOGUE

Gold Creek, California

The Present

Prologue

Some men you never forget.

Heather Leonetti parked her Mercedes beneath a deep green canopy of pine branches. Her head pounded and her heart beat an icy tempo. Through the windshield, she stared at the calm waters of Whitefire Lake and wondered how she would find the strength to undo the string of lies that had started six years before—lies she hadn't meant to utter, lies that weren't supposed to hurt anyone, lies that had her so bound, she didn't know if she could untangle them.

Her mother had said it all, years ago. "The trouble with lyin' is, once you start, you never can seem to stop. Your father, for example. Just one lie after another, one Jezebel of a woman after the next...."

Heather closed her eyes and rubbed her temples. Soon her mother would know the truth, as would everyone in Gold Creek. As would Turner.

She had to tell him first. He deserved to know. Too late, she realized. He should have known six years before. She should have found a way to reach him, to let him know that he had become a father. Instead, after a few feeble attempts to reach him, she'd taken the easy way out. And now, Adam, her son, her reason for living, was paying. It just wasn't fair.

Tears collected behind her eyes and clogged her throat, but she wouldn't give in to the pain. Not yet. Not while there was hope. She squeezed her eyes shut for a minute and sent up a prayer for strength. Somehow she had to undo all the wrongs; somehow she had to give her boy a chance to live a normal life. And Turner might be the answer. Although the horrid disease was now in remission and the doctors seemed to think that Adam had as good a chance as any for beating leukemia, Heather was scared to death...as she had been for nearly two years. It was time to face Turner.

Gritting her teeth, she forced her eyes open and knew she had to face Turner again.

Some men you never forget. Turner Brooks was that kind of man—all bristle and gruffness with brown hair streaked with gold, a rugged profile too cynical for his years and eyes that saw far too much. A cowboy. A rodeo rider. A penniless no-good, as her mother would say.

Heather hadn't seen him in six years. She couldn't imagine his reaction when she showed up on his doorstep, trying to undo those cloying lies, and begging for his help. She knew that he hadn't returned her calls, that her letter had gone unanswered. He obviously didn't want her to be a part of his life. But he couldn't reject his son.

Or could he?

Heather's heart cracked, because she didn't really know the man who was her son's father, had barely known him six years before.

"Help me," she whispered, refusing to break down. Pocketing her keys, she climbed out of the car and left the door ajar. A quiet bell reminded her that she should close and lock the Mercedes, but she didn't care. Pine needles muted her footsteps as she stuffed her hands into the pockets of her jacket and walked the short distance to the shore.

From the boughs overhead a hidden squirrel scolded brashly and a flock of quail rose in a thunder of feathers into the thin fog. The lake was quiet; there were only a few fishing boats in the misty dawn. Heather was reminded of the old legend about the waters of Whitefire Lake as she crouched down among the sun-bleached stones of the bank and ran her fingers through the cool depths. Her left hand mocked her. Naked, stripped of her diamonds when she and Dennis were divorced nearly two years before, it waved ghostlike beneath the clear surface.

She sent up a silent prayer for her son, then skimmed a handful of the lake water and drizzled it against her lips. She'd been greedy in the past and she'd taken too much from life—too much for granted. Her expensive car, her house in San Francisco, her studio and all her clothes and jewels meant nothing to her now. All that mattered was Adam.

She didn't really believe in the legend of the lake, but she was willing to try anything, *anything,* to save her son's life.

Even if it meant confronting Turner.

She shivered, feeling a tiny icicle of dread against her spine. As she stared into the clear waters of Whitefire Lake, she remembered the summer of 1986 so clearly, it was almost as if she were still eighteen and working at the Lazy K Ranch. . . .

BOOK ONE

Lazy K Ranch, California

Six Years Earlier

Chapter One

The air was thick and sultry, filled with horseflies and bees that buzzed around Heather's head as she shook the old rag rug. Dinner was long over and the guests of the Lazy K had broken into groups. Some had retired early, others were learning to play the guitar in the main hall and still others were involved in games of checkers or poker in the dining room. Laughter and music spilled from the windows, floating on a thin evening breeze.

Every bone in Heather's body ached from the twelve-hour days she worked in the kitchen. Her feet were swollen and she smelled as bad as some of the ranch hands. Deep down, she knew she wasn't cut out for ranch life, and yet here she was, kitchen maid at an obscure dude ranch in the foothills of the Siskiyou Mountains. Well, things could be worse. She could be back in Gold Creek.

Shuddering at the thought of the sleepy little town where she'd been born and raised, she stared at the distant hills.

There were too many painful memories in Gold Creek for her to ever want to stay there. Even though some families like the Fitzpatricks and Monroes seemed to spawn generation after generation of citizens of Gold Creek, Heather wasn't planning on putting her roots down in a town so small... so full of gossip.

Her family, the Tremonts, had been the subject of the Gold Creek gossip mill for years. First there had been her father and his affair with a younger woman. Eventually her parents had divorced, her mother bitter and unhappy to this day, her father involved with his new young wife. And then there had been the incident involving Heather's sister, Rachelle, and the boy she'd been involved with—Jackson Moore.

Heather remembered all too vividly some of her mother's "friends" and how they'd whispered just loud enough so that Heather could catch a few of the key words. "...Never believe...all their hopes on that one, you know...no scholarship now...so hard on Ellen. Poor woman. First that no-good skirt-chasing husband and now this...and the younger one doesn't have a lick of sense...if there's a God in heaven *that* one will marry the Leonetti boy and give her mother some peace!"

Heather's cheeks had burned as she'd heard the wagging tongues in the checkout line at the Safeway store, in the dining area of the Buckeye Restaurant and Lounge, and even on the porch of the church after services. There was no way she was going to spend the rest of her life trapped in Gold Creek!

But ranch life? It wasn't a lot better. Though she planned on staying only for the summer. Only until she had enough money to enroll in art school. Only so that she didn't turn out to be one of those weak women who marry a man for his money, to get what she wanted. Only so she didn't feel compelled to marry Dennis Leonetti, son of one of the wealthiest bankers in Northern California.

Heather tossed the old rag rug over the top rail of the fence and stared across the vast acres of the Lazy K. Horses gathered in the shade of one lone pine tree, their tails switching at bothersome flies, their coats dull from rolling in the dusty corral. Sorrels, bays, chestnuts and one single white gelding huddled together, picking at a few dry blades of grass or stomping clouds of dust.

A hazy sun hovered over the ridge of mountains to the west, and she spied a lone rider upon the ridge—one of the ranch hands, no doubt. Squinting and shading her eyes with her hand, she tried to figure out which of the hands had chosen a solitary ride along Devil's Ridge. He was tall and wide-shouldered, though his broad chest angled to a slim waist. Against the blaze of a Western sunset, he sat comfortably in the saddle—as if he'd been born to ride a horse. She could see only his silhouette, and try as she would, she couldn't recognize him. Her mind clicked off the cowboys she'd met, but none of them seemed as natural in the saddle as this man.

A breath of wind tugged at her hair and caused goose bumps to rise on her skin as the stranger twisted in the saddle and seemed to look straight down at her. But that was impossible. He was much too far away. Nonetheless, her heart leapt to her throat and she couldn't help wondering who he was.

He kicked his mount and disappeared into the forest, leaving Heather with the impression that he hadn't even existed, that he was just a figment of her healthy and romantic imagination.

Her palms had begun to sweat. Nervously she wiped her hands down the front of her apron.

"Heather—you about ready to help clean this kitchen?" Mazie's crowlike voice cawed through the open window of the ranch house.

Heather jumped. Guiltily she yanked the rug off the fence and shook the blasted thing frantically, as if the fabric were infested with snakes. Dust swirled upward and caught in her throat. She coughed and sputtered and beat the life out of the rug.

"You hear me, girl?"

"In a minute...." Heather called over her shoulder. "I'll be right there."

"Well, mind that you git in here afore midnight, y'hear?" Mazie insisted, mumbling something about city girls more interested in cowboys than in hard work. She slammed the window shut so hard the panes rattled.

Swiping at her sweaty forehead, Heather hauled the dusty rug back to the ranch house. She hurried up the steps, through the long back porch and into the kitchen where other girls were scouring pots and pans, washing down the floor and scrubbing the counters with disinfectant. No dirt dared linger in Mazie Fenn's kitchen!

"'Bout time you got back here. Why don't you take care of the leftovers—take those pails onto the back porch for Seth's pigs," Mazie suggested. Seth Lassiter was one of the cowboys who worked at the Lazy K during the day, but lived on his own place where he raised pigs and his own small herd of cattle.

Jill, a redheaded waitress who was one of Heather's roommates, smothered a smile as she glanced at the two heaping buckets of slop. Carrying out the heavy pails was one of the worst jobs on the ranch, and it tickled her that Heather seemed to always inherit the job. Jill bit her lip to keep from giggling, then threw her shoulders into her own work of mopping the yellowed linoleum until it gleamed.

Heather gathered the heavy buckets of milk, corn bread, potatoes and anything else that was edible but for one reason or the other hadn't been consumed by the guests and staff of the ranch. Without spilling a drop, she hoisted both pails to the porch and told herself not to linger, though she couldn't help staring at the ridge where she'd seen the lone rider.

All her life her mother had accused her of dreaming romantic fantasies, of being "boy crazy," of living in an unreal world of heroes and heroines and everlasting love. Her older sister, Rachelle, had been the practical nose-to-the-grindstone type, and time and time again their mother had shaken her head at Heather's belief in true love.

"If you want to fall in love, then why don't you let yourself fall for Dennis Leonetti?" Ellen had asked her often enough. "He's cute and smart and rich. What more could you want?"

Heather sometimes wondered herself. But there was something about Dennis—something calculating and cold that made her mistrust him. Why he wanted to marry her, she didn't know; she only knew that deep in her heart she didn't love him and never would. Marrying him seemed like admitting defeat or becoming a fraud or, at the very least, taking the easy way out. Heather, despite her fantasies, didn't believe that there were any free rides on this earth. She had only to look at her mother's hard life to see the truth.

"Heather?"

Drat! Mazie again. Heather couldn't afford to look lazy; she needed this job. She dashed back to the kitchen.

"I thought we lost you again," Mazie said as she lit a cigarette at the little table near the windows. "Mercy, I've never seen anyone whose head is higher in the clouds than yours!"

"I'm sorry," Heather said as she wiped the top of the stove to look busy. Most of the polishing and cleaning was done, and three girls were huddled together near the swinging doors that separated the kitchen from the dining room.

"It's all right. Your shift's over." Mazie honored Heather with a rare smile. "Besides, you're missin' all the fun." Taking a puff on her cigarette, she motioned to the girls crowded around the swinging door. "The boys are back."

"The what?"

". . . I told you he was gorgeous," Jill whispered loudly.

Mazie chuckled.

"They all are," another girl, Maggie, said, her eye to the crack between the two doors. She let out a contented sigh. "Hunks. Every one of them."

"But they're trouble," Sheryl added. She was a tall, thin girl, who, for the past six summers, had worked at the Lazy K. "Especially that one—" She pointed, and Jill shook her head.

"What's going on?" Heather couldn't hide her curiosity.

"The cowboys are back for a while. Between rodeos," Jill explained a trifle breathlessly.

Cowboys? Heather wasn't particularly interested in the rough-and-tumble, range-riding type of man. She thought of Dennis, the banker's son, and he suddenly didn't seem so bad. But dusty, grimy, outdoorsmen smelling of tobacco and leather and horses...? Well, most of her fantasies were a little more on the sophisticated side.

However, she remembered the ridge rider and her heart did a peculiar little flop. But he was a man of her dreams, not a flesh-and-blood cowpoke. She didn't bother peeking through the crack in the door. Instead, to atone for her earlier idleness, she hauled the sacks of potatoes and onions back to the pantry where she double-checked that the plastic lids on huge tubs of sugar and flour were secure.

Cowboys! She smiled to herself. If she were to believe the image on the silver screen, cowboys spit tobacco juice and tromped around in filthy scraped leather boots and tattered jeans. They loved the open range as well as horses and booze and country music and loose women in tight denim skirts.

And yet there was something appealing about the cowboy myth, about a rugged man who was afraid of nothing, about a man who would die for what was right, a man who disdained city life and health clubs and sports cars.

Even Rachelle—stalwart, sane, levelheaded Rachelle—had fallen for a rogue of sorts. Jackson Moore, the reputed bad boy of Gold Creek, the boy whom everyone believed had killed Roy Fitzpatrick. Rachelle had stood up for Jackson when the whole town had wanted to lynch him; Rachelle had given him an alibi when he had desperately needed one; and Rachelle had stayed in town, bearing the disgrace and scandal of having spent the night with him, while he'd taken off, leaving her alone to face the town.

And that short love affair had scarred her and their parents forever.

"I'm not going to sit around and watch you make the same mistake your sister did," Ellen had told Heather as she'd nervously taken a drag from her cigarette. "And she was the levelheaded one! You, with all your fantasies and silly notions about romance...ah, well. Unfortunately, you'll learn in time." She'd stubbed out her cigarette, and concern darkened her eyes. "Just don't learn the hard way. Like Rachelle did. That no-good Moore boy used her, he did. Spent one night with her, then left town when he was accused of murder. Left her here alone to defend him and mend her broken heart." Ellen had shaken her head, her loose brown curls bobbing around her face. "You listen to me, Heather. Romance only causes heartache. I loved your father—was faithful to him. Lord, I had supper on the table every night at six... and what happened? Hmm? He flipped out. Wanted a 'younger model.'" Ellen scowled darkly. "Don't fool yourself with thoughts of romance. Make life easy for yourself. Marry Dennis."

Heather frowned at the memory. Closing the pantry door behind her, she crossed the kitchen and headed up the back stairs to the room she shared with the other girls. She changed quickly, stripping off her apron and uniform and sliding into a pair of shorts and a T-shirt.

Within minutes, she'd caught and saddled her favorite little mare, Nutmeg, and was riding along a dusty trail through the pines. Telling herself she needed the ride to cool off, that her interest in exploring the trails had nothing to do with the rider she'd seen, she urged Nutmeg steadily upward, through the foothills. The sun had disappeared, and a handful of stars was beginning to wink in the evening sky. For the first time that day, Heather felt free and content. Her blond hair streamed behind her, and she even hummed along to the tempo of Nutmeg's steady hoofbeats. She met no one, didn't so much as hear another horse neigh.

So much for the solitary ridge rider.... Another fantasy.

Clucking gently to the mare, Heather followed the trail that led to the river. The air was fresher there, though the drone of insects was constant. She smiled as she spied the natural pool she'd discovered, a deep hole that collected and slowed the water where the river doglegged toward the mountains.

"I deserve this," she told Nutmeg, as she slid to the ground, and without a thought to her horse, stripped quickly out of her clothes, dropping them piece by piece at the river's edge. She ran along the rocky shelf that jutted over the dark water and with a laugh, plunged into the cold depths.

Frigid. So cold she could barely breathe, the icy water engulfed her, touching every pore on her body, sending a shock wave through her system. The river sprouted from an underground spring and the water was close to freezing. She didn't care. After battling the heat of the kitchen oven and the hot summer sun all day, the cold water was refreshing. She felt alive again.

Surfacing, she swam to the far shore, feeling the tension slip from her muscles as she knifed through the water. As the sky darkened, she dived down again, touching the rocky bottom with her fingers before jetting upward and breaking the surface. Sighing happily, she tossed her hair from her eyes and nearly stopped breathing.

She wasn't alone.

A tall, rugged man stood on the shelf of rock jutting over the water's edge. Dressed in dirty jeans, scratched boots and work shirt that was unbuttoned to display a rock-hard chest, he stared down at her with eyes the color of gunmetal. His lips were thin and compressed, his tanned face angular and bladed.

Without a doubt, this was the very man she'd seen earlier riding the ridge.

Her heart nearly stopped.

Romantic fantasies fled.

She didn't know this man, didn't know what he was capable of. He could be dangerous, and from the looks of him she didn't doubt it for a moment. Though his brown hair was streaked with gold, there was something about him, something about the arrogant way he stood in front of her bespoke trouble.

He was nearly six feet or so and looked to be in his mid-twenties, and Heather wanted to crawl behind the nearest rock and hide. But, of course, it was too late. In one hand he held the reins to his mount, a huge buckskin gelding, in the other, he dangled her clothes off one long, callused finger.

Heather swallowed hard and wondered just how menacing he really was. She didn't want to find out.

"Lose something?" he asked in a lazy drawl.

She rimmed her lips with her tongue. What could she say? She was obviously naked—the clothes had to belong to her. She decided to take the offensive before things really got out of hand. "Just put them down," she said, eyeing her shorts swinging from his finger. She treaded water in the deep part of the pool, hoping he couldn't see too much of her body through the darkening ripples of the river.

"I'm not talking about these." He tossed her shorts, T-shirt, bra and panties close to the water's edge—almost within her reach.

He was playing with her! Dear God, why hadn't she told anyone where she was going? Feeling a fool and very much afraid, Heather swallowed back a lump of fright in her throat and studied him more carefully. A cowboy, no mistaking that. His Stetson was pushed back on his head, displaying a ring of grime that matted brown hair to his forehead. His jean jacket was torn and dirty, his Levi's faded and tight, his shirt, a plaid cotton that was open to display a dusting of hair on a sun-bronzed chest. He looked hot and tired and disgusted. "Your horse," he prompted, and her gaze flew to the edge of the forest where she'd left Nutmeg grazing only minutes before. The mare was nowhere in sight.

"Oh, no—"

"She's halfway back to the stables by now," he said, and his flinty eyes showed just a flicker of amusement. "Looks like you have to hike or hitch a ride with me."

For a fleeting instant she thought he was handsome, almost sexy, in a coarse sort of way, but she didn't dwell on his looks as she was busy trying to keep herself covered.

"Don't worry about me. I'll make it back," she said, knowing that riding with him would only spell trouble.

"Will ya, now?" he drawled in a voice as rough as sandpaper.

"Yes." She eyed her clothes and prayed for the cover of darkness.

"What's your name?"

Did it matter? "Heather." Anything to get rid of him so she could fetch her clothes and get dressed.

"Hmmm. You work in the kitchen?"

"That's right." So he was one of the men the girls were fawning over.

He didn't say anything to this bit of news, just stared down at her, and she wondered at the picture she must make—pale skin beneath the dark ripples, hair wet and plastered to her head, face awash with embarrassment, white legs moving quickly as she tried to stay afloat. "Look, if you don't mind, I really could use some privacy."

A slow smile spread across his chin. "What if I do mind?"

Drat the man! Her fists curled for one frustrated second and she started to sink, her chin sliding under the water's cool surface. Sputtering, she accused, "You're no gentleman."

"And I doubt that you're much of a lady," he said, working the heel of his boot with the toe of the other.

Heather nearly jumped out of her skin. He wasn't really thinking of diving in and joining her, was he? To her horror, he kicked off both boots, yanked off a pair of dusty socks and started pulling his arms out of the sleeves of his jacket. "Wait a minute," she said, surprised at the breathless tone of her voice.

"Wait for what?"

"Whatever it is you think you're going to do—"

He stripped his jacket and shirt from a torso as tough and lean as rawhide. There wasn't an ounce of fat on him and only a smattering of gold-brown hair that arrowed down over a tanned, hard chest and a washboard of abdominal muscles. *Lean and mean.* Even in the darkness she saw a bruise, purple and green, discoloring the skin across one shoulder. "I don't think I'm gonna do anything. I *know* I'm goin' for a swim."

"But you can't—" she cried, as his shirt and jacket fell onto the pile of boots and socks.

"Why not? I've been swimmin' here since I was ten."

"But I'm here and . . ."

"You won't bother me." A devilish, off-center smile flashed in the coming darkness and he didn't pause once at the waistband of his jeans. They fell away with the *pop, pop, pop* of buttons.

Heather averted her eyes. She'd never seen a naked man before, and she was certain this man wasn't a good one to start with.

"You're not the first girl to swim here with me."

"That's comforting," she said, her voice filled with sarcasm. "And I'm not a girl—"

"That's right. My mistake. You're a *lady*."

Heather felt a tide of color wash up her neck. She was out of her element. Way out of her element. And yet she was fascinated as, from the corner of her eye, she saw him yank off his jeans and in one lithe motion, dive into the river. She caught a glimpse of white—his underwear as he dove—and that was all it took. As quickly as he was in, she was out, scrambling into her clothes.

Dear God, how had she gotten herself into this mess? One minute she was fantasizing him and the next he was there, taunting her, teasing her with his smile, playing dangerous games with his gaze.

Her hands were cold, her body wet and her clothes clung to her skin. She didn't bother with her bra or panties; she was only interested in covering up as much as possible in the shortest amount of time. Heart thundering, icy fingers fumbling, she found the tab of the zipper of her shorts just as she heard him break the surface of the water. All she wanted to do was get out and get out fast!

She started for the path.

"Leavin' so soon, darlin'?" he yelled across the rush of the river. "I didn't scare ya off, now, did I?"

Miserable beast!

He still thought this was a game! She tried to ignore the challenge in his words. "I was done anyway."

"Sure," he taunted.

"I was." What did it matter? *Just take off, Heather. Leave well enough alone!*

"Well, you sure as hell weren't troublin' me."

"Good. Because you troub—you bothered me."

He chuckled, deep and low. "I'll take that as a compliment."

"Take it any way you please," she threw back, not understanding the emotions that seemed to have control of her tongue. The man scared her half to death, yet she was fascinated by him. He couldn't be more than twenty-five or -six, and yet he wore the jaded cynicism of a man twice his age.

"You'd better be careful of that tongue of yours," he said and, from the corner of her eye, she saw him swim closer, his head above water, his gaze never leaving her. "Could get you into a heap of trouble."

"Thanks for the warning."

"My pleasure." Again that deep, rumbling chuckle. At her expense. He reached the ledge and threw his elbows onto the rocks, content to stretch in the water. Heather was mesmerized by his sinewy forearms as they flexed.

There was something about him that got under her skin, something irritating, like a horsefly caught under a saddle that just kept biting the horse. Though she knew she was playing with fire, she couldn't just walk away, letting him think that he'd bested her—by seeing her naked and forcing her, for propriety's sake, to leave.

A plan of revenge started to form in her heart. Oh, but was she willing to pay the price? He obviously worked at the Lazy K. If she angered him, he might make the next two months of her life miserable. But it was worth the gamble. "I didn't catch your name."

"Didn't give it to you." His gaze found hers again, and for some reason she had trouble finding her breath. "Turner Brooks."

Not just one of the cowboys. Turner Brooks was nephew to the owner of the Lazy K. A drifter who followed the rodeo circuit. A man with a past that she'd only heard snatches of. Something about his father and a woman...maybe a girlfriend... Then there were the rumors of all the hearts he'd broken over the past few years— women along the rodeo circuit waiting for his return. "What're you doing back at the Lazy K?"

"Got to work between rodeos," he said.

"Aren't you good enough to make a living out of riding broncos?" She heard the sarcasm in her voice, but he didn't seem to mind. In fact, damn him, he grinned again—that irreverent I've-seen-it-all kind of grin that caught her by surprise and made her heart beat unsteadily.

"I'm good," he said, his dark gaze moving slowly up her body and causing a tingle to spread through her limbs. "Very good."

Her throat turned to dust. She swallowed with difficulty.

"I just came here to help out and earn a little extra spending money. Hurt my shoulder a while back and it's givin' me some trouble. Thought I'd take a rest." His gaze hadn't left her face, and she felt as naked as she had in the water. Though she was dressed, she knew that she had no secrets from him; her clothes were little shield. He'd seen her completely unclothed, had his fun at her expense; now it was time to turn the tables on him. She eyed his pile of clothes, wondering how he would feel if she took his worn jeans and work shirt. As if he guessed her intent, he clucked his tongue. "Don't even think about it unless you want more trouble than you can even begin to imagine." She bit her lower lip. Stealing his jeans seemed too childish and not punishment enough. Besides, he would catch her. But not if she took his horse. What more humiliation for a cowboy than to have a mere woman steal his pride and joy? No more had the thought entered her head than she turned and caught the gelding by the reins.

"I wouldn't do that if I were you," he warned. "Sampson doesn't like people he doesn't know."

"Then I guess I'd better introduce myself," she ridiculed. She wasn't going to let him bluff her. She climbed into the saddle and kicked the big buckskin, pulling hard on the reins. In a ripple of muscles, the horse whirled and leapt forward, covering the open ground at a breakneck pace. Heather clung to his mane and leaned forward as Sampson's long strides carried her into the woods. Trees rushed by in a blur. Heart pounding madly, she prayed the gelding's hooves were sure because the forest was gloomy, the trail uneven. She felt a quick little thrill of showing up the cowboy, and yet she knew that what she'd done was dangerous. Turner would never forgive her.

She glanced over her shoulder, half expecting to find Turner, wet and naked and furious, yelling and running barefoot through the trees. But Turner didn't start hollering or giving chase, and that worried her. He didn't seem the kind of man to roll over and accept defeat so easily.

She could imagine the consternation in his gray eyes, the anger holding his features taut.

A loud, low whistle pierced the forest. Heather's skin crawled. The gelding slammed to a stop, nearly pitching her over his head.

"Hey—wait a minute," Heather whispered, giving the buckskin a quick kick.

Another whistle curdled the air and sent a shiver of dread down Heather's spine.

With a snort, Sampson wheeled and Heather was nearly thrown to the ground. She wound her fingers more tightly in the gelding's coarse mane and pulled hard on the reins with her other hand, but the stubborn rodeo horse had a mind of his own.

"No, you don't," Heather commanded, as Sampson broke into a lope and headed back to the river. Back to Turner. Back to whatever terrible punishment he intended to mete out. She could do nothing but hold on. "You miserable lump of horseflesh," she muttered, still yanking on the reins, but the gelding had the bit in his teeth and he didn't even break stride.

Damn, damn, damn and double damn! Now what? Within seconds the forest seemed to part and the river rushed before her, a night-dark swirl that cut through the canyon. Turner, dressed only in his jeans and boots, was sitting on the rocks, his face a stony mask, fury blazing like lightning in his eyes. Drops of water still clung to his hair and drizzled down his chin.

"Nice try," he said to Heather's mortification.

"You *are* a bastard."

"Just as long as I'm not a gentleman," he drawled, shoving himself to his feet and dusting his hands.

"Never."

"Good. Glad that's settled." He walked over to the gelding, and before Heather could scramble off, he'd hopped onto Sampson's broad back, wedging his thin hips between Heather's rump and the back of the saddle.

"Hey—just a minute—"

"At least I'm not a horse thief."

"It was only a prank." Heather's mind was racing and her heart pumped wildly. "Look, I'm sorry. Now, I'll walk back to the ranch—"

"Too late. We're doin' this my way," he said, clucking to Sampson and taking the reins from Heather's reluctant fingers. His arms surrounded her, his scent filled her nostrils and his breath, hot and wild, seemed to caress the damp strands of her hair. Lord, what a predicament!

Her heart was drumming so loudly, she was sure he could hear its loud tattoo. The back of her shirt, still damp, was pressed into the rock-solid wall of his chest and his legs surrounded hers, muscle for muscle, thigh to thigh, calf to calf. Worst of all, her buttocks were crushed intimately against the apex of his legs, moving rhythmically as the horse headed home. One of his hands held the reins, the other was splayed firmly over her abdomen, his thumb nearly brushing the underside of her breasts.

"I'll walk," she said again, her voice a strange whisper.

"No way."

"Then *you* walk."

"Sampson can handle us both."

But I can't handle you! she thought, clenching her teeth in order to keep her wild tongue silent. She'd just try to pretend that he wasn't slammed up so close to her that she could feel the tickle of chest hair through her T-shirt. She'd attempt to ignore the scents of river water mingling with musk and pine as he swayed in the saddle so intimately against her. She'd disregard the fact that his breath blew gently against the nape of her neck, causing delicious tingles to spread along her skin, and she wouldn't even think about the fact that his body was molded so closely and intimately to hers that she could scarcely breathe.

They rode in silence. The sounds of the night—the flurry of air as bats took flight, the gentle *plop* of Sampson's hooves, the drone of insects and the steady rush of the river fading in the distance—were drowned out by the rapid beat of her heart and her own ragged breathing. This was crazy! Being alone with him was dangerous and tricking him had been asking for trouble. Why, oh why, had she been so impulsive and foolish?

"Look, really, I can walk...." She glanced at him from the corner of her eye and caught the hard line of his lips.

"And have me be accused of not being a gentleman?" he replied with more than a trace of derision. "I don't think so."

"But—"

Sampson broke free of the woods, and beyond a few dry fields the ranch loomed before them. Harsh security lamps flooded the parking lot, drenching the barns and stables in an eerie blue-white illumination, and the ranch house, two stories of sprawling night-darkened cedar, was surrounded by dusky pastureland and gently rolling hills. The windows were patches of warm golden light. The French doors were swung wide and on the back deck several couples were learning the Texas Two-step to a familiar country tune by

Ricky Scaggs. Some of the soft notes floated on the breeze and reached Heather's ears.

The couples laughed and danced, and Heather wished she were anywhere else in the world than imprisoned in the saddle with this cowboy. How could she ever have thought of Turner as a romantic figure, riding alone along the ridge this afternoon?

A few animals stirred as they passed the corrals, and Heather noticed some of the ranch hands. Their boots were propped against the lowest rail of the fence, the tips of their cigarettes pinpoints of red light that burned in the night. A thin odor of smoke mingled with the dust and dry heat.

Turner rode into the main yard, and several of the cowboys, lingering near the paddock, glanced their way and sniggered softly amongst themselves.

Great. Just what she needed—to be branded as Turner's woman. No doubt they made an interesting sight, both half-dressed and wet, wedged tightly into the saddle.

She didn't wait for an invitation. When Sampson slowed, she swung one leg over the gelding's neck and half stumbled to the ground. Without a word, she spun and started for the back of the house.

"Aren't you gonna thank me?" Turner called.

She stopped, her hands clamped into tight little fists. "Thank you for what?" she asked, inching her chin upward as she turned to face him again. "For humiliating me? For forcing me to ride with you against my will? Or for being a voyeur while I swam?"

"Don't flatter yourself," he said lightly, but his eyes didn't warm and his jaw remained stiff.

"Go to hell!"

"Oh, lady, I've already been," he said with a mocking laugh that rattled her insides.

Heather turned again, and without so much as a backward glance, she hurried up the back steps to the kitchen and tried not to hear Turner's hearty laughter following after her like a bad smell.

She barely got two steps into the kitchen when Mazie, seated at the small table in the corner, glanced up from balancing the kitchen's books. "Trouble?" she asked.

"No—"

"Your horse came back alone. Zeke's none too happy about that and he was worried sick about you. He was just about to send out a search party. You'd better talk to him."

"I will," Heather promised. She wanted to drop through the floor. Mortified already, she didn't need to be reminded of her carelessness with Nutmeg. "Where is he?"

"In his office," Mazie replied, staring for a second at Heather's state of dress and tangled hair before turning back to her books and chewing on the end of her pen.

Heather ran up the back steps and slid into her room. Jill was on her bed, reading some teen-idol magazine. She glanced up when Heather shut the door behind her.

"What happened to you?" she asked, eyeing Heather with a curious gleam.

"I went swimming."

"In your clothes?"

"No," Heather said managing a smile. "I just didn't have a towel to dry off."

"Heard you lost your horse."

"That's the abbreviated story." In the mirror, her reflection stared back at her. Without makeup, her hair wet and limp, she looked about twelve years old. Turner Brooks probably thought she was just a kid. *Except he's seen all of you—breasts, the triangle of hair . . .*

"Great," she muttered, swiping a towel from the vanity and rubbing it hard against her long blond hair.

Jill tossed her magazine aside. "So what happened? And I don't want the *Reader's Digest* condensed version."

"It's boring," Heather replied, lying a little.

"I doubt it."

Heather stripped out of her dirty clothes and stepped into clean underwear, a denim skirt and pale blue shirt. She clipped a silver belt around her waist, combed her hair into a quick ponytail and contented herself with fresh lipstick.

"Does this have anything to do with Turner Brooks?" Jill asked. She drew her knees beneath her chin and smiled knowingly up at her roommate. "I saw Turner ride out that way."

"Did you?" Heather turned her attention back to the mirror in order to hide the tide of embarrassment she felt climbing up the back of her neck.

"Isn't he something?" Jill sighed contentedly.

In the reflection, Heather saw the girl close her eyes and smile dreamily.

"He's just the kind of man I'd like to marry."

"Turner Brooks?" Heather was aghast. The same slow-talking, sarcastic man she'd met? What kind of a husband would he make?

"God, he's beautiful."

"But there are rumors...about his past."

"I know, I know, but I don't care." Jill grinned wickedly. "Besides, a man with a past is a little more interesting, don't you think?"

"What I think is that Turner Brooks is a conceited, self-centered jerk who—"

"So you did run into him!" Jill's eyes flew open. "Oh, I wish I'd been there with you."

"Me, too," Heather replied under her breath. Before Jill could say anything else, she hurried out of the room and clambered down the stairs. She had to face Zeke and explain that she hadn't meant to lose Nutmeg, and hope that he wasn't too angry with her.

Zeke's office was in the front of the house and with each step Heather felt a mounting sense of dread. She couldn't lose this job. She just couldn't! All her dreams of art school and escaping Gold Creek would turn to dust if she didn't save enough money to move away from her mother's little cottage.

Steeling herself, Heather tapped lightly on the door.

"It's open."

Mentally crossing her fingers, she entered. The room was small and cozy. Filled with rodeo trophies, Indian blankets and worn furniture, the office smelled of tobacco, lingering smoke and leather. Antlers of every shape and size were mounted on the plank walls, and sprawled in one of the cracked leather chairs in front of the desk was none other than Turner Brooks himself. He turned lazy eyes up at her, and Heather nearly stumbled on the edge of the braided rug.

"Come on in," Zeke ordered, his voice softer. He was a man few people forgot. With snowy-white hair and thick muttonchop sideburns, he was a big man—over two hundred and twenty pounds and six foot one or two. Though he was huge in comparison to Turner, Heather barely noticed the older man. All her senses were keyed in to Turner—the slant of his knowing smile, the mockery in his gray eyes, the smell of him, a scent that seemed to cling to her nostrils. "You've already met my nephew."

Turner nodded in recognition and Heather swallowed hard. "Yes. Earlier." She forced her unwilling eyes back to her boss. "Look, Mr. Kilkenny, I need to talk to you."

Zeke leaned back in his chair and the old springs creaked. "So talk."

"I mean in private."

Zeke smiled. "We got no secrets here, Heather. At the Lazy K, we're all family." He waved her into the chair near Turner's. "Sit down and tell me what's on your mind."

Balancing on the edge of a chair, Heather tried not to think about the fact that Turner was only bare inches from her, that at any moment his hand could brush hers. "I...I'm sorry about losing Nutmeg. I was careless. It won't happen again."

"No harm done," Zeke said, rubbing his chin. "Nutmeg hightailed it back here for her supper. But it could've been worse."

"I'll be more careful," Heather promised, surprised she was getting off so easy. The horses were the life and blood of the ranch, and Zeke Kilkenny had a reputation of caring more for his animals than he had for his wife of twenty-odd years.

"Well, I know you haven't been around horses much— you livin' in town and all—and you're a good worker. Mazie says you're one of the best helpers she's had in the kitchen and she's trained more'n her share, let me tell you."

Heather could hardly believe the praise. From Mazie? The woman who single-handedly was trying to work her to an early grave?

"I could warn you off the horses, but, the way I see it, that's unnatural. Horses and men—or women—they just go together." Zeke leaned forward, and his smile was friendly. "Turner here came up with the perfect solution to our little problem."

Heather's blood ran cold. A suggestion from Turner? She tried to say something but for once her tongue tangled on itself.

"Why don't you tell Heather your idea," Zeke invited.

Turner leaned closer to her. "I thought that you might need some lessons handlin' a horse."

"I don't—"

"And Turner here's offered to teach you," Zeke cut in, so pleased he beamed. "You couldn't get a better teacher. Lord, Turner could ride before he could walk!" He chuckled at his old worn-out joke, and Heather felt as if her life were over.

She imagined the grueling lessons where Turner would take his vengeance and his pleasure in making her ride so long, she'd be sore for weeks, by having her groom every horse in the stables, by having her clean out every stall and shed on the ranch. The summer would never end. When she found her voice again, she held on to the arms of her chair in a death grip and said, "Surely Turner has more important work here—"

Zeke waved off her reasoning. "Always time to get someone in the saddle. So that's it. Starting tomorrow, right after you work your shift, you're Turner's!" He slapped the desktop and the phone jangled.

The meeting was over. Heather stood on leaden feet as Zeke picked up the receiver. Riding lessons with Turner Brooks? She'd rather die! He'd be merciless. Life as she knew it would end. She'd spend too many grueling hours with Turner the Tormenter!

"Cat got your tongue?" he asked as he followed her to the door.

"You'll regret this," she warned.

"Oh, I don't think so," he drawled with a sparkle of devilment lighting his eyes. "Matter of fact, lady, to tell you the truth—I'm lookin' forward to it!"

Chapter Two

Turner slapped his hat against his thigh and dust swirled to the heavens. Why in God's name had he told Zeke he'd like to show Heather how to handle a horse? She must've made him crazy last night, because this was the worst idea he'd come up with in years! It didn't help that he hadn't slept a wink the night before. Nope. All night long he'd thought of her, how her white skin had looked in the darkening water. He'd seen her nipples, hard little buds in the frigid depths, and he'd grown hard at the sight. She'd done her best to cover up, but he'd noticed the slim length of her legs as she'd tried to tread water and cover her breasts at the same time. The sight had been comical and seductive. Had she been a different kind of woman, he'd have spent the night with her.

But Heather Tremont had been like no woman he'd ever met before. She'd been indignant when she'd spied him and when he'd tried to tease her, she'd refused to laugh. But she'd challenged him. By taking his horse. And he'd never yet come up against a challenge he hadn't taken and won.

Now, as he watched her try to keep her balance upon a high-strung gelding, he almost grinned. Served her right for keeping him up all night wondering what it would feel like to kiss her lips, to drown in her sky-blue gaze, to touch her man to woman in the most intimate of places.

He shifted, resting his back against the fence and forcing his thoughts away from his sudden arousal.

"Pull back on the reins," he said. "Let him know who's boss."

"That's the trouble," she threw back at him. "He already knows! And it's not me!"

Turner swallowed a smile. She had guts—he'd give her that. She'd blanched at the sight of Sundown, a burly sorrel with a kick that could break a man's leg, but other than inquire about Nutmeg, her usual mount, she'd climbed into the saddle and gamely tried to command a horse who was as stubborn as he was strong.

"Uh-uh. No hands on the saddle horn," he reminded her as Sundown gave a little buck of rebellion and her fingers searched frantically for any sort of purchase. "That goes for the mane, as well."

"I know, I know!" she snapped.

She pressed her legs tighter around the gelding, and Turner's eyes were drawn to the tight stretch of denim across her rump. Her waist was tiny, but her hips were round and firm, in perfect proportion to her breasts. He saw the stain of sweat striping her back and the resolute set of her mouth.

He wondered what she would taste like. Yesterday, riding so close to her, the scent of her skin had driven him mad and he'd thought long and often about pressing his lips to hers. But, so far, he hadn't gotten close enough or been stupid enough to try to kiss her.

"How long is this going to take?" she asked, yanking hard on the reins and swearing under her breath when Sundown didn't respond.

"As soon as I think you're ready to take him out of the paddock."

"Humph." She set her tiny little jaw and a gleam of determination flared in her eyes. She worked the reins again and the gelding reared, but she hung on, refusing to be dismounted.

Turner forced his mouth to remain grim, though he wanted to smile. Crossing his arms over his chest, he settled back against the fence to enjoy the show.

Heather decided the lesson was a disaster.

While he leaned his back against the rails of the fence and watched her put her mount through his paces, she tried to stay astride Sundown, who fought the bit and pranced this way and that.

"You know, I'd work a lot better with Nutmeg," she grumbled when Sundown tried to buck her off for the third time. She managed to stay in the saddle, but only because she finally grabbed hold of the saddle horn.

"You'll never make a rodeo queen," Turner said. He shifted a piece of straw from one side of his mouth to the other.

"Oh, gee, all my dreams, down the drain," she tossed back, but laughed a little. She was hot and dirty and tired. After spending most of the day in the kitchen, she'd changed into jeans and had been astride Sundown for two hours, and her legs ached.

"You know, Heather, you might like me if you let yourself."

She nearly fell off the horse. The last thing she expected was any conversation from him about their relationship—or lack of one. "Me? Not like you? Whatever gave you that impression? Just because you invaded my privacy, forced me to ride with you and then came up with this harebrained idea of having you teach me, on *my* free time, mind you, all I wanted to know about horses but was afraid to ask, now, why would you think I didn't like you?''

A bevy of quail suddenly took flight and Sundown leapt high. Heather scrabbled for the reins and the saddle horn, but the horse shifted quickly. She pitched forward. The ground rushed up at her and she hit the dirt with her shoulder, landing hard. Pain exploded through her arm, and she sucked in her breath.

Turner was there in a second. Concern darkened his eyes as he reached to help her to her feet. ''Are you okay?''

''You're the teacher,'' she snapped. ''You tell me.'' But her arm throbbed and she held it against her body.

''Seriously, Heather.'' With a gentle touch she thought he reserved only for horses, he poked and prodded her shoulder. Eyebrows knit, he watched her reaction. ''Hold your arm up, if you can.''

Wincing, she forced her elbow high into the air. Like fire, pain shot through her bones. She gritted her teeth. Again his fingers touched her shoulder. ''Ooh!''

''That hurt?'' he asked.

''It all hurts.'' Especially her pride. The last thing she wanted to do was fall off in front of him. She sent Sundown a scathing look. ''Idiot.''

''Well, I see your sweet temper is restored,'' he said, and relief relaxed the hard contours of his face. For a second she was lost in his silvery gaze and her silly heart skipped a beat. His hands were warm and tender, and beneath his rough cowboy exterior Heather spied a kinder, gentler man—a man with a sense of humor and a man who did seem to care.

"Good as new," she said sarcastically, for she didn't want to glimpse into Turner's soul. It was easier to hate him than to have a current of conflicting emotions wired to her heart.

He tried to help her up, but she ignored his hand and found her feet herself. The less he touched her, the better.

"I think that'll do it for tonight."

"Oh? You're not one who believes that you have to climb right back on a horse if you fall off?"

He eyed her speculatively, his gaze searching her face, and her breath was suddenly constricted in her throat. "You enjoy putting me down, don't you?" When she didn't answer, he stepped closer and the twilight seemed to wrap around them. "What is it you've got against me, Heather?" he asked, and his hand reached upward, barely touching her chin.

"I don't have anything against you," she lied.

"Oh, yes you do, lady, and I intend to find out just what it is." His thumb stroked the edge of her jaw and she felt as if she might collapse, so weak went her knees. Instead, she knocked his hand away.

"Don't touch me," she said, her voice breathless.

"Afraid?"

"Of you? No way."

"You're a liar, Heather Tremont," he said slowly, but didn't touch her again. "And I don't know what you're more scared of. Me or yourself." He whistled to Sundown and caught the gelding's reins in the hand that had so recently touched her skin. "You'd better go into the house, Heather, and have Mazie look at your shoulder." His lopsided grin was almost infectious. "Unless you need the paramedics, I'll see you same time, same place tomorrow."

"How long will these lessons last?" she asked, rubbing the pain from her upper arm.

His gaze focused on hers again—hot, flinty and male. With a sardonic twist of his lips, he said, "We'll keep at it for as long as it takes."

Heather's heart dropped to her stomach and she knew she was in trouble. Deep, deep trouble.

Luckily, her shoulder wasn't sprained. Mazie clucked her tongue, Jill was absolutely jealous that Heather was spending so much time with Turner, Maggie didn't much care, but Sheryl, the girl who'd been with the Lazy K longer than any of the others in the kitchen aside from Mazie, seemed to grow more quiet. Heather caught Sheryl staring at her several times, as if she wanted to say something, but the older girl would always quickly avert her eyes and hold her tongue. Heather didn't pay much attention.

Even with her bruised upper arm, Heather was still able to do her kitchen duties, sketch without too much pain and meet with Turner every evening. Despite telling herself that being with him was a torture, a punishment she was forced to endure, she began looking forward to her time alone with him.

They rode through the forest on trails that had been ground to dust by the hooves of horses from the Lazy K. He showed her an eagle's nest, perched high over the ridge where she'd first spotted him astride his horse all those days ago.... It seemed a lifetime now. He pointed out the spring that fed the river and let her wade in the icy shallows. They raced their horses across the dried pastureland, laughing as grasshoppers flew frantically out of their way; and they watched the sun go down, night after night, a fiery red ball that descended behind the westerly mountains and brought the purple gloaming of dusk.

Often he touched her—to show her how to hold the reins, or tighten the cinch, or guide the horse, but the impression of his fingers was always fleeting and he never showed any inclination to let his hands linger.

One night, when they were alone in the woods, standing at a bend in the trail, she felt the tension that was always between them—like a living, breathing animal that they both ignored.

He was on one knee, pointing to a fawn hidden in the undergrowth. Heather leaned forward, for a better view and her breast touched his outstretched arm. He flinched a little, and the tiny deer, which had stood frozen for so many seconds, finally bolted, leaping high as if its legs were springs, and making only the slightest sound as it tore through the scrub oak and pine.

The wind died and the hot summer air stood still. Heather felt droplets of sweat between her shoulder blades, and she moved a step back as Turner stood. "I—uh, guess we scared him off," she said, her throat as dusty as the trail.

"Looks that way." He was so close, she could smell the scents of leather and horse that clung to his skin.

She moistened suddenly dry lips and wondered why she didn't walk back to her gelding, why she didn't put some distance between herself and this man she barely knew. There was something reckless about him, an aura that hinted at danger and yet was seductive. He touched her shoulder, and she nearly jumped at the heat in the pads of his fingertips. From the corner of her eye, she noticed the raw hunger in his stare.

She expected him to yank her close, to cover her yielding lips with his hard mouth, to feel the thrill of passion she'd read about in so many books. The naked hunger in his expression tightened her diaphragm about her lungs.

"We'd better get back," he finally said, his hands dropping.

Disappointment ripped through her.

"It'll be dark soon." Still he didn't move.

Heather's throat constricted at the undercurrent of electricity in the air. She licked her lips and heard his breath whistle past his teeth.

"Come on!" Grabbing her arm roughly, he strode back to the horses. "We don't want to be late."

"No one's waiting up for us," she replied, surprised at her own boldness as she half ran to keep up with him.

"For the love of Pete," he muttered. Stopping short, he pulled on her arm, whirling her so that she had to face him. The darkness of the forest seemed to close in on them and the night breathed a life all its own as the moon began to rise and the stars peeked through a canopy of fragrant boughs. "You're playing with fire, here, darlin'," he said, his voice tinged with anger.

"I'm not playing at all."

He dropped her arm as if it were white-hot. "Then let's go home, Heather, before I start something neither one of us wants."

She wanted to argue, to protest, but he scooped up the reins of his horse, climbed into the saddle and kicked Sampson into a gallop.

Heather was left standing in the darkening woods, wondering why he seemed to want her desperately one second, only to reject her the next. She was certain she hadn't misread the signals. Turner wanted her; whether for just a night or a lifetime, she couldn't begin to guess. But he wanted her.

Yet he wouldn't break down and admit it.

She hoisted herself onto Sundown's broad back and followed Sampson's angry plume of dust. Turner was probably right, drat it all. Whatever there was between them was better left untouched.

The next morning, Heather and Sheryl were assigned to inventory the pantry. The room was close and hot and

Heather counted while Sheryl wrote down the information.

"Sixteen quarts of beans... three tins of beets... five carrots—"

"You've been spending a lot of time with Turner," Sheryl said suddenly, causing Heather to lose track of her tally of the corn.

"I—well, I've been taking riding lessons from him."

Sheryl lifted an arched eyebrow. "And that's all?"

"Yes—"

"Good," she said, seeming relieved. "The man's trouble, you know."

Heather bristled a little. "His reputation doesn't interest me."

"Well, it should, because Turner Brooks is bad news. He doesn't care about anyone. I've seen the girls come here, year after year, and without fail, one of them falls for him. They get all caught up in the romance of loving a cowboy, and he ends up breaking their hearts. Not that he really intends to, I suppose. But they all start seeing diamond rings and hearing church bells and the minute they start talking weddings and babies, Turner takes off. He's out for a good time and that's it," Sheryl said, shaking her head. "And it's not really his fault. His dad's a drunk and his mother's dead. Some people say that the old man killed her—either from neglect or booze, I'm not really sure. But she's gone, and before she died, they had horrible fights. Turner never lets himself get too involved with any woman."

"Is that so?" Heather responded, wanting to close her ears. Why should she believe this girl?

Sheryl's eyes were suddenly clouded, as if with a private pain. She touched Heather lightly on the shoulder. "Look, for your own good, stay away from Turner Brooks. He'll cause you nothing but heartache. You can't expect a commitment from a man who'd rather sleep on a bedroll in the snow and cook venison over an open fire than enjoy the comforts of a feather bed and hot shower. You like the good life—I can tell. You want to be an artist and live in a big city and show your work in some fancy gallery, don't you?''

Heather could barely breathe, but she managed to nod.

"And Turner? What do you think he'd do in the city? Take you to the theater? Do you see him standing around an art festival and listening to jazz music? Or do you see him dancing in a tuxedo in an expensive restaurant?''

"No, I don't think—''

"He belongs to the open range, Heather, and to the mountains. His idea of a wild time is having a couple of beers after a rodeo in a small town in the middle of nowhere. He'd never be happy in the city.''

Heather's heart nearly stopped. She wanted to say something, to defend herself, but her tongue was all tied in knots.

"There was a time when I thought I could change him,'' Sheryl said softly. "I've been working here since my senior year in high school and I guess I had a crush on him.'' She fingered her pencil nervously and avoided Heather's eyes. "I thought…well, that given enough time…he'd grow up or away from ranch life. I was wrong. I've been here six summers. This spring I'll have my masters in architecture. I've already started looking for jobs in L.A. Two years ago, I gave up on Turner. I knew I couldn't change him.'' Tears filled her eyes. "God, he's got a girl in just about every town from here to Alberta! I was crazy. I…I just don't want you to make the same mistake I did.''

"I'm not—'' Heather protested, but knew she was lying.

"You belong in the city, Heather. Don't kid yourself.'' Clearing her throat, Sheryl motioned toward the cans of corn stacked on one of the deep shelves. "How many tins have we got?'' she asked, and Heather, shaking inside, her dreams shattered, started counting again.

* * *

In the next couple of days, Heather thought about Sheryl's warning, but she couldn't help herself where Turner was concerned. She knew she was beginning to care about him too much, looking forward to their time alone together, and she refused to let Sheryl's confession change her. Besides, she couldn't. She'd waded too far into emotional waters and there seemed to be no turning back.

Every evening, when the heat of the day fused with the coming night, Heather felt that she and Turner were alone beneath a canopy of ever-growing stars. They weren't alone, of course. Laughter and the rattle of the coffeepot could be heard from the ranch house and every so often one of the hands would come outside to smoke or play harmonica or just gaze at the stars. But it truly *seemed* as if nothing else existed but the horse, Turner and herself. Silly, really. Nonetheless she did feel a change in the atmosphere whenever she was with him, and she began to notice him not so much as an adversary or a teacher, but as a man.

The lone rider on the ridge.

Yet he never so much as touched her again.

"He's such a hunk," Jill said after work one evening as Heather changed for her lesson. "God, Heather, you're so lucky! I'd give anything to spend a few hours alone with him."

Heather fought down a spasm of jealousy. "I'm sure he'd like that," she said, brushing her hair and noticing the little lines between her eyebrows. Those little grooves always seemed to appear when Jill was gushing about cowboys in general, and Turner in particular.

"Oh, no. He's half in love with you." From her bed, Jill sighed enviously.

Heather nearly dropped her brush. It clattered on the bureau. "You're crazy," she said, but felt a warm glow of contentment at Jill's observation.

"No way." Ripping a black headband from her hair, Jill offered Heather a conspiratorial smile before tossing the headband onto the bureau and rummaging under her bunk for a well-worn magazine. "I've seen it before."

Turner? In love with her? Absolutely ridiculous! Still, the idea had merit. "He doesn't like me any more than I like him."

"That's what I said. He's half in love with you," Jill replied, licking her fingers and flipping the page. In the mirror, Heather saw the wash of scarlet that was causing her cheeks to burn just as Sheryl walked into the room. Her lips were pressed into a hard line, and if she'd heard any of the conversation, she pretended she hadn't.

However, Jill thought Heather cared about Turner. Heather glanced at Sheryl, but the girl was fiddling with her Walkman and fitting the earphones over her head. Heather fingered her brush and tried to convince herself that Turner wasn't her type. Too cynical. Too hard. Too…threateningly male. His sensuality was always between them, always simmering just below the surface of their conversations, always charging the air. And yet she'd wanted him to kiss her when they were alone at the deer trail. She wouldn't have stopped him.

The next few lessons were more difficult than ever.

Though she tried not to notice, Heather found herself staring at the way his jeans rode low on his hips, the magnetism of the huge buckle that fit tight against his flat abdomen, the insolent, nearly indecent curve of his lips and his eyes…. Lord, his eyes were damned near mesmerizing with their cynical sparkle. Worse yet, whenever she had a few moments alone and she began to sketch, it was Turner's face she began to draw, Turner's profile that filled the pages of her book.

Was she falling in love with a man who was only interested in the next rodeo? A cowboy who had seen too much of life already? He was a little bit mystery, and a lot rawhide and leather.

It was dusk again—that time of day she seemed destined to spend with Turner. A few stars dappled the sky and the wind, blowing low over the Siskiyou Mountains, tugged wayward locks of her hair free of her ponytail. Clouds had gathered at the base of the mountains and the air felt charged, as if a storm were brewing.

Turner was waiting for her in the corral, arms crossed over his chest, back propped against the weathered fence. His eyes were dark and serious, his expression hard as granite.

"You're late."

She felt the need to apologize, but shrugged and said, "Large dinner crowd."

As she reached the corral, he opened the gate. Sundown stood in the far corner, no bridle over his head, no saddle slung across his broad back.

"Aren't we going to ride?"

"You can—soon as you catch your horse."

"Oh, no way..." She started to protest, knowing how stubborn the sorrel could be and how he hated to be saddled. Always before, Turner had seen that the gelding was ready to start the riding lesson. Tonight was obviously different. "What if he decides that—"

"Do it." Turner yanked the bridle from a fence post and threw it at her.

She caught the jangling piece of tack by the bit and, stung by his attitude, said crisply, "Anything you say, *boss*."

His lips flattened a little, but he didn't reply. Arms over his chest, a piece of straw in one corner of his mouth, eyes narrowed, he glared at her.

"Are you angry with me?"

"Has nothin' to do with you."

"What doesn't?"

His eyes flashed fire for a second, then he tamped down his anger and glanced pointedly at his watch. "I don't have all night. Go on—get him."

The task was an exercise in futility. Sundown had it in his thick skull that he wasn't going to let Heather touch him. In fact, he seemed to enjoy the game of having Heather chase him around the corral. Nostrils flared, tail aloft, he pranced around the corral as if the evening wind had rejuvenated his spirit.

"Come on, you," she said, clucking softly to the horse, but no matter how she approached him, he let her get just close enough to nearly touch his sleek hide, then he bolted, hoofs flying, as he sent a cloud of dust swirling in his wake. Heather was left standing in the middle of the corral, her hand outstretched, the bridle dangling from her fingers.

"Nice try," Turner remarked on her third attempt.

"Look, I'm doing the best I can."

"Not good enough."

Damned cowboy! Who did he think he was? How in the world had she fancied herself in love with him? Humiliation burned bright in her cheeks, and she decided right then and there that she'd show Turner Brooks what she was made of. Even if it killed her. Gritting her teeth, she started after Sundown again, slowly clucking her tongue, her gaze hard with determination. He breezed by, nearly knocking her over.

"I'm gonna win," she told him, and again the horse took off in the opposite direction.

By the time she finally cornered the horse and threw the reins over his neck, the big sorrel was soaked with lather and she, too, felt sweat clinging to her skin and beading on her forehead. "You useless piece of horseflesh," she muttered, but gave him a fond pat. Despite his temperament, or maybe because of it, she felt a kinship with this hard-headed animal.

She adjusted the chin strap of the bridle and led a somewhat mollified Sundown back to the side of the corral where Turner was waiting.

"'Bout time," Turner had the gall to remark as Heather tossed the blanket and saddle over Sundown's glistening back. She tightened the cinch, making sure the horse let out his breath before buckling the strap. Thrilled at her small victory, she climbed into the saddle and picked up the reins. This was the part she loved, when she was astride the horse and she and Turner rode the night-darkened trails. "Now what?" she asked, her hopes soaring a bit.

"Now take his gear off and groom him."

"But—"

Turner looked pointedly at his watch and swore under his breath. "I can't hang around any longer." Without another word, he put two hands on the top rail of the fence and vaulted out of the corral. Once in the yard, he strode straight to a dusty blue pickup and hauled himself into the cab. There were a few silent seconds while Heather, still astride Sundown, sat stunned, disbelieving; then the pickup's old engine turned over a few times and finally caught with a sputter and a roar of blue smoke. Turner threw the rig into gear and, spraying gravel, he drove off.

"Terrific," Heather muttered, patting the sorrel's shoulder as the pickup rounded a bend in the lane and disappeared from sight. The rumble of the truck's engine faded through the trees. "Just terrific!"

Turner had been different tonight and Heather wondered if she'd pushed him too far in their last lesson, but she couldn't think of anything she'd said or done that would provoke this kind of treatment. True, they had nearly kissed—she was certain of it—but nothing had happened. She kicked Sundown gently in the sides and rode him the short distance to the stables. Why did she even care what was going on with Turner?

She spent the next half hour grooming the gelding and stewing over the cowboy who had touched her heart. Her emotions seemed to change with the wind that blew off the mountains. One minute she was angry with him, the next perplexed and the next she fantasized about loving such an unpredictable man.

Telling herself to forget him, she walked back to the ranch house and swatted at a bothersome mosquito that was buzzing near her face. Muttso, a scraggly shepherd with one blue eye and one brown, was curled up on a rug on the porch near the screen door. He yawned lazily as she passed. Inside the kitchen, Mazie was washing a huge kettle she'd used to cook jam. The fruits of Mazie's labor, twelve shining jars of raspberry preserves, were labeled and ready to be stored in the pantry.

"How'd the lesson go?" Mazie asked as she twisted off the taps. The old pipes creaked and the faucet continued to drip. "Damned thing." Mazie swiped her hands on her apron, then mopped her sweaty brow with a handkerchief. Her face was the color of her preserves and she was breathing hard.

"The lesson? It was fine," Heather hedged.

"Turner take off?" Mazie asked. Without waiting for a reply, she shoved aside the muslin curtains and looked out the window to the parking lot and the empty spot where Turner usually parked his truck. Absently, she reached into a drawer for her cigarettes. "That boy's got a lot to carry around," she said as she lit up and snapped her lighter closed. Letting out a stream of smoke, she said, "His pa's got himself in trouble again." Mazie untied her apron and hung it on a peg near the pantry door, then turned toward Heather.

"Booze. Old John can't leave it alone, and when he goes on a bender, look out!" Mazie pressed her lips together firmly and looked as if she was about to say something else, but whatever secret she was about to reveal, she kept to herself. "It's a wonder that boy turned out to a hill of beans. You can thank Zeke Kilkenny for that. Never had a son of his own—took his sister's boy in when he needed it."

"So Turner went to meet his father tonight?"

"Your guess is as good as mine. Long as I can remember, Turner's been bailing John out of jail. Looks like nothin's changed." Mazie, as if suddenly realizing she'd said too much, waved toward the preserves. "Now, you put those jars where they belong in the pantry. I don't have all night to sit around gossipin'."

Heather did as she was told, but she couldn't help wondering where Turner was and when he'd be back.

Later, she climbed into her bunk bed and picked up her sketch pad. Gazing through the window, she began to draw idly, her fingers moving of their own accord. Soon, Turner's face, scowling and dark, was staring back at her.

Sheryl, face scrubbed, walked into the room. She glanced up at Heather, her gaze slipping quickly to the sketch pad propped by Heather's knees. Sadness darkened her eyes. "I heard that Turner left," she said, flopping onto her bed. The old mattress creaked.

"That's right," Heather replied.

"Is he gone for good?"

Heather's heart froze. "For good?"

"For the season. His shoulder's healed up and I thought he'd entered a few more rodeos—that he'd be leaving soon."

"I—I don't know," Heather admitted, her insides suddenly cold.

"Well, even if he comes back, he'll be leaving soon. Believe me. He always does."

There was no riding lesson the next day, nor the following evening, either. Turner hadn't returned, and Heather silently called herself a fool for missing him. Was Sheryl right? Had he just taken off without saying goodbye? Her heart ached as if it had been bruised. She hadn't realized how much she'd looked forward to their time together.

"You must really be bored," she told herself on the third evening when Turner's pickup rolled into the yard. Her heart did a stupid little leap as she watched through the dining-hall window and saw him stretch his long frame out of the cab. He looked hot and tired and dusty, and the scowl beneath three days' growth of beard didn't add to his charm.

He spent the next hour with his uncle in the office and when he emerged, Heather, from the kitchen window, saw him head straight for the corral. Though she still was supposed to wipe down the tables, she tore off her apron and ran upstairs. Within minutes she'd changed into jeans and a blouse and was racing down the back staircase. She practically flew out the back door, nearly tripping over Muttso. The old dog growled and she muttered an apology as she flew by.

But the corral was empty and her heart dropped.

Turner's pickup was still parked in the yard, but she didn't think he'd gone to the bunkhouse. "Damn," she muttered under her breath. Why she felt so compelled to talk to him, she didn't understand, and yet compelled she was. She hurried to the stables, flipping on the lights and disturbing more than one anxious mare.

A sliver of light showed beneath the tack room door, and Heather hurried past the stalls and through the short hallway. Her boots rang on the concrete floor and she ripped the door open. Billy Adams, a boy of about nineteen, and one of the younger ranch hands who worked at the Lazy K, was seated on an old barrel and furiously polishing a bridle. He looked up and his freckled face split with a smile at the sight of her.

"Have you seen Turner?" she asked, and tried not to notice that Billy's boyish grin wavered a bit.

"He just took off."

"To where?"

"I don't know. He just saddled his horse and headed into the hills."

"North?" Heather asked, her mind racing.

Billy lifted one scrawny shoulder. "Guess so."

"Thanks!" She didn't pause to hear if he responded, just headed back to the stables. Sundown was a range horse and wasn't put in each night and Nutmeg was sadly missing, as well. But Heather wasn't to be thwarted. Bridle in one hand, she ran back to the kitchen, slunk into the pantry and stole several sugar packets. Feeling like a thief, she raced back to the paddocks and spied Sundown lazily plucking grass in the pasture.

"Come on, you old mule," she said with an affectionate smile. "Look what I've got for you."

Sundown nickered softly and his ears cocked forward. His eyes were still wary, but he couldn't resist the sweet temptation she offered, and soon Heather snapped the bridle over his head. "Your sweet tooth's going to be your downfall," she chided.

She didn't bother with a saddle, just led the big sorrel out of the pasture, and closed the gate. Swinging onto his broad back, she gave a soft command, and Sundown, bless him, took off. She didn't know where Turner had gone, but she crossed her fingers, hoping that he'd returned to the bend in the river where they'd first met.

Her heart was racing in tandem to the thud of Sundown's hoofbeats as he tore through the forest, along the trail, guided by the fading light of a dying sun. She didn't think about what she would say when she caught up with Turner, didn't dwell on the disappointment of not finding him at the swimming hole. She knew only that she had to see him.

The smell of the river was close, and the hint of honeysuckle and pine floated on the air. Heather pulled hard on the reins as the trail widened and the trees gave way to the rocky bank where Sampson was tethered.

Heather's gaze swept the river and she spotted Turner as he broke the surface near the rocky ledge that jutted over the water. His eyes met hers for a brief instant before he placed both hands on the shelf and hauled himself out of the water. Naked except for a pair of ragged cutoff jeans, he tossed the water from his hair and wiped a hand across his face.

Heather's throat went dry at the sight of his wet, slick muscles moving effortlessly as he shifted to a spot where he could sit comfortably. She noticed for the first time a purple scar that sliced a jagged path across his tanned abdomen.

"You lookin' for me?" he asked, his gaze piercing and wary, every lean muscle taut.

She would have liked to lie, but couldn't very well deny the obvious. "We, uh, we haven't had a lesson for a few days." Dismounting quickly, she tied the reins of Sundown's bridle to a spindly oak and wondered how she was going to reach Turner and why she bothered to try. He wasn't happy that she'd shown up; in fact, he seemed to be trying to tame a raging fury that started a muscle leaping in his jaw.

"Thought you hated the lessons," he observed.

"Thought you did, too."

The ghost of a smile touched his lips. "I've been busy."

"I heard."

He froze, and his eyes drilled into hers. "You heard what?" he said, his voice so low, she could barely hear it over the rush of the river.

She wanted to squirm away from his stare, and yet she stood, stuffing her hands into her pockets for lack of anything better to do, trying to keep her chin at a defiant angle. "I heard you had some trouble."

"That damned Mazie," he growled. "Doesn't know when to keep her mouth shut."

"Seems as if it's common knowledge."

"Or common gossip. Christ, I hate that." He picked up a smooth stone and flung it so hard that it flew across the river and landed with a thunk against a tree trunk on the opposite shore. Throwing his arms around his knees, he glowered mutinously across the rushing water. "What is it you want, lady?" he said without so much as tossing her a glance.

"I just thought you might want to talk."

"I don't."

"But—"

He swiveled around so fast to stare at her that she nearly gasped. "You made it perfectly clear what you thought of me the first time we met, and every day thereafter. Now you'd better climb on that damned horse of yours and ride out of here or I might just show you how much of a gentleman I ain't."

"You don't scare me," she said, though her insides were quivering.

"Well, I should."

"Why?" She walked up to the ledge where he was sitting and stared down at his wet crown. Drops of river water still clung to his hair, causing the gold streaks to disappear. He leaned back, his eyes focused on her so intently that her heart nearly stopped. With eyes that smoldered like hot steel, he studied her for a long, breathless moment.

"Because," he said, rising to his more than six feet and taking his turn to stare down at her. "Because I think about you. A lot. And my thoughts aren't always decent."

Oh, God. Her knees threatened to crumble.

"So, what're you really doing here, Heather?" Reaching forward, he touched the edge of her jaw, drawing along the soft underside with one damp finger. She trembled and swallowed hard as his gaze searched the contours of her face. "Because we both know that you and I, alone, can only mean trouble."

Her heart was pumping, its erratic beat pounding in her eardrums and her skin, where he touched it, felt on fire. Knowing she was stepping into dangerous, hot territory, she decided to plunge in further. "I came here because I care, Turner."

He snorted in disbelief.

"Mazie said that you were having a rough time of it, and I thought I . . . I hoped that I could help."

He barked out a hard laugh, and the finger that was traveling along her chin slid lower, down her neck, pausing at the slope of her shoulder before sliding down between her breasts. "And how did you think you'd do that, eh?" he asked, but his own breathing seemed suddenly as uneven as her own.

She grabbed his wrist and held his hand away from her. "Don't try to cheapen this, okay? I'm here as a friend."

"Maybe I don't need a *friend* right now. Maybe I need a lover."

Her stomach did a flip. Sheryl's warning flitted into her head then disappeared like morning fog. "Maybe you need both."

He eyed her silently, his gaze moving down her body slowly, then up again. "I think you'd better get on your horse and leave, little girl, while you still can."

"I said it before, Turner Brooks. I'm not afraid of you."

"Then you're a fool, Heather." Reluctance flared in his eyes for just a second as he grabbed her and yanked her body hard against his. Before she could utter a word of protest, he pressed his hot lips to hers, molded his wet body against her own and kissed her with such a fevered passion, she thought she might pass out. His arms were strong and possessive, his body as solid and hot as she'd imagined.

Closing her eyes, she swayed against him. The river seemed to roar in her ears and the thunder of her heart was only eclipsed by the sound of his, beating an irregular tattoo. His tongue pressed hungrily against her teeth, and she opened her mouth, feeling the sweet pressure of his hands against the small of her back. She felt weak and powerful all at once as emotion upon emotion ripped through her.

She thought of denial, of surrender, of love and of hate, but she was powerless to do anything but return his kisses with her own awakening passion which exploded like a powder keg at his touch. One of his hands lowered, cupping her buttocks, lifting her from her feet so she could feel his hardness, his desire. Still she wasn't frightened, and all her doubts seemed to float away into the twilight. She was a virgin, a girl who had never experienced the thrill of a man's passion and for the first time in her life, her virginity seemed no longer a virtue, but a prison.

With Turner, she could be freed of the bonds. She ran her fingers down his shoulders, feeling the corded texture of his skin, tasting the salt on his lips, smelling the powerful scents of maleness and river water.

Lifting his head, he stared down at her for a second. His eyes no were longer angry but glazed. A red flush had darkened the color of his skin. "Do you know what you're doing?"

"I don't care...."

"This is insane—"

She kissed him again, and with all the strength he could muster, he grabbed her forearms and held her at arm's length from him.

He was breathing hard now and his lips were pale with strain. "Listen to me, damn it! We're playing with fire, here, and one of us is gonna get burned."

Her senses were spinning wildly out of control, but slowed instantly as she realized that he was rejecting her. She, who was ready to offer him her body as a means to balm his wounds, was being told that he didn't want her. Tears, unwelcome drops of misery, suddenly filled her eyes. "Turner—"

"Don't you see, Heather? I'm just using you!" he said, though the pain in his eyes wouldn't go away.

"I don't believe—"

"I don't want *you,* I just want *someone.*

Got it? Any woman would do."

Her heart crumbled into a million pieces; he couldn't have hurt her more if he'd thrust a white-hot knife into her chest. "You don't mean—"

"We're not the same, you and I. Men don't think like women. So if you want me just because you want to experiment with sex, or you don't really give a damn and just want to get laid, then we're okay. But if you think that what's happening here has anything to do with love or romance, then you'd better get on that damned horse and hightail it out of here.''

A small cry escaped her lips.

"I mean it, Heather," he said, squeezing her arms so hard that they hurt. Pain swept through his eyes, but he didn't back down.

"I...I...I just wanted to help you," she whispered, tears drizzling down her face.

"Don't sacrifice yourself. I'm not worth it," he said bluntly as he dropped her arms. "No one is. Save yourself for your boyfriend back in Gold Creek."

"I don't—" she said, but bit off the rest. Somehow he'd heard about Dennis. "We broke up."

"Then don't *use* me to get even with him."

Without thinking, she raised her hand and slapped him so hard the smack echoed through the canyon. "I'm not using you."

"You're right about that, darlin'," he drawled, rubbing the side of his face.

Emotions all tangled, her vision blurred, she ran and stumbled blindly. The horse was where she'd left him, and she threw herself across his back, swung one leg over and kicked with all her might. Holding back sobs of humiliation, she headed back to the ranch house.

Turner watched her go, with a mixture of anger and relief. He'd almost lost himself in her. It wouldn't have taken much more to forget about his father, forget about his problems and make love to Heather Tremont.

It had taken all of his worthless upbringing to be able to say the cruel things—the lies—that had forced her away. He kicked at a stone and swore under his breath, not sure that he'd made the right decision. His face still stung where she'd hit him. He may have hurt her, but he kept telling himself he'd done the right thing. She was a small-town girl with dreams of the good life, a cute little thing who was bored to tears on the ranch. He'd become her distraction, and though she might have had the best intentions in the world, he didn't trust her. No more than she trusted him. And he wasn't going to treat her like a whore, not even if she wanted it. Because, deep down, when all was said and done, he did believe she was a lady.

Chapter Three

Heather, her pride wounded beyond repair, managed to avoid Turner for the rest of the week. She heard the gossip surrounding him, knew his father had been hurt in a barroom brawl and tossed in the local jail. Turner had been absent several days, without explanation, but the gossip was that he was trying to help his old man dry out and avoid another jail sentence.

Only Sheryl didn't buy into it. Peeling apples at the sink, the water running slowly, Sheryl shook her head. Her lips compressed and she attacked the apples with a vengeance. The Rome Beauties were on the soft side—having wintered over in the fruit cellar. While Sheryl worked to remove the Romes of their skins, Heather was at the next sink, slicing the apples into thin slivers for the pie filling.

"If you ask me," Sheryl said, "Turner took off because of woman trouble."

Heather's stomach knotted, and Jill, mixing sugar and cinnamon, shot her a knowing glance.

Sheryl went on. "Oh, his father might have got into some trouble, Lord knows that's possible, but I'll bet there's a woman involved— Oh! Damn." She dropped the apple peeler and sucked in her breath. "Cut myself." Snatching a kitchen towel, she blinked back sudden tears, then dashed up the stairs toward the bathroom.

Mazie sighed. "If you ask me, she never got over him." Clucking her tongue, she picked up the dropped peeler and started stripping the apples of their tough skins. "Turner and Sheryl were . . . well, I don't think you'd say they were in love. Leastwise he wasn't, but Sheryl, I'm afraid she fell for him." Mazie smiled sadly. "Just like half the other girls around here."

Jill, suddenly red-faced, handed Mazie the bowl of sugar and cinnamon, then set about wiping down the wood stove, which was only used when the power went out.

Heather bit her lip and kept working, afraid that if she said anything, she'd look as foolish as the other girls who'd thought themselves in love with Turner Brooks.

With her tongue still clucking, Mazie dried her hands quickly and left the rest of the apples to Heather. "Yep, that Turner . . . he's somethin'. I don't know how many girls fall for him." She grabbed her old wooden rolling pin and a bowl of pie dough from the refrigerator. Measuring by handfuls, she dropped several lumps of dough onto a flour-covered board, then started stretching and flattening the dough. "Well, speak of the devil," she said, glancing up as Turner's pickup wheeled into the yard.

Heather's stomach dropped to the floor as she watched the headlights of the pickup dim and Turner step down from the cab. Averting her eyes, she continued working on the remaining small mound of apples while Jill turned her attention to filling the salt-and-pepper shakers for the next day.

Mazie frowned as Turner started for the house. "He's got his share of troubles, that one."

"I heard his dad will spend a year in jail," Jill said, eager for gossip.

Mazie frowned. "I doubt it. Seems old John's always slippery enough to get off." She worked the dough to her satisfaction and folded the flattened crust in half.

"So Turner's father is an outlaw," Jill whispered with a deep sigh.

"Nothing so romantic. John Brooks is a drunk and a crook who depends upon his son to get him out of one jam after another." Scowling, Mazie draped several pie plates with the unbaked crusts. "If he were my brother-in-law—"

"Mazie…" Zeke Kilkenny's voice was soft but filled with quiet reproof. Heather's head snapped around and Mazie's spine stiffened.

She started shaping the edges of the crust as if her very life depended on it. "Well, it's true, and if you won't admit it, Zeke, I will!" She finished with one pie, and started working on another, twirling the pan as she cut off the excess crust. "Margaret might have been your sister, but she was my cousin, damn it, and my best friend and that…that drunk of a husband of hers killed her!" Mazie's chin wobbled, and she turned toward the window, dropping the pie pan and spilling the crust onto the floor. "Oh, God, now look—"

"I'll get it," Heather said quickly, grabbing a broom and dust pail and scraping away the ruined crust.

Zeke shoved his hat off his head and ran a hand through his thick white hair. "You girls go on," he said, as Heather did her best to clean up the fine film of flour on the floor. "You're finished for the night. Mazie and I—we'll take care of this.'' The look he sent them brooked no argument. Heather didn't waste any time. She was up the stairs like a shot. She yanked the band from her ponytail and stripped out of her apron. Jill followed her into the room, but Sheryl was missing.

"Wow! Can you believe what we just heard?" Jill said. She walked to the mirror and plucked a contact lens from her eye. "Melodrama at the Lazy K! Just like a soap opera!"

"You hear so much around here, you really can't believe it all."

But Jill wasn't listening. "No wonder Turner's so... distant. Such a rebel."

"You're making more of it than there is," Heather said, trying to think of a way to change the subject.

"I don't think so." Jill removed her second contact and found her glasses. "What do you think? Turner's dad killed his mother? But how? Did he take a gun and shoot her or beat her or—"

"Enough! I...I don't think we should talk about this. It's just gossip!"

"Where there's smoke, there's fire!" Jill said. "And Mazie said—"

"Mazie talks too much," Heather replied, inadvertently paraphrasing Turner as she hurried down the stairs. She avoided the kitchen and slipped through the dining room where some of the guests were watching television, or playing checkers or cards.

The French doors were open, and a breeze filtered into the ranch house, stirring the crisp muslin curtains as she dashed outside. Muttso growled from the bushes somewhere, but Heather didn't pause. She ran down a well-worn path leading to the stables and corrals. Outside she could breathe again. The claustrophobia of the ranch house with its gossip and conjecture slowly ebbed away. Heather slowed her footsteps and closed her eyes for a second. She needed to be calm, because beneath her determination to see Turner again, she felt a sense of dread. What if he rejected her again? Not that she was going to throw herself at him, of course. But he needed a friend. And she was willing to be that friend.

And how much more? her mind niggled, but Heather shoved that nasty little thought aside. She pressed her palms to her cheeks and waited for the heat to disappear from her skin. Her breathing was normal again, though her heart was pounding about a thousand beats a minute.

She found him in the stables, pitching hay into the mangers of the brood mares. He'd taken off his jacket, and the sleeves of his work shirt were rolled over his forearms, showing off strong muscles and tanned skin. He didn't look up when she entered, but his muscles flexed, his jaw grew tight and he hurled his pitchfork into a bale of straw. The seconds ticked slowly by. Heather hardly dared breathe.

"Didn't you get the message?" he finally asked as he turned and faced her. His eyes were the color of flint and just as explosive.

"I didn't think we were through with our lessons."

He let out a long, low breath and forced his eyes to the rafters where barn swallows swooped in and out of the open windows.

Again the silence stretched between them—as if they were awkward strangers. Heather fidgeted.

Turner hooked a thumb in his belt loop. "You know enough about horses to get by."

"Do I?"

He trained his eyes on her, and his expression was a mixture of anger and desire. "Look, Heather, I just don't think it's such a good idea—you and me."

"All I was asking about was riding lessons..." Her voice drifted off when she noticed the tic at the corner of his eye. The lie seemed to grow between them.

"Don't play dumb," he said, his jaw shifting to one side. "'Cause I won't buy it. You and I both know what's going on here and I'm just tryin' to stop something that you'll regret for a long, long time."

Unconsciously, she bit her lip. "I didn't come here to try and seduce you, if that's what you're getting at."

A thin smile touched his lips. "Good."

"I just thought you could use a friend. Someone to talk to."

"And that's what you want to do. Talk...oh, and ride, of course."

She shrugged. "Why not?"

"I can think of a million reasons." But he didn't voice any of them, and despite all million, he muttered a curse under his breath, threw her a dark, brooding look and saddled their two mounts. "I should be hung for this," he said, as he led the horses from the barn and swung into the saddle.

"Not hung. Shot, maybe, but not hung," she said, offering a smile, and Turner laughed out loud. Some of the strain left his features as they headed through a series of paddocks to the open pastureland.

Soon, the horses were loping along the westerly trail, skirting the pastures and keeping to the edge of the forest.

"Where're we going?" she asked, hardly daring to break the companionable silence that had grown between them.

Turner's grin widened. "Wait and see."

"But—"

He spurred his horse forward, and Heather had no choice but to follow. The path thinned as it wound upward, through the hills and along the rocky banks of Cottonwood Creek.

Turner didn't say much and Heather didn't dare. The night was too perfect to be broken with words. The moon, full and opalescent, hung low over the hills and thousands of stars studded the sky like tiny shards of crystal. Every so often, a shooting star would streak across the black heavens in a flash of brilliance that stole the breath from Heather's lungs.

The hum of traffic along a distant highway melded with the chorus of frogs hiding in the shallow pools formed by the creek.

All the while they rode, Heather couldn't take her eyes off Turner. Tall in the saddle, his shoulders wide, his waist narrow, his hips moving with the easy gait of his horse, he rode as if he belonged astride a horse. She imagined the feel of his hard thighs pressed against the ribs of the horse and her mouth turned to cotton.

"Here we go," he finally said, when the trees parted to reveal a clearing of tall grass and wildflowers. A lake shimmered, reflecting the black sky and tiny stars. Moonlight streamed across the surface in a ghostly ribbon of white, and fish jumped at unseen insects, causing splashes and ripples along the glassy surface.

Lithely, Turner hopped to the ground and tethered his horse on a nearby sapling. The animal snorted, then buried his nose in the lush grass.

"What is this place?" Heather asked, mirroring Turner's actions by tying Sundown to a scraggly pine.

"My mother's favorite spot in the world. She brought me up here a lot in the summer." He stared across the night-darkened landscape and a sad smile crossed his lips. "The Lazy K was where she and Zeke grew up. It was just a working ranch then—no boarders or tourists. But then my grandparents died and left the place to Zeke." He glanced over his shoulder. "They cut Mom out of the will because she married my old man."

"Oh," Heather said weakly.

"That's what this is all about, isn't it?" Turner shoved his hands into the back pockets of his jeans. "You heard some gossip about me and you want to know what's true."

"No, I—I just wanted . . ."

He turned and faced her, his hair ruffling in the slight breeze, his face taut and hard. "What, Heather? You wanted what?"

Time seemed to stand still. The air became suddenly quiet aside from her own frightened breathing. Swallowing hard, she decided that she had to be honest with him. "I just wanted to be alone with you," she whispered, feeling an odd mixture of shame and excitement.

"Don't you think that's dangerous?"

No time for lies. "Probably," she admitted.

"I don't get involved—"

"I know, Turner," she snapped. "Listen, I didn't want to like you and I hated the first few times we had lessons, but. . .day after day, I started to look forward to being with you."

"Because you're bored."

Licking her lips, she shook her head. "I don't think so, Turner. I think I . . . I think I'm falling for you." Her voice, though a whisper, sounded deafening.

He didn't move. Aside from the breeze tugging at the flap of his shirt, he stood stock-still, as if carved in stone.

She took a tentative step forward, walking close enough to touch him.

"What about the guy in Gold Creek?" he asked.

"I told you. It's over."

Biting her lip, she reached upward, touching the thin curve of his lips. With a groan, he grabbed her hand, holding it away from him. "You're playing with fire here, Heather."

"I know what I'm doing."

"I don't mess with women who are involved with other men."

"I'm not!" She turned beseeching eyes up to him. "Believe me, Turner. Just trust me."

He wanted to. She could see the passion stirring in his night-darkened eyes. And yet he held back, his fingers surrounding her wrist in a death grip, his emotions twisted on his face. "Don't play with me."

"I wouldn't," she said, and all at once his arms were around her, his lips molded over hers in a kiss that robbed the breath from her lungs. His lips were warm and supple and his tongue gained easy access to her mouth when she parted her lips.

Her thoughts swirled and blended with the night and a warm ache started somewhere deep in her abdomen. He explored and tasted and she moaned softly, unconsciously winding her arms around his neck, pressing her body closer still, feeling her nipples grow taut.

Groaning, he dragged them both to the ground, to the soft bed of bent grass and fragrant flowers, and still kissing her, he slowly removed her T-shirt, kissing the tops of her breasts, rimming the circle of bones at her throat with his tongue, creating a vortex of heat in her center that she didn't protest as his hand slid beneath the waistband of her jeans and toyed with the lacy edge of her panties.

"You're sure?" he asked, his breath ragged against her ear.

She kissed him hard on the lips and he let out a deep sigh, the flat of his hand pressed intimately to her lower abdomen.

"I mean it, Heather, because if we don't stop now, I won't be able to."

It was already too late for her. The fires within her had been stoked and now were white-hot and ready to explode. She pulled his head back to hers and kissed him with parted lips. "Don't ever stop," she whispered into his opened lips.

His hand slid deeper into her jeans, teasing the apex of her legs, creating a liquid need so intense that she was squirming and writhing beneath him. In the darkness, he smiled. "Take it easy, darlin'," he drawled, kissing the beads of sweat dampening her forehead. "We've got all night."

His lips found hers again, and he began his magic. Hands, callused and rough, were gentle as they unclasped her bra and held her breasts, pushing the soft mounds together, kissing her skin and causing her nipples to turn to hard little nubs.

"That's a girl," he whispered before his mouth closed over one dark peak and he teased and played, his tongue and teeth nipping and laving until the pressure within her was so hot she bucked beneath him.

He stripped her of her jeans, his large hands sculpting her buttocks, his face buried in the soft flesh of her abdomen.

Heather's mind was spinning; she'd never been so reckless, never wanted more of the touch, feel and taste of any man. He guided her fingers to the buttons of his shirt, and she quickly undressed him, her hands running eagerly over the sinewy strength of his muscles.

His fingers tangled in her hair and she ran her palms down the springy hair that covered parts of his chest. His lips were on hers again and he kicked off his jeans. The back of her throat tightened at the sight of him—she'd never seen a man completely naked before. A warning pierced her mind, but she ignored it.

"I've wanted you since the first time I saw you skinny-dipping in the river," he admitted, kissing her eyes, her lips, her throat and moving lower still.

"And I wanted you," she whispered, her mind racing in romantic fantasies of a cowboy and his lady. She wound her arms around his neck as he settled over her, gently prodding her knees apart.

"You're sure about this?" he asked again, though his voice shook and his control seemed held by a rapidly fraying thread.

"Oh, yes, Turner. Yes."

He kissed her forehead and eyes before his mouth claimed hers with a possession that reached to her very soul. She felt him shift, the tensing of the muscles of his back as he entered her. She cried out, for the pain was blinding, but he didn't stop, and with each thrust thereafter the pain lessened, balmed with pleasure, driving all thoughts from her mind as she gazed up at him. His hair fell over his forehead and his body was backdropped by the jewel-like stars. She met each of his strokes with her own increasing tempo, and without realizing it, she clung to him, her fingers digging into his shoulders.

With a shivering explosion, he climaxed. She, too, convulsed in a shattering, dizzy burst of color and light that erupted behind her eyes and sent shock waves through her limbs.

"Heather, sweet lady," he whispered between tattered breaths.

"Oh, Turner, I love you," she cried, holding him close, listening to the wild cadence of his heart, smelling the earth and water and wind on his skin.

"Shh." He kissed her so tenderly that she thought she would die.

Tears sprang to her eyes for the cowboy and all the pain he'd suffered. She would change things—change him. No longer would he have to wear a cynical shield . . . she would be there.

Slowly he rolled off her and cradled her in his arms. Together, without a sound, they watched the shooting stars streak through the heavens and listened to the soft sounds of their horses plucking grass, bridles jangling quietly, hoofs muffled by the thick turf of the meadow.

"You didn't tell me you were a virgin," he finally said.

"You never asked."

"I just assumed that . . ." His voice drifted off.

"You assumed that because I'd been engaged, I'd experimented with sex," she finished for him. "Well, it didn't happen."

"Why not?"

She levered up on one elbow and stared down at him. "Does it matter?"

"Just curious." His gaze touched hers, and her heart missed a beat.

"I wasn't interested."

He lifted a skeptical eyebrow.

"I only really dated Dennis and . . . well, our relationship wasn't all that physical."

"What's wrong with the guy?"

"Nothing! Everything! I mean—I just knew it wasn't right."

He snorted. "But with me?"

"I love you, Turner," she said again, hoping to hear the magic words returned. Instead she felt him stiffen and the arms that had held her so tenderly suddenly seemed like lead.

"You don't."

"Yes . . . I love you."

"You don't even know me."

Her heart turned stone cold. "But I...we...I thought..."

"You thought what?" he asked, his arms slowly withdrawing from her as he sat and stared at her. "That we had something special? That we were in love?" His voice was filled with a cold incredulity that drove a spike straight into her soul.

"Of course—"

"Hey, wait a minute. I like you and hell, yes, I wanted you, I mean wanted you in the worst way. Damn thing of it is, I still want you. But love... Heather, you're kidding yourself."

Her throat seemed strangled and she wanted to die.

"Look—" He reached forward as if to touch her, but she drew away, as if he'd burned her. "I care about you and we can be friends, but—"

"Friends?" she whispered, her throat catching in disbelief. "Friends? I don't make love with my friends!" Oh, God, what a mess! What had seemed so remarkable, so incredible only moments before, now seemed cheap. And to think of how she'd thrown herself at him. She thought of her sister, Rachelle, and all the pain and embarrassment she'd suffered at the hands of Jackson Moore, a boy she'd slept with only one night, a boy who had left her with her reputation in tatters.

"Don't get me wrong," he said. "I care for you. I do—"

"But you don't love me."

"I don't love anyone," he said flatly. "I don't believe in it."

She closed her eyes on the horrid words, felt hot tears in her eyes. "Then I feel sorry for you, Turner," she said flatly.

He tried to touch her again and she recoiled. How could she have been so stupid? After Sheryl had warned her, how could she have thought she would be the one who could change him?

"I don't know what you were expecting, Heather, but I'm not the kind of man to settle down with a wife and kids and picket fence and station wagon. I ride rodeo. In two weeks, I'll rejoin the circuit. I'll be in Oregon, Colorado, Wyoming and Alberta. And then—"

"I don't need to know what you'll do after that," she said.

He grabbed her then, and though she tried to squirm away, he held her tight. Aware of her nudity, of his strength, of the love she still felt deep in her heart, she closed her eyes.

"Look at me, damn it," he said, shaking her a little.

When she lifted her lids, she found his face only inches from hers, his expression filled with concern, remorse dark in his eyes. "What do you see?"

"I don't underst—"

"What do you see?"

"You," she said, her throat tight.

"And what am I?"

"A..."

"A cowboy, right? The kind of man you wouldn't really want to be caught dead with, not to mention spend the rest of your life following around. I have nothing, Heather. Nothing except a drunk for a father and part of a ranch with a mortgage against it that rivals the national debt. I own a broken-down pickup, a saddle, a damned good horse and the shirt on my back. That's it. Is that what you want?"

She didn't answer, couldn't speak past the dam of tears that filled her throat.

"Well, is it?"

"Yes," she cried, tears streaming down her cheeks.

"Oh, lady," he whispered, and suddenly she was deep in his arms again. They were warm and tender and loving, and the kisses he placed in her hair and on her cheeks eased the pain in her heart. She tasted the salt of her own tears when his lips found hers again and she didn't think about the future as she kissed him back and made love to him again. Tomorrow didn't matter. As long as she could have him this one night, she'd live with her memories forever locked in her heart.

Chapter Four

Turner gave himself a mental kick. Astride Sampson, he threw out his arm and sent the lasso whizzing through the dusty air. The rope loop landed with a thud on the ground, inches away from his target, a bawling Hereford calf. It was the second time he'd missed, and several of the guests as well as some ranch hands were watching.

"Hey, Brooks, he's gittin' away," Hank hooted from the other side of the fence.

"Yeah, maybe you should stick to tying something you can handle—like your shoes!"

Color washed up the back of Turner's neck. He gritted his teeth and hauled the rope back. With lightning-quick speed, he spun the rope again, urging Sampson forward with his knees as they chased the calf and, just at the right moment, he let loose. The lasso snaked through the air, landing squarely over the surprised calf's neck.

Sampson started stepping backward instinctively, tightening the loop as Turner vaulted from the saddle, ran through the dust, and over the cheers and jeers of the onlookers tied the Hereford neatly.

Damn, what a job! He stepped back from the struggling calf and yanked his hat from his head. His life seemed to be turned upside down. Ever since making love to Heather, he hadn't been himself. He'd been gruff and surly with some of the hands, his duties at the Lazy K had suffered and the skills in which he'd prided himself for years seemed to have escaped him. All because of some female!

But not just any female. No, Heather Tremont was different from all the women Turner had known. A small-town girl who had dreams of fame and fortune and the glitter of the city life. A woman who wanted to be an *artist* for God's sake. A female who believed in romance and love. Hell, what a mess! What he needed was a drink and maybe a good hard kick in the head to make him wake up.

"'Bout time you roped him," Bud yelled, cupping his hands around his mouth.

Turner ignored the gibe. He deserved it. A few days ago he could've lassoed that calf with his eyes blindfolded. But not now. Not since Heather had wormed her way into his heart.

He knocked his hat against his leg, sending dust up in a cloud, then jammed the Stetson back onto his head and walked back to untie the calf. He didn't know what he was going to do about Heather. Had no idea. He didn't believe in love or marriage, and even if he did, he realized she'd never be satisfied with him. So that left him with the obvious option of continuing the affair he'd so reluctantly started. But his reluctance was now long gone. Even now, just thinking of her, he ached. Never, *never* had he experienced such intense passion with a woman, never had he felt so sated. And yet, he couldn't stop thinking and plotting how he was going to get her alone again.

"Miserable bastard," he muttered at himself. Everyone who heard him probably thought he was talking to the calf. With a flip of his wrist the rope fell away and the Hereford was free. Bawling and scrambling to his feet, the whiteface ran to the far end of the corral.

"Y'all done?" Bud hollered. "We were hopin' for another demonstration. These here guests paid good money to see you miss that calf."

Turner grinned lazily. "Maybe I should practice a little more."

"Ah, hell. Ya got a lot on yer mind," Hank said as he opened the gate and Turner, leading his buckskin, walked through.

"That I do," Turner agreed, letting Hank and Bud and the others think that his problems all stemmed from his father. Not that John Brooks wasn't on his mind. The old man had given him nothing but grief over the years, but right now his problem was Heather.

He'd never planned on marrying or even settling down with one woman. But Heather turned his thoughts around. He suddenly was questioning everything he'd ever believed in.

After turning Sampson out to pasture, he brushed the dust from his jeans and started for the kitchen. But he stopped short when he saw the black Porsche roar into the yard. The car looked like liquid ebony under the sun's hot rays. It rolled to a stop, and the engine, along with a hard-rock song that had been thrumming from the sports car's speakers died.

Turner stopped short and he felt the ghost of dread crawl up his spine as a tall man about his own age rolled out of the plush leather seats. Mirrored glasses, a smooth leather jacket, polo shirt, slacks and expensive shoes covered the man from head to foot. A gold watch strapped to the man's wrist glinted in the sun's rays.

Turner had never seen the guy before in his life, but he wasn't surprised to watch as Heather, wiping her hands on her skirt, ran out of the house to greet him.

Turner's gut twisted. Heather didn't run to the man's open arms, but didn't protest too much when he grabbed her and spun her off the ground. He caught her lips in a kiss and she pushed away.

So this was the man she was supposed to marry. Dennis something or other—Italian sounding, if he remembered right. His back teeth ground together and he wanted to wring the man's neck. Turner started toward the couple, then thought better of it. What did he have to offer Heather? Nothing. But this guy—he could give her the world.

His mood as dark as the Porsche's gleaming finish, Turner swung toward the ranch house, washed his hands in the basin on the back porch and, feeling dirt-poor and ranch-bred, dared walk into Mazie's kitchen.

She was smoking at the table, going over some sort of list. "What's on your mind, Turner?" she asked, eyeing his boots critically as if to make sure he didn't drag any dirt or manure into her kitchen.

"Nothing." He checked the cooler and found a bottle of beer. "Just a little thirsty," he said, slamming the door shut and twisting off the top from his bottle.

"You don't want to talk about anything?"

"Nah." In the past, he'd confided in Mazie. She was kin and the only mother figure he could remember. Zeke's wife had left him years before and eventually died and Turner's mother had been killed when he was twelve. That left Mazie. His mother's cousin. And a woman who had trouble keeping her mouth shut.

"Thinkin' of movin' on?"

Turner took a long pull on his beer. "In a couple of weeks." Funny, the thought wasn't as appealing as it had been. When his old man had been thrown into the slammer, Turner had sworn to leave the Lazy K as soon as his shoulder was well, but since he'd become involved with Heather... He glanced out the window and saw Heather and her boyfriend. They were standing several feet apart and she looked guiltily over her shoulder. The rich guy took a step toward her, but she held up her hand, said something and spun on her heel, running back to the house.

"You could stay on," Mazie said, as she always did, and Turner barely heard her his heart was slamming so loudly.

"What? Nah. I don't think so."

"Zeke needs good hands."

"Not me." His heart was beating like a drum as the man, his face dark red with fury, climbed into his fancy car and started the engine. With a spray of gravel, the sleek car and its driver were gone. The front door slammed shut and quick footsteps pounded up the stairs. Heather!

"And you'd be closer to your ma's place," Mazie pointed out.

Turner didn't look at her, could barely concentrate. She'd pushed the city boy out of her life! But why? For him? Pride mingled with self-disgust; he knew he would never be able to make her happy.

"Turner? You listening to me? I said 'you'd be closer to your ma's place!'"

Forcing his attention back to the conversation, Turner frowned and took a long swallow from his beer. While his mind was occupied with Heather, Mazie was talking about the run-down ranch where his father lived. Turner had grown up there and his father had rented the place from Thomas Fitzpatrick, a wealthy Gold Creek businessman who had gotten the ranch by some shady means. John Brooks had always wanted to own that miserable scrap of earth and when his wife had died, he'd managed to buy out Fitzpatrick with the life insurance proceeds coupled with a huge mortgage from the Bank of The Greater Bay.

Turner had done his best to pay off the mortgage. He scowled as he thought of it.

"Someday, son," his father had told him when he was barely thirteen, "this will all be yours." John Brooks had waved expansively to the acres of green grass and rolling hills. "And that's the way your ma, rest her soul, would've wanted it. Oh, I know she took out that policy for you, so you could go to college, earn yourself a degree, but she would've known that you weren't right for schoolin', that you needed some land, some roots." He'd slapped Turner on his shoulder. "That's right, boy. Your ma, now she was a smart woman. Had her own degree, y'know. In music. Could've been a teacher, but she married me instead—and me, I wasn't about to have my wife workin' and supportin' me. No way!" John had leaned over the fence rails, cradling a beer and smiling into the western hills. The tears in the corners of his eyes were probably from the intense light of the afternoon sun. Those telltale drops probably had nothing to do with remorse for being drunk behind the wheel of the pickup when it had rolled down an embankment, flipped over and killed his wife. "She would've wanted you to own something, kid, and there's nothing more valuable than land. Yesirree, Margaret would've approved."

Turner doubted it. He finished his beer in one long swallow and tossed the empty into the garbage can. In his peripheral vision, he caught Mazie studying him through a cloud of cigarette smoke.

"It won't work, y'know," she said kindly, and in that instant he realized that she could read his mind. "She wants the fine things in life, has her sights set upon being an artist."

"I don't know what you're talking about."

"Sure you do. I see the way you look at Heather when you think no one's watchin'. And she feels the same. But it won't last, son. Think of your poor ma—"

He rammed his hat back onto his head. "I'll be leavin' before the end of the month," he said suddenly. "Don't want to miss the final days of the rodeo season." Without waiting for a reply, he headed back outside and refused to think about Heather. Mazie was right. Heather complicated his life, and right now he had more than his share of complications.

Heather couldn't sleep. Dennis's surprise visit had caught her off guard. He'd come hoping to patch things up and she'd had to be firm. She didn't love him. Never had. Never would. She'd tried to be gentle, but he'd understood and he'd been angry when he'd left. Dennis Leonetti was used to getting what he wanted.

What had she ever seen in him? Compared to Turner...well, there was just no comparison. Sighing, she threw off her blankets and let the brisk night air that stole through the open window cool her body.

Her roommates didn't share her problem with insomnia. They were all tucked under their covers, snoring softly, dreaming whatever dreams filled their heads. But Heather was restless. She tossed and turned.

Ever since the night she and Turner had made love, he'd been avoiding her. She was hurt, and the ache in her heart wouldn't go away. Getting through the days had been difficult, and she'd just gone through the motions of her work. Mazie had been forced to scold her more than once and even Jill had noticed her bad mood. Sheryl hadn't said a word, but her blue eyes had been filled with silent accusations.

All because of Turner.

What a fool she'd been. She loved him. She was sure of it now. The fact that he was a cowboy was no longer repulsive—she even found his livelihood intriguing and romantic. "You're being as silly as Jill," she muttered to herself as she climbed from her bunk. She felt bottled up—claustrophobic—and she had to get outside for some fresh air. Throwing a robe over her nightgown, she stole down the back stairs.

The ranch house, filled with noise during the day, seemed strangely quiet. The hall clock ticked, the refrigerator hummed, the old timbers groaned and creaked, but still the house was different, the dark shadows in the corners seeming close.

Holding her robe together with stiff fingers, Heather dashed through the kitchen and outside. Muttso growled from somewhere in the bushes, but she ignored him and ran to the paddocks, her bare feet scraping on the stones and packed earth of the paths and walkways. The air was filled with the drone of insects and an owl hooted from an upper branch of a mammoth pine tree situated behind the pump house.

Heather breathed deeply of the pine-scented air. She ran her fingers through her hair, shaking the loose, tangled curls that fell down her back. The notes of an old country ballad drifted from a forgotten radio left on the windowsill of the tack room.

She wondered about Turner. Was he in his bed—sleepless as she? Was he packing to leave, for she'd heard he would soon rejoin the rodeo circuit? Or was he sleeping soundly, maybe with some other woman in his arms? That thought caused a particularly painful jab in her heart.

"Don't you know it's dangerous slinking around here in the middle of the night?" Turner's voice was soft and close, and for a minute she thought she'd imagined it, had conjured the deep sounds as her thoughts had drifted to him.

Turning, she saw him, shirt open and flapping in the gentle breeze, Levi's riding low over his hips. She forced her gaze to his face, expecting hard censure. She wasn't disappointed, his gaze was stony, his jaw set.

"I couldn't sleep," she said, hoping her voice didn't betray her.

"Seems to be contagious." His voice was low and supple and seemed to whisper up her spine.

Heather gripped the top rail of the fence so hard she felt splinters against her fingers. "Did you think about the other night?"

"Can't think of much else."

Her heart took flight. "Me, neither."

He hesitated a second. "You had a visitor today."

Her stomach turned over and she bit her lip.

"Your boyfriend."

"Ex," she said automatically.

"He didn't seem to think so."

"Look, Turner, it's over. I know it and I think he does now, too."

He turned halfway, leaning an elbow on the fence rail and studying her face as if it held a vast secret he hoped to expose. "You're a hard woman to forget."

"Is that a compliment?" she asked, her voice tremulous.

"I'm just pointing out that your 'ex' didn't look like the kind who gives up easily."

"He's not."

"But you convinced him?" His voice was edged in skepticism.

"All I can tell you is that it's over between me and Dennis. It has been for a long time. And now..."

"Now what?"

Curling her fists, she sent up a silent prayer for strength, for honesty took more strength than she knew she possessed. "And now I only want you."

He let out a long low whistle. "You don't—"

She stepped forward, touching the rough stubble on his face with her hand. "I do, Turner. I want you."

She felt him smile in the darkness, a slow, sexy grin that brought an answering smile to her own lips.

"So what're we going to do about it?" he drawled.

She turned and looked across the rolling acres of night-darkened grassland. Her throat felt thick and tight. "You tell me," she finally whispered, swallowing hard and afraid that he would tell her that he didn't want her again, that it would be best if they stopped seeing each other. Her heart was knocking against her ribs, her hands sweating.

"I think the less we talk about it, the better." His arms suddenly surrounded her. He pulled her backward a bit, so that her buttocks pressed against his thighs, and he bent his head and kissed the crook of her neck. She went liquid inside, her knees giving way as his hands slipped beneath her robe, wrapping possessively around her abdomen. Through the thin fabric of her nightgown, she felt his fingertips, the hot pinpoints stretching from beneath her breasts to the top of her legs.

"I've missed you, Heather," he murmured, his lips hot and hungry.

"I...I've missed you, too."

His hands moved, stroking the skin over her belly, the thumb of one hand grazing the underside of her breasts, the fingers of his other swiping the apex of her legs.

Her blood began to pulse as he shifted, his hardness firm against her buttocks.

Closing her eyes, she knew she couldn't resist, that as long as Turner and she were together, she would surrender to him, even seduce him, time and time again. As they tumbled into the dry grass, she realized that loving him was her destiny as well as her curse.

For the first time in her life, Heather felt weak. She knew she should avoid Turner, for he would certainly leave and leave soon.

"You're making a big mistake," Sheryl told Heather as they basted chicken with tangy barbecue sauce. Over fifty fryer quarters sizzled over the huge barbecue pit in the backyard. Tonight was the last evening at the ranch for many of the guests. Balloons and torches lined the back porch and a huge barbecue and dance were planned.

"What kind of a mistake?" Heather asked innocently as the sweat ran between her shoulder blades. She picked up the tongs and began turning each quarter. The sun was blindingly hot. Grease spattered loudly and smoke billowed into the blue sky.

"You know what I mean. About Turner. You should avoid him. He'll only cause you heartache."

Jill, balancing a tub of sauce on her hip, heard the last of the discussion. "I don't know," she said, sending a wistful glance in the direction of the corral where some of the cowboys were branding calves. "I'd take his kind of heartache any day of the week."

"That's crazy," Sheryl muttered, as she brushed more sauce onto the chicken.

"Crazy like a fox," Jill replied, tossing her head and lowering her voice. "But I tell you, if I wanted to tie Turner down, I'd trick him."

"I don't want to tie anyone down," Heather snapped, hating the conversation. "I don't think we should be talking about—"

"Trick him?" Sheryl repeated. "How?"

"By telling him I was pregnant."

Heather dropped the tongs.

"Oh, God," Sheryl whispered. "That's insane."

"Not if you really want a man. You know what they say, 'all's fair in love and war.'"

"But he'd find out—" Sheryl said.

"By then it'd be too late, or I would be pregnant," Jill replied with a smile.

Sheryl and Heather stared at each other as Jill flounced up the stairs. "She'd do just about anything to leave home, I guess," Sheryl said, biting her lip. "Even trap a man."

Heather felt sick. She finished basting the chicken, then helped bake corn bread as Mazie stood over a massive tub of chili. Even with the windows thrown wide, the kitchen seemed well over a hundred degrees. Heather tried to keep her concentration on her job, but her eyes kept wandering to the window and beyond where calves bawled and sweaty men tended a small fire and pressed the hot brand of the Lazy K into living rawhide.

Turner was there. She could see him leaning over a frightened calf, talking softly, untying quick, flying hooves and stepping back swiftly as the calf scrambled to its feet.

"If you don't watch out, that bread'll rise three feet," Mazie admonished. "Just how much baking powder you figure on adding?"

Heather jumped, nearly dumping the contents of the baking powder can into her mixture of cornmeal, flour, milk, sugar and egg. "Sorry," she said, recovering.

"Just keep your mind on what you're doing."

That wasn't easy advice to follow. For the next few hours, her eyes worked as if they had a mind of their own, searching the corrals, always seeking out Turner. Just as some of the guests were leaving tonight, Heather had a horrible premonition that Turner, too, would try to say goodbye. He'd been hinting at it for the past two days. It was only a matter of time.

The girls were given time to change after the food had been served, and they, along with the hands and guests, danced on the plank deck while the flames of the torches gave off a flickering light. The music was a blend of country and old rock and roll, and Heather danced with several of the ranch hands and guests before she found herself in Turner's arms.

The lead singer, as if on cue, started singing a slow ballad by the Judds that nearly broke Heather's heart.

Turner's arms folded around her and she clung to him with a desperation born of fear. Tears burned behind her eyes. Soon he would leave. As surely as the sun would rise in the east, Turner would be gone.

And what was she supposed to do? Live her life as if she'd never met him? Pretend that their affair hadn't existed? Save enough money for art school and find an apartment in the city? She thought of her sister's life-style, once so envied, that now didn't have the same fascination for her. The bright lights of the city, the dazzle of theater openings, the glitter of dance clubs had dimmed as she'd come to know and love Turner.

She snuggled deeper in his arms, closing her eyes as his scent enveloped her. Leather and denim and smoke from the branding fire mixed with soap and horses to create a special male aroma. His body molded against hers, and beneath the sundress she wore, her skin turned warm. His lips pressed against her bare neck and she tingled all over....

The song ended, and Turner whispered, "Meet me in the barn at midnight," before they parted and found new partners. She fell into the arms of a hefty guest name Ron, who stepped on her toes, and Turner wound up dancing with Sheryl. Heather gritted her teeth and forced a smile and tried not to watch as Sheryl smiled up at Turner and whispered something in his ear. Turner laughed and Sheryl cast a superior glance in Heather's direction.

Heather turned her attention back to her partner and started counting down the minutes until midnight.

Turner was waiting for her. His silhouette was visible against the window as she stepped into the darkened barn.

"I thought you might have changed your mind," he said.

"Never." Running to him, she threw herself into his open arms and met his hot lips with her own.

"Not here.... Come on," he whispered, taking her hand and leading her to the ladder that stretched to the hayloft. He followed her into the bower of fragrant hay and together they tumbled onto a mattress of loose straw. His lips found hers again and the hunger in his kiss told her that he would leave soon. There was a surrender in his movements that she'd never felt before, as if he hoped in one night to take his fill of her.

She met his fevered lovemaking with her own flaming desire. She closed her mind to the future, lost herself in the here and now and made love to him with all the passion and fear that tortured her heart.

"I love you," she whispered recklessly, as she straddled him and her hair fell around her face and shoulders in thick golden waves.

Turner gazed up at her, his eyes glazed, his face flushed with desire. "Don't say—"

"But I do, Turner," she gasped.

He placed a finger over her lips, and she caressed it with her mouth and tongue, convulsing over him as he bucked upward and released himself deep within her. "Heather," he cried, "Sweet, sweet, lady." His arms were around her and he pulled her sweat-soaked body down to rest on his.

She felt tears fill her eyes, but she wouldn't cry, not in front of him. Together they lay, entwined, their hearts beating rapidly, their breath mingling in the warm summer air. Turner's arms were wound possessively around her and his lips touched her hair. They lay on their backs, staring through the open window near the apex of the roof, and watched the stars wink in the dark sky.

"I can't stay here forever," Turner said as he kissed her temple and plucked a piece of straw from her hair.

Her throat was so tight, she could barely whisper, "Why not?"

"I've got a life out there."

Oh, God, not now! Please not now! Her world seemed to crack. "So you're just a ramblin' man," she said, fighting tears and the sarcasm that poisoned her words. She'd promised herself that when he wanted to leave, she wouldn't tie him down, but now she felt desperate to do anything, *anything* to stop him.

"I guess."

She squeezed her eyes shut and told herself she wouldn't break down, wouldn't shed one solitary tear for this man whose heart was hard enough that he could walk away.

"You'll leave soon anyway, too," he said calmly, though his voice was rougher than usual. "You've got school in the fall—"

"It doesn't matter now."

"Sure it does." He levered up on one elbow and studied the features of her face so intently she looked away. "Heather, you have a chance—to do what you want. Go for it. Don't let anyone take your dreams away from you."

"Like someone took yours from you?" she guessed, and he stiffened.

"I always wanted to be a cowboy."

"Little boys want to ride horses and shoot guns," she said, touching his arm, feeling the downy hair beneath her fingers. "Grown men like to sit in offices, order their secretaries around and play golf."

"Not this one." He flopped onto his back and stared at the dusty rafters where a barn owl had tried to roost. "That's the problem, Heather. I *like* my life the way it is. I'd die in a three-piece suit and a tiny office on the forty-third floor of some high rise. I'd rather hassle with my old pickup than drive a Mercedes. And I'd take a camp stove and a tent over a house in the suburbs any day. I wouldn't be any good at frying hamburgers on the backyard grill and I don't see myself coachin' Little League."

"You're telling me there's no room in your life for me."

"Nope. I'm telling you there's no room in *your* life for *me*."

"I love you, Turner."

"You don't—"

"Shh." She pressed a finger to his lips and fought back the urge to cry. He didn't love her. Oh, he cared for her. That much was evident. But to him she was no more than his girl at one of the many places he called home. He probably had women waiting for him in every rodeo town in the West.

Tears clogged her throat and burned her eyes. She leaned over and kissed him.

He responded, but his eyes were open and he saw the tears that she fought so bravely. With a sad smile, he wiped a tear from her cheek. "Don't cry for me, darlin'. Believe me, I'm not worth it," he said before his lips found hers again and he showed her a way to forget the pain.

Heather didn't see Turner the next day. He didn't come in for meals and his pickup wasn't in the yard. If Mazie knew anything, she was keeping her lips buttoned and Zeke wasn't around.

All day long Heather's stomach was queasy and her heart felt as if it had turned to stone. But he wouldn't have left without saying goodbye.

The day dragged endlessly, and when finally she was finished shaking the rugs, hanging the kettles and mopping the floor, she tossed her apron into a hamper and ran outside. Heart in her throat, she walked to the stables.

Sampson was missing.

And Turner's saddle wasn't slung over the sawhorse near the corner of Sampson's stall. She hurried down the cement walkways, her boots ringing hollowly beneath the glare of single bulbs.

In the broodmare barn she found Billy, pitchfork in hand, tossing fresh hay into a manger.

"Is—have you seen Turner?" she asked when Billy glanced her way.

"Not since daybreak. He's gone."

"Gone?" she replied, panic causing her heart to beat so fast she could barely breathe. Maybe Billy meant that Turner had driven into town for supplies with Zeke. Or maybe he meant that Turner had taken some of the guests on an overnight campout. Or maybe his father had gotten himself into trouble again and Turner had to bail the old man out. That was probably it. John had gotten drunk, thrown a few punches in a bar and—

"He took off just after dawn," Billy volunteered, jabbing another forkful of hay.

"When will he be back?"

Billy's jaw tightened. He stuffed the pitchfork into a bale of straw and yanked off his gloves. "I don't reckon he's comin' back. Leastwise not this summer."

Her heart dropped to the cold cement floor. "You're sure?"

"Hell, I don't know." Billy shrugged and tossed his hair out of his eyes. "But his shoulder isn't hurt anymore and he paid a lot of money for entry fees and everyone knows he likes to keep some distance between himself and his old man, so you figure it out."

He yanked on his gloves and began spreading straw in some of the empty stalls. Heather's throat squeezed shut and tears stung her eyes. So he'd gone. Without telling her. Well, maybe he'd tried last night, but she'd expected more than a "I'll be leaving soon."

She battled tears all the way back to the ranch house. She wanted to throw herself onto her bed and kick and scream and sob until all her tears were wrung from her body. But she couldn't go upstairs and run into Sheryl or Jill or any of the girls who worked at the ranch. No, she'd have to do her grieving by herself. Maybe he'd call. Or write. She could cling to those frail hopes.

Feeling more miserable than she'd felt in all of her life, she saddled Sundown and rode to the bend in the river where she'd first spied Turner. "The beginning of the end," she whispered, patting the gelding's neck and hopping to the ground while tears streamed down her face.

She tried to be strong because she faced more than a single fear. Not only did she realize that he'd used her, that she'd been nothing more than one of the girls he'd met on the road, that he'd never loved her, she also suspected that she might be pregnant.

She touched her flat abdomen and tried not to cry for the baby who would never know his father. For the baby, she had to be strong; for the life beating within her, she had to find a way to survive. Without Turner.

BOOK TWO

Badlands Ranch, California

The Present

Chapter Five

The bronc leapt high, twisted in midair and kicked toward the sun, but Turner held on, his fingers twined in the bridle and mane of his furious mount. "That's it, you bastard. Show me what you've got," he gritted out. His hat flew off, skimming through the dry air to land in the center of the paddock. The roan, a nasty beast named Gargoyle, landed with a bone-jarring thud before he became airborne again, bucking and rearing, fighting to dislodge his unwanted rider.

Turner gritted his teeth and ignored the grime and dust of a day's work. This ugly stallion was the best of the lot he was to train, a fiery-tempered quarter horse who didn't give up, the kind of do-or-die animal that Turner had always found a challenge.

Hooves found earth again and the roan took off, running the length of the paddock, kicking up dust and nearly smashing Turner's leg against the shaved poles of the fence.

Grinning wickedly, Turner clamped his thighs tighter, shifting his weight, letting the horse know who was boss.

Gargoyle careened to a stop, wheeled on back legs and took off again, running and bucking and tearing up the arid ground.

"I think that's enough." Turner reined in, and while the horse took a minute to shift gears, Turner hopped to the ground and wrapped the reins around the top pole of the fence. Man and beast were both sweating and breathing hard.

Turner retrieved his Stetson and slapped the dirty hat against his thigh. A cloud of dust swirled upward. "Tomorrow," Turner promised.

The horse glowered at him, flattening his ears and shifting his rear end to get a clean shot at Turner's shin.

Sidestepping quickly, Turner avoided the kick. "You lazy no-good son of a bitch," Turner muttered, though he was amused by the stallion's spirited antics. With a little work, this quarter horse would be one of the best he'd ever ridden—ugly or not. "You won't win, y'know." With an eye to the horse's back legs, Turner loosened the cinch and slid the saddle from the roan's back. "And I'm considering changing your name to Silk Purse. You know the story, don't ya?"

Gargoyle swung his broad head around and tried to take a nip from Turner's butt, but the reins restrained the stallion and he was left to stomp the hard earth in frustration.

"Serves you right." Turner hoisted the saddle to the fence rail, then quickly unsnapped the bridle. Gargoyle didn't need any more encouragement. He took off, bucking and kicking across the dusty paddock, snorting and galloping with as much speed as any stallion Turner had come across in a long while.

"Remember—tomorrow!" Turner called out as he vaulted the fence. The roan huffed, fire in his eyes, as if he were already anticipating the outcome of their next encounter. Turner laughed. "Yeah, well, I'm lookin' forward to it, too."

"Quite a show you put on."

The voice was soft and feminine, and Turner glanced up sharply to find Nadine standing in the shadow of the barn. He'd forgotten this was her day to come and clean his place. "Didn't know anyone was watchin'," he drawled as she crossed the gravel lot, her red hair catching fire in the sunlight. She was a pretty woman with big green eyes, an easy smile, and a smattering of freckles across the bridge of a straight little nose. Divorced, with two small children, Nadine made her way in the world alone.

"I thought you might need this." She handed him a cold bottle of beer, right from the refrigerator. "And I didn't want you tracking dirt on my floor."

"And here I thought that floor was mine," he replied, taking the bottle and twisting off the cap.

"Not until the wax is dry, it isn't." She reached into the pocket of her denim jacket and withdrew a stack of envelopes. "Mail call." Slapping them into his callused palm, she motioned toward the stallion. "Not too handsome, is he?"

"He'll do." Turner couldn't help baiting her a bit. "Don't you know that the uglier they are, the better they look flyin' out of the chutes?"

"He flies all right. I'll give him that." She squinted up at Turner, and for a minute he caught a glimpse of some emotion she usually hid. She'd been his housekeeper for four years, long before she was divorced from Sam Warne, but lately he'd gotten the feeling that she was interested in more than wiping the grime from his windows. "By the way, she called again,'' Nadine added, and Turner's gut turned to stone.

"Who?"

"As if you didn't know. Heather, that's who. Seems as if she's trying pretty hard to reach you."

Turner didn't respond. No reason to. As far as he was concerned, Heather didn't exist—hadn't for a lot of years.

"And the Realtor for Thomas Fitzpatrick hasn't let up. He phoned, too. Fitzpatrick wants this ranch back in a bad way."

Turner's glower increased. "I already told him—it isn't for sale."

"Thomas Fitzpatrick doesn't give up easily."

"He doesn't have a choice."

She lifted a shoulder. "Just thought you'd want to know."

"Only good news. That's all I want to hear about," Turner said, his eyes narrowing.

"Well, you may be waiting a long time."

Though she was only teasing, he knew she was right. He closed his eyes for a second. Damn, he didn't need either Heather Tremont Leonetti or Thomas Friggin' Fitzpatrick fouling up his life. He was capable of fouling it up himself without anyone else's help. When he opened his eyes again, he watched Nadine as she waved and moved toward her car, a beat-up old Chevy filled with mops, brooms, soap and wax.

Turner's gaze followed after her as she climbed behind the wheel, fired the engine and tore off down the lane, leaving a plume of dust behind her. She was a good-lookin' woman, a woman any man would be proud to claim as his wife, but Turner wasn't interested. Besides, she deserved better. He took a long swallow of the beer and wiped the sweat from his brow. Leaning both arms over the top rail of the fence, he eyed the stallion. "You are a mean beast, you know," he said.

A soft nicker whispered over the dry fields, and Gargoyle lifted his head, nostrils extended, ears pricked forward, in the direction of the sound. Turner followed the stallion's gaze to the small herd of mares, sleek hides gleaming in the afternoon sunlight as they grazed near the ridge. Backdropped by a copse of cedar and pine, they plucked at the dry grass, oblivious to the stallion's interest.

Gargoyle tossed back his head and let out a stallion's whistle to the mares. Beneath his dusty, reddish coat, his shoulder muscles quivered in anticipation.

"You poor bastard," Turner said with genuine regret because he liked the feisty roan. He watched as Gargoyle pranced along the fence line, whinnying and snorting, head held high, tail streaming like a banner as he showed off for the lackadaisical females. "So you like the ladies, do you? It's a mistake, you know. Can only get you into trouble."

The stallion nickered again and the mares, flicking their ears toward the noise, continued to graze and swat at flies with their tails.

Turner had seen enough. Wiping his hands on the thin denim covering his thighs, he started for the small ranch house he called home. It wasn't much, but it was bought and paid for and all Turner needed now that his old man was gone. The mortgage had nearly sucked the life blood from him, but he'd used every penny he'd earned to pay back the bank—Leonetti's bank. Dennis's grandfather and father had owned and run the bank and when old John had taken out the mortgage, Turner hadn't yet met Heather or known of Dennis Leonetti. But once he'd figured it all out, he couldn't pay off his debt fast enough. The thought that he owed any Leonetti money galled the life out of him.

What comes around goes around, he thought. Now Thomas Fitzpatrick was interested in the ranch again—wanted to run some geological tests on the land beneath the ridge, scouting around for oil—but Turner held firm. This was his place, bought with his mother's tears and his own blood and sweat. He wasn't going to allow the likes of Thomas Fitzpatrick to get his hands on it again.

As he headed along the weed-choked path, his body, jarred from two hours in the saddle, ached. Old pains, "war wounds," as he referred to them, reappeared. His hip hurt so badly he nearly limped again, but he gritted his teeth against the pain. He was barely thirty, for God's sake—he wasn't going to start walking like a run-down old man.

Kicking off his boots on the back porch, he swatted at a bothersome yellow jacket, then shoved open the screen door to the kitchen. The house reeked of lemon, pine and cleaning solvent—in Turner's opinion, a stench worse than horse dung and sweat.

He didn't breathe too deeply, but as he crossed the gleaming floor, he noticed the white rose propped in a cracked vase, giving the kitchen "a woman's touch." As usual. And as usual, the rose would wither and die until Nadine came back and put another flower of some sort in its place. As if he cared.

Settling into one of the chairs at the table, he took a long swallow from his bottle. The beer was cold and slid easily down his parched throat. A little too easily. He wiped his mouth with the back of his hand.

He was careful with liquor, because of his old man. He knew how the beast in the bottle could drive a man—how it could break him. But, though he hated to admit it, he had a fondness for beer. One of his weaknesses. His first was—or had been—a woman. He'd given up on one, so he felt no compulsion to forsake the other. But he'd be careful. No way was he going to end up like John Brooks—in and out of the drunk tank all of his life, dying before he was fifty because his overworked liver just gave up and quit.

He took another pull, drained half the bottle and felt his muscles relax. Shuffling through the mail, his hands leaving smudges on the white envelopes, he eyed the sorry stack of bills, advertisements, a magazine and one lone letter—written crisply in a woman's hand. Heather's hand.

The return address was San Francisco—where she'd moved to escape the small-town poverty and boredom of Gold Creek. For that, he didn't blame her. Nothing but trouble ever came out of Gold Creek, California. Including himself.

Memories of Heather skittered like unwanted ghosts through his mind. He finished his beer and reached into the refrigerator before curiosity overcame good sense.

His mouth went dry for just a second.

Heather Tremont. No, Heather Tremont Leonetti. She was married now. Had been for years. Her husband was Dennis Leonetti. Big name; big money. A slick-talking banker who had inherited his money, could give his beautiful young wife anything her heart desired—as long as it had a price tag attached. Even an art gallery. And a son. The same SOB she was supposed to have broken up with when he'd come careening into the yard of the Lazy K in his rich boy's machine. Well, Heather had shown her true colors, hadn't she? All that talk about not caring about money. About trust. About love. All BS!

Not that it mattered. Not that he cared. He let the door of the refrigerator swing shut.

Peeling the label from his empty bottle, he noticed the message written on a notepad by the phone—Heather's name and phone number written in Nadine's no-nonsense scrawl. In his mind's eye, he compared Heather to Nadine.

Nadine was so simple, so earthy, so straightforward. Heather had always been complicated, beautiful and manipulative. An *artist* for God's sake—with the temperament to match. So why was it always Heather's gorgeous face that disturbed his dreams? Why couldn't he take a chance on a simple, good-hearted woman like Nadine Warne?

He reached again for the refrigerator. This time he didn't stop when he opened the door. He pulled out a tall, dewy bottle and twisted off the top as he glanced again at the letter.

Heather.

He wondered if she'd found happiness with all her money. Not that he gave a damn. Crumpling the letter in a grimy fist, he lobbed the wadded, unread note into a corner where it bounced off the wall and landed on the gleaming floor, six inches from the basket. Well, he'd never been good at basketball. In fact, he hadn't been much good at anything besides staying astride a stubborn rodeo bronc. Now, even that was gone.

He glanced through the window to the rolling hills of his ranch; he'd kept it running with the stubborn grit that told him he had to make something of himself, something to break the legacy that he'd inherited from John Brooks. He had all he wanted right here.

He didn't need Heather Leonetti or her money to remind him of that.

Frowning darkly, Turner took another long tug from his beer. He'd finish this one, take a shower and maybe drive into town—do anything to stop thinking about Heather.

Heather had never been to Turner's ranch. Never had the guts. She'd put their past in a neat little package of memories that she'd locked in a closet in her mind and had never dared examine. Until recently.

She'd been married and tried to make the marriage work. It, of course, had been doomed from the beginning. Without love, the walls of her marriage had cracked early on only to crumble later. Now, as she squinted through her sunglasses, her hands were sweating on the wheel of her Mercedes. She'd let the top down and felt the wind tug at her hair and whip across her face.

The landscape was dry; the grass already bleached gold, the dust a thin layer on the asphalt as the wheels of her Mercedes flew over the country road leading north from Gold Creek to Badlands Ranch. Once called Rolling Hills, Turner had renamed it for who knew what reason. Heather didn't understand why and didn't care.

She only had to face Turner again because of Adam. At the thought of her son, she caught her lip between her teeth. His disease wasn't, at the moment, life threatening. But at any time his remission could be reversed and then...oh, God, and then... She shuddered though the interior of the car was warm.

Her own bone marrow didn't match that of her son. And, of course, Dennis's wouldn't, either. That left Turner. For, if Adam should need a donor and was unable to donate enough good tissue to himself, Turner was the next logical choice.

He deserved to know.

She pushed a little harder on the throttle, and her car leapt forward, exceeding the limit. She couldn't seem to get to Turner fast enough. She'd been in Gold Creek long enough to know that he wasn't married, that no woman openly lived with him, but she wasn't sure that he wasn't in love with someone and that whoever the woman was, she wouldn't want Heather showing up on Turner's doorstep with the news that not only was he a father, but that the boy needed him.

She tasted blood and forced herself to relax, removing her teeth from her lip and easing up on the throttle. The ranch was just ahead. She spotted the turnoff to a long dirt-and-gravel lane that wound through a thicket of trees. The ranch house was probably beyond. She turned into the lane. The tire of the Mercedes hit a pothole and shuddered, and Heather sent up a prayer that when she faced Turner again, she wouldn't break down.

The temperature in the barn hovered around a hundred degrees. Dust filled the air that was acrid with the smells of manure and oil from the broken-down tractor. Yellow jackets buzzed near the filthy windows and swallows flew in and out the open door. The light from the lowering sun seeped through the cracks in the old siding and faded in the recesses of the interior. A headache thundered behind Turner's eyes. He needed a shower and a drink and then maybe a woman. Not necessarily in that order. He'd be lucky if he got the shower.

Sweat ran down the back of his neck and over his bare back as every one of his muscles strained while he pitted his will and strength against that of the stallion.

Gargoyle wasn't going to win this round, Turner decided as he held the roan's bent foreleg tightly between his thighs and carefully, so as to avoid being nipped in the rear, tapped the nails of the horseshoe back into Gargoyle's hoof. The roan snorted, shifting his weight against the man and looking for a way to take a piece out of Turner's hide.

"Relax," Turner muttered around a mouthful of nails. His muscles ached, but he didn't give in. For his efforts, he was flicked in the face with the coarse hairs of the horse's tail. "Cut it out!"

Tap, tap, tap. He drove the nails into the hoof. The horse was nervous. Lather greased his coat and his ears were flat with hatred for the man intent on taming his wild spirit. "You'll live. Believe me," Turner told the roan as he drove the last nail into place.

"Turner?"

The feminine voice, so familiar in his distant memory, caught his attention. He looked up and saw her silhouetted in the open door, her figure dark in contrast to the fading sunlight, her skirt moving slightly in a tiny ghost of a breeze. The hairs on the back of Turner's neck lifted one by one. It couldn't be . . .

"Turner Brooks?" she repeated, stepping into the shadows of the barn, closer now so that he could see her face, the same damned face that he'd tried so hard to forget.

Gargoyle shifted, his head swinging around. And Turner, thighs still clamped over the horse's foreleg, sidestepped the nip. He spat the nails into his hand, all the while never letting his gaze wander from the doorway. "Well, well, well," he heard himself saying. "If it isn't Mrs. Leonetti?" She winced a little at that, and he wondered where was the satisfaction he should have felt in wounding her. Letting the roan's leg drop, he vaulted easily over the railing of the stall. She was still a few feet away, but he noticed her eyes widen a bit, and the quick intake of her breath, as if she were frightened. "You know, I never thought I'd see you again."

"I . . . um . . . I know." She licked her lips—from nerves or in an effort to play coy, he couldn't guess. His gut tightened, warning him that she was trouble. Always had been. Always would be. Her blond hair, the color of winter wheat, stirred in the breeze, and in the half light of the barn her eyes were as dark as the stone cold hue of an arctic sky. Fitting. "You haven't returned my calls," she accused, though her words weren't harsh.

"Nothin' to say."

"And my letter?"

One edge of his lip lifted sardonically. God, she was beautiful—frigidly so. The layer of sophistication she'd so carefully wrapped around her made her seem ice-cold and untouchable—like a marble statue. She'd changed over the years, and not for the better. "You sent me something? Must've got lost," he drawled, and they both knew it was a lie.

"You should've read it."

"Why?" He folded his arms over his chest, waiting with measured patience.

Her mouth moved, but she didn't speak.

"Look, lady," Turner said irritably as he remembered using that very word as an endearment in the past. She froze for a second and he mentally kicked himself. "Is there something you want? If so, just spit it out and then leave me the hell alone."

"I just . . . I . . . Oh, drat!" She rolled her eyes to the ceiling, and for the first time he noticed the lines of strain near her mouth. Maybe being married to Mr. Big Bucks wasn't all it was cracked up to be. "I had to see you again."

His body turned rigid. Every sweat-soaked muscle grew taut with suspicion. She was playing with him. A bored housewife looking for a quick thrill. "So now you've seen me," he said, with as much malice as he could muster. May as well have a little fun with her. She deserved it. "Now what?"

"I, um, thought we could talk."

He sauntered closer to her, aware that he smelled of sweat and horse and dirt. He hadn't shaved in three days, and his faded jeans, threatening to bust through in the knees and butt, were streaked with grime. A pretty sight he made, he thought as he stopped only inches from her and stared down into her cobalt-blue eyes. In his peripheral vision, he caught a glimpse of a sleek, silver Mercedes—a rich woman's car.

"Talk?" He lifted a dubious eyebrow and smiled inwardly when her pulse, visible in her throat, leapt. So she was either scared or nervous. Good. "I'm not in the mood to talk. There's only one thing I've ever wanted to do with you," he said cruelly, keeping his voice low while sliding one long finger along the V of her neckline. "And you know what that is. So, let's either get down to it or you can get the hell out of my life."

Shuddering, as if from revulsion, she drew in a long breath and focused her eyes directly on his. "Don't try to scare me, Turner. It won't work."

So she did still have some gumption. She tossed her thick blond hair away from her face and didn't flinch, not even when his finger slipped beneath the clear button and the blouse opened a slit. He told himself she could never arouse him again, but the pad of his fingertip pressing against the taut skin over her sternum caused a reaction elsewhere in his body, and when he noticed that her expensive white blouse was dirty where he'd touched the lapel, his groin tightened. He always had liked a challenge and she seemed intent on giving him one.

So what the hell? Even if she were here for a quick roll in the hay—why not? So she was married. He'd always drawn the line at married women before, but with Heather, when she was practically begging for it . . .

He grabbed the front of her blouse in his fist and drew her close, intent on kissing her.

"Don't even think about it," she warned as he lowered his head.

"No?"

Her own fingers wound around his wrists. "I didn't come here to seduce you, Turner and, in fact—" she managed to rake her gaze down his filthy body "—if I were in the mood, you'd be the last man I'd want."

"I doubt that," he replied, his eyes slitting as he stared down at this rich little bitch who had the nerve to stride onto his ranch, uninvited, and insult him.

"I'd heard that you were a broken-down cowboy, a man who was on the verge of pouring his life into a bottle, but I didn't believe it. But now—" she skated that haughty gaze over the rough planes of his face "—I see that I was wrong."

He wasn't going to argue with her. So he'd inherited his old man's reputation. Big deal. He knew that he'd never, *never* follow the same path as John Brooks. What other people thought—including Heather Leonetti—didn't matter.

"Then why the hell are you here, *lady?*" he asked, spitting out the final word.

"Because I need your help!"

His fist uncoiled and he stepped away from her, noticing the fire in her eyes. "From a 'broken-down cowboy'? From a man who's on his way to 'pouring his life into a bottle'? I don't think so." He glared at her as if she were dirt. His lip curled in disgust. He was tired of the game and furious that just the sight of her could arouse him. "Go home, Heather. Go back to your fat-cat husband. I don't really give a damn what you want. I wouldn't help you if you crawled back to me on your hands and knees."

"Well, think about it, Turner, because that's exactly what I'm doing," she said, holding her wobbling chin a little higher. Tears filled her blue eyes and he felt his pride start to shatter. "I'm begging you because I need your help."

"I don't think so—"

"We have a son, Turner," she said quickly, and all sound inside the barn seemed to cease. He stared at her as if she had gone stark, raving mad. "He's five. His name is Adam. And regardless of what you think of me, he needs you very much."

Chapter Six

Beneath his tan, Turner's face drained of color. "A son," he repeated, when he finally found his tongue. Disbelief clouded his eyes and his voice was deadly. "I have a son?"

"Yes and—"

"And you haven't told me about him for six years and now, all of a sudden, out of the clear damned blue, I have a son." He looked at her long and hard, his face harsh and flushed with fury. "Come on, Heather, you can do better than that. Just try."

"I'm telling the truth!" She didn't panic. Not yet. She'd known he wouldn't believe her, not at first.

"Sure. Well, for your information we have three daughters, too. I just never got around to tellin' you 'bout 'em." He offered a cold smile, and it was all Heather could do not to grab him by his filthy collar and shake some sense into him.

"It isn't impossible, you know."

His cruel grin faded, and she knew he, too, was remembering all the times they'd made love that summer.

"Why would I lie?"

"You tell me." Yanking a handkerchief from his pocket, he wiped the sweat and grime from his face. His hands shook a little and she knew she was finally reaching him.

"I wouldn't be here if I didn't have to be, Turner. You know that."

Time seemed to spin backward six long, lonely years. The air was thick with old, tangled emotions that seemed to creep into the barn and bring sweat to Heather's brow. Turner's expression turned from wary to a thundering rage that knotted his features as the truth finally hit home. "Are you trying to tell me that I've had a kid for five years and you've kept it a secret?"

Heather's heart ripped.

"That you married a rich banker so that my kid wouldn't have to be raised by a poor cowboy? Is that it?"

She choked, her throat swollen, her heart shredding.

"Are you trying to convince me that you're so callous— so friggin' manipulative that you would pass off another man's son as his?"

She couldn't help herself. With a smack that resounded to the dusty rafters, she slapped him hard across his dirty face. He caught her wrist, and the ugly horse in the stall snorted and stamped impatiently. "It wouldn't be wise to get physical with me, lady," he warned, the tension in the barn snapping as with the current of an electric storm.

But Heather barely heard his warning. She yanked back her hand and glared at him. "You weren't interested in commitments, Turner, remember? You didn't want a family. No strings to tie you down. You were too busy chasing cows and riding bucking horses and being a loner to think about...about..."

"About the fact that I had a kid? How the hell would I know?"

"You didn't stick around long enough to find out, did you?" she accused. Her fury suddenly grew to a living, breathing beast that roared within her. All her pent-up rage exploded. "You don't think I wanted to tell you? I tried, Turner. But you were gone."

"Seems to me you found yourself a patsy."

"A patsy? All I wanted was a father for my child! A man who would care for him, a man who *wanted* him—"

"All you wanted was a rich man, Heather. That's all you've ever wanted. I knew it then and I know it now. But I'm warning you, if you're lyin' to me—"

"I'm not. Adam's your son," she said flatly. "And believe me, if I could change that, I would."

For the first time, he actually seemed to see past his anger. A vein ticked in his forehead and sweat drizzled down his neck. "And why, after six years, do you want to see me now?"

Her stomach knotted with the pain of the truth. "Adam's sick, Turner," she said, her voice barely a whisper.

His spine went rigid and his eyes turned black as night. "Sick?"

"He has leukemia," she said, deciding that it was now or never. She saw the fear flare in his eyes. "The disease...it's in remission. He's been through hell fighting it, but the drugs have seemed to work. Now the doctor is talking about a possible bone-marrow transplant. But Adam has no siblings and...well, I don't match. Even though it's a slim chance, I was hoping...I thought that you might..." She threw her hands up toward the rafters and tears filled her eyes. "Oh, Turner," she whispered, her voice cracking as she thought about losing Adam. "I wouldn't have come, but you're Adam's best hope."

"*If* I'm his father," he said coldly.

"You are, damn it! Do you honestly think I would've wasted my time driving up here, dredging up everything again?" Blinking rapidly, she fingered the clasp of her purse. "I've got a picture—"

"I'll need more proof than that."

"Anything," she whispered, glad that at least they were making headway.

Turner's gaze shifted around the barn quickly, as if he were sizing up his own operation. Nervously, he rubbed the top rail of the stall. "They have tests now—genetic tests that would prove without a doubt—"

"I *know* that, Turner. That's why you should trust me. If I'm lying, I'll be found out. But I'm not. Believe me, I wouldn't have bothered."

That stopped him. His fidgeting hands quit moving. "Does your husband know?"

"Of course my *ex*-husband knows. He knew I was pregnant when we got married. I told him about you." She thought fleetingly of Dennis, of his reaction when she'd first told him she was pregnant with another man's child. He'd been angry, even wounded, and he'd left her mother's house with a screech of tires. But he had come back. Swearing that he loved her. Vowing to look after her and the baby. Promising to give the infant everything it could ever want. And she'd stupidly believed Dennis Leonetti, a man obsessed with her. It all seemed like such a long time ago. And now, staring at Turner, she wondered how she'd ever let the world think that Adam had been Dennis's son.

Turner's jaw tightened, and before he could say anything hateful, she said, "I didn't really know that I was pregnant until you were gone. Then I tried to contact you...but it was impossible. I called the Lazy K. Zeke wouldn't say where you were and for once Mazie kept her mouth shut. Even the other ranch hands played dumb.''

''So you married Leonetti,'' he said, his voice cold as stone.

Why bother explaining? He'd set himself up as judge and jury, tried her and found her guilty. But she couldn't expect much more, she supposed. She dug into her purse, found the picture of Adam and held it out to him. ''This…this is our son,'' she said.

Turner swept the snapshot out of her fingers, and in the half-light within the barn, he squinted at it. His eyebrows knotted in concentration.

Can't you see it, Turner? Doesn't the resemblance leap out at you? He has the same straight, light brown hair, the same gray eyes, the same little cleft in his chin? Oh, God, Turner, he's yours!

A dozen emotions flickered in Turner's eyes. Emotions that were dark and dangerous. His voice, when he spoke, was thick. ''How do you know?'' he asked, and though she'd been prepared for the question, it startled her.

''I was a virgin, remember? You were the first. The only.''

His mouth tightened. He remembered all right. Everything about her. Loving any other woman had never felt so right. Even now, in her expensive clothes and soft leather shoes, she was as attractive to him as she had been as a girl in cutoff jeans and halter tops. ''There could have been others.''

Her steady blue eyes held his. ''There weren't.''

''How do I know—''

''You don't. You have to trust me on this one, Turner. I never made love to anyone but you until I married Dennis—two weeks after the doctor confirmed my pregnancy. You can think what you want of me, but that's the God's honest truth. Adam's yours.''

His heart was pounding so hard he could hear the blood pumping at his temples. She leaned closer to him, and he could see the golden crown of her head, could smell the provocative fragrance of her perfume. Just as before, he found her impossible to resist.

"I wouldn't have come here unless you were my only hope, Turner. It's just that I'm out of options and I would risk anything, even facing you again, to help my boy. I was hoping you'd feel the same way."

Turner's guts twisted. Leukemia! Wasn't that fatal? His mouth turned to sand as he thought about a boy he'd never had the chance to know, a son that he could lose before he'd ever really found him. Damn Heather and her lies! She should have told him. She'd owed him that much. His fingers curled possessively over the slick snapshot. "What if he hadn't gotten sick? Would you have ever told him about me—or let me know I had a kid?" he asked, rage beginning to swell inside him.

"Yes."

"When?"

She hesitated just a second. "When he was eighteen."

"Eighteen!" She had it all planned out. And she'd intended to rob him of ever seeing his boy as a kid. So that they'd never play catch, never ride trails and camp out on the river, never even meet. "Eight-friggin'-teen?" he said in a voice so low he saw the fear register in her eyes.

"He'd need to know someday."

"And me? Did I need to know?"

She shook her head, and there was a trace of sadness in her cold blue eyes. "You gave up that right when you walked away from me and acted as if what we'd shared never existed," she said as icily as if she meant every word.

He started to argue with her. To ask why she'd never returned his calls, why she'd never answered her mail, but he already knew the reasons. By the time he'd returned and started looking for her, she'd already married the son of one of the richest men in the bay area.

Pregnant or not, she'd realized even then what she'd wanted and it had come with a price tag. A price tag he could never afford. He handed her back the picture of Adam and watched as the disappointment registered on her face. "I want to see him," he said, trying to keep his voice level. "Face-to-face. I want to meet my son."

"You will."

"You'll bring him here?"

She was startled. Again, fear registered across her beautiful features. Nervously, she licked her lips, and Turner's diaphragm slammed up to his ribs. "I thought in the city, in the hospital..."

"Does that have to happen immediately?"

"No, right now he's better, but—"

"Then I want to meet him, but not in some sterile hospital room with a bunch of doctors and nurses stickin' tubes and needles in him."

To keep his hands busy, he grabbed a pitchfork and tossed hay into Gargoyle's empty manger. He felt trapped, felt as if he had to move on, and yet he wouldn't have it any other way. If the kid was his, and he was starting to believe Heather, then Turner planned to include the boy in his life.

He shoved the pitchfork in a split bale and leaned upon it. Heather was waiting, her elegant features tense. "Look, no matter what happened between us, I'll do what you want," he said, his heart twisting as the tension left her pretty face. "I'll go to the city, have the tests done. No reason to hold this thing up. If the kid needs a donor and I'm a match, I'll do whatever I have to. No problem."

Relief brought a tremulous smile to her lips, and he anticipated the words of gratitude that were forming on her tongue. She misunderstood and he had to set her straight.

"But that's not the end of it, Heather. As soon as he's well enough and the tests have proven that he's mine, then I want you to bring him back here...and not for an afternoon."

The color in her face turned pasty and her fingers curled into tight little fists. "That might take a while. I don't know when he'll be well enough. The doctors might decide to do the transplant—if it's possible—and he'll need a long recovery."

"Then I'll meet him at your place, but not the hospital. Afterward, when it's all done, and he's well enough to come to the ranch, I want to spend some time with him. Two, maybe three weeks—enough time to get to know the boy."

"That's impossible—"

He picked up the pitchfork and hung it on a nail on the wall. "The way I figure it, you've had him for five years. Now it's my turn."

Panic registered in her eyes. "But he's sick—"

"I wouldn't do anything to jeopardize his health, Heather, but I have a right to know my own boy."

She swallowed hard and sweat collected on her forehead. His reasoning was sound, but a deep fear started to grow deep within her, a fear that if she didn't lose her son to this horrid disease, she might very well lose him to his father. But it was a chance she had to take. She was all out of options. "I...I...suppose if the doctor will approve."

"He will."

She licked her lips and glanced anxiously around the rundown old barn. "But he can't stay here alone."

"I'll be here."

"I know, but he'd be frightened. He doesn't even know you!"

"Whose fault is that?"

"We're not talking about laying blame, Turner. We're talking about my son's well-being!"

"You're not going to bring up some damned nanny to this ranch," he warned, and watched as she squared her shoulders.

"No, Turner, I'm not. But if Adam stays here, so do I."

He started to argue. Hell, the last thing he wanted here was Heather Tremont Leonetti. She'd be in the way. She'd be a distraction. She'd interfere with him getting to know the boy, always overplaying the part of the mother. But he could see by the set of her small jaw that it was all or nothing, and he wasn't enough of a bastard to barter with the boy's health. No way could he say that he'd only agree to the tests if the kid would be allowed to come here alone. A son! He had a son. The very thought knocked the breath out of his lungs. He noticed her watching him and rubbed a hand over his chin.

"All right, lady, you've got yourself a bargain," he said, letting a slow, lazy grin drift across his face. Deliberately, he let his gaze rest for a long moment on the hollow of her throat. "But it's not going to be easy."

"With you, nothing is," she said, not backing down an inch. He approached her and she didn't move; in fact her eyes widened and she parted her lips ever so slightly. If he didn't know better, if he didn't still feel the sting of her hand against his cheek, he'd swear she was coming on to him. But that was crazy, or was it?

The look she sent him fairly sizzled. "I'll call and set up an appointment with the doctor and the hospital," she said, and impulsively he touched her arm.

"I think we should talk some more."

She paused just a second, as if deliberating. "I don't see what good that would do."

"Give me a break, Heather. It's been six years. I think we have a lot to discuss."

"I—I don't know—"

"We'll call a truce. Temporarily at least. There's a lot I want to know." The fingers curling over her forearm tightened and she stared deep into his eyes. "You *owe* me this much."

Quickly, she yanked her arm away. "Let's get something straight, Turner. I don't *owe* you anything. But I know that you have a lot of questions. I—I'll be back later. Right now, I've got to go into town and talk to my mom. Good enough?"

"I guess it'll have to be."

"What time?"

"I'll be through with my chores around seven."

"I'll be back at seven-thirty." With that, she was gone. In a cloud of tantalizing perfume, she stormed away, never even looking down at her blouse where the dirt from his fingertips still stained the silken fabric.

She'd gotten tougher over the years as well as more sophisticated. To Turner's mind, she was more deadly than before, because now, unless she was lying through her beautiful teeth, she had his son!

Heather squinted through the dust that collected on the windshield. Badlands Ranch was located to the northwest of Gold Creek, and the main road leading back to the town was a narrow ribbon of asphalt that wound around the western shore of Whitefire Lake. Through the trees, Heather caught glimpses of the water, now blue and pristine, unlike the white misty lake from which she'd taken a long sip this morning. It had been a foolish ritual, and now, if she hadn't felt so desperate, she would have laughed at herself. But she could barely concentrate on anything except Turner and the fact that he wanted to make love to her again. She'd seen it in his eyes—the passion rising to the surface. And he'd even tried in a crude way to suggest that they could make it happen again. He'd been bluffing at that point, trying to force her out of his life by proving he wasn't the kind of man she wanted.

But he hadn't known how desperate she was. And he hadn't known that this would have been the perfect time to make love to him. And he hadn't known that should she make love to him and become pregnant with his child, she would be giving their only child another chance for survival. But she hadn't been able to do it. She couldn't deceive him so coldly, nor could she plan to conceive one child just to save the life of another.

Or could she?

She'd always wanted another baby. The fact that Dennis had been unable to father children had been a big disappointment for them both. And the thought of giving birth to another son or daughter with Turner as the father touched her in a romantic way that bordered on lunacy. Just because Adam had turned out so well was no reason to think that another child would fit into the life she'd carved out with her son.

But a sibling could save his life. Every doctor she'd talked to had stressed that donors for bone marrow are usually a brother or sister of the recipient. The more siblings a recipient had, the better the chance for a match. Already she knew that she couldn't help her son; there was a strong chance Turner couldn't, either. But a sibling...

The thought turned her stomach. She wouldn't, *couldn't*, even think about another pregnancy, another child.

But if it means Adam's life? And why not have another baby to love? Adam needs a sister or brother and you need another child.

"Another child without a husband. No way," she told herself as she approached Gold Creek. She followed the road past the dip beneath the old railroad trestle and through the sprawling suburbs that were growing eastward into the foothills of the mountains. Several homes were for sale, white-and-red signs for Fitzpatrick Realty posted on the front lawns. She drove past the park where children played in the playground and concrete paths crossed the green, converging in the center where a white gazebo had become a shrine to Roy Fitzpatrick, eldest legitimate son of Thomas Fitzpatrick and the boy Jackson Moore had once been accused of killing.

But that was a long time ago, and now Heather's sister, Rachelle, was planning to marry Jackson. His name had been cleared and some of the scandal of the past had been erased.

She slowed for a stoplight, then turned onto Main Street, past the Rexall Drugstore where, sometimes after school, she and Rachelle and Rachelle's friend, Carlie, had bought sodas at the fountain in the back. Rachelle hadn't much liked Heather tagging along, but Carlie, whose mother had worked at the fountain for years, hadn't seemed to mind that Rachelle's younger sister was always hanging around.

A few blocks farther and she passed the Buckeye Restaurant and Lounge. Her stomach tightened as she heard the country music filtering through the open doors. More than once she'd had to wait at the back door while a busboy or kitchen helper had searched out her father, who, smelling of cigarette smoke and liquor, had stumbled into the parking lot and walked the few blocks back to their house with her.

She pulled up in front of the little cottage where she'd grown up. One story, two bedrooms, cozy but in need of repair, the bungalow had been home, but Heather had only wanted out. Away from a mother and father who bickered continually, and later, away from the scandal that had tainted her family.

Her mother didn't live here now. In fact, Heather owned half the cottage, so all that running hadn't done anything. This still could be her home. She shuddered at the thought. Could she bring Adam here, to grow up riding his bike along the same cracked pavement where she'd cruised along on her old hand-me-down ten-speed?

She didn't stop to think about it for too long. There was a lot to do. Her insides were still in knots because of her having seen Turner again and presenting him with the truth; now she had to do the same with her mother.

"God help me," she whispered as she turned around in the driveway and drove the two miles to her mother's small house on the other side of town. Recently separated from her second husband, Ellen Tremont Little would be in no mood to hear about her youngest daughter's problems.

"I don't believe you!" Heather's mother reached into the drawer where she kept a carton of cigarettes. "This . . . this story you've concocted is some crazy fantasy." She clicked her lighter over the end of her cigarette and took a long drag.

"It's the truth, Mom."

Ellen wrapped one arm around her thickening middle and squinted through the smoke. "But Dennis—"

"Dennis isn't Adam's father."

"He *knew* about this?"

"Yes. From the beginning. Remember the night he left here so angry with me. It was right after I got home from working at the Lazy K. I told him about Turner—"

"Turner?" Ellen's head snapped up. "Not—"

"Turner Brooks."

"Oh, God." She sank into a chair at the table and cradled her head, her cigarette burning neglected in her fingers. "John Brooks's son."

"Yes."

Her mother let out a long, weary sigh, then drew on her cigarette. Smoke drifted from her nostrils. "How will I ever hold my head up in church?" she asked, staring out the window to the bird feeder swinging from the branch of a locust tree. Several yellow-breasted birds were perched on the feeder. "Cora Nelson will have a field day with this. And Raydene McDonald... Dear Lord, it will probably be printed in the *Clarion!*"

"I don't think so," Heather said, and saw her mother attempt a trembling smile.

"Why would you ever want a boy like Turner Brooks when you had Dennis?"

"Don't start with me, Mom," Heather said with a smile, though she meant every word.

"He's never done anything but ride horses and get himself busted up."

"He took care of his father."

Ellen stubbed out her cigarette. "I suppose he did."

"He's not a bad man, Mom."

"So where was he when you were pregnant? He didn't marry you, did he? No... Dennis did." Shoving herself upright, she turned to the dishwasher and started taking out the clean dishes. "We Tremont women have a great track record with men, don't we?" she said, her words laced with sarcasm. "Well, without us, what would the gossips in town do?"

"I'm not ashamed that Turner is Adam's father."

"No, I suppose you're not. But what were you thinking, Heather? Why fall for a rodeo rider when you could have had any boy in town including..." Her voice drifted off. "I guess I'm beginning to sound like a broken record, aren't I? Well...we'll just have to change that. After all, nothing matters but Adam's health, and if Turner's willing to do what he can to save my grandson, then I'll just have to quit bad-mouthing him."

Heather chuckled. "Do you think that's possible?"

"I don't know. But I've accepted Jackson. I *never* thought that would happen."

"Neither did I."

"And he and Rachelle are getting married." She stacked two glasses in the cupboard and wiped her hands. "You know, I was wrong about Jackson—the whole town was wrong about him. Maybe I'll be wrong about Turner, too."

"You are, Mom," Heather said with more conviction than she felt.

"I hope so. For everyone's sake. I hope so." She hung her dish towel on a rack. "Now tell me, what happens if Turner's tissue doesn't match Adam's?"

"Don't even think that way."

"But it's a possibility."

A good one, Heather thought to herself. *What Adam needs is a sister or brother... Oh, God, not this again!*

"He's not in any immediate danger," Heather heard herself say as she repeated the pediatrician's prognosis. "His remission could last for years. If so, he won't need a transplant."

"But if he does?" Ellen persisted.

"Then we'll cross that bridge when we come to it," Heather replied, while she tried to tamp down thoughts of a sibling for her son.

Ellen's brow was drawn into a worried frown. "We'll have to talk to your father and anyone else in the family—any blood relation—who might be able to help the boy."

"Turner will be the most likely donor," Heather said, and tried to still the beating of her heart. She thought of facing him again and her insides went cold. There was still the attraction; she'd felt it in the barn. Now she had to decide how she would deal with him. Would she keep him at arm's length or try to seduce him?

Chapter Seven

Turner was waiting for her. Seated in a worn-out old rocking chair on the front porch, a bottle of beer caught between his hands, he watched as she parked her Mercedes near the barn. "It's now or never," she told herself as she climbed out of the car and slung her purse over her shoulder. She'd changed into a pair of white slacks and a wine-colored T-shirt, pulled her hair back into a ponytail and left her jewelry in her makeup bag back at the cottage.

The evening air was heavy, weighted with the coming night. Insects droned and lavender clouds shifted across the darkening sky. Twilight. A summer evening and she was alone with Turner. Just as she had been six long years before. But now they had a son—a son with an illness that could be fatal. Oh, God, why?

"I thought maybe you'd chicken out," he said, the old chair creaking as he stood.

"Not me." She forced a smile she didn't feel and realized just how isolated they were. No bunkhouse full of ranch hands, no attic rooms with kitchen help, no guests dancing or laughing or playing cards in the dining hall, no Zeke, no Mazie. Just Turner and the windswept hills that were Badlands Ranch.

Her heart drummed loudly and she only hoped that he couldn't hear its erratic beat over the sigh of the wind.

"You didn't have to show up," he said, finishing his beer and setting the empty bottle on the rail of the porch. As he walked down the stairs, she noticed his limp, barely visible, but evidence of the pain his body had endured for a life he loved. "I would have gone through with the tests, anyway."

"I figured I owed you this much," she said, trying not to observe his freshly shaven jaw, or his slate-colored eyes, or the loose-jointed way he sauntered across the hard earth. Or his limp. The reminder of the life he led. In jeans and a faded shirt, with a backdrop of a run-down ranch house and acres of grassland, he was, without exception, the sexiest man she'd ever seen. That was the problem. What they'd shared had been sex—in its young, passionate, raw form. Naively she'd thought she'd loved him; that he'd loved her, but all that had been between them was a hunger as driven as the winds that blow hot through the California valleys in August. Even now, as she tried to seem relaxed, she felt that tension between them, the tug of something wild and wanton in her heart, the hot breath of desire tickling the back of her neck.

"Tell me about Adam," he said. "Where is he now?"

"He's with the baby-sitter, Mrs. Rassmussen. She lives two houses down from mine."

"How sick is he?"

Her heart twisted. "He's in remission. It could last indefinitely, but then again…" She shook her head and bit on her lower lip. "Adam's pediatrician's name is Richard Thurmon—he's the best in San Francisco. I've told him about you and all you have to do is call him. He can tell you anything you want to know."

"I will."

They stood in awkward silence and Turner stared at her, sizing her up, as if he still didn't believe her. "I tried to call Zeke today."

"To check my story."

His lips twitched. "He's in Montana. Won't be back for a couple of weeks."

"What about Mazie?"

"She doesn't remember much about that summer, but she does think you called, that you wanted to talk to me."

"She doesn't remember me practically begging her for your address—for a phone number where I could reach you?" Heather said in disbelief. Though she hadn't confided in Mazie, she'd been near tears, her voice choked with emotion. But Mazie had probably taken more than her share of teary phone calls from women Turner had left behind.

"She didn't say."

"Well, it's the truth, damn it!" Heather cried, then threw her hands up in despair. Turner still acted as if she were a criminal, and she was no better about trusting him. One minute she was fantasizing about him, the next she wanted to wring his neck. "Why don't we go for a ride," she suggested.

"A what?"

"A trail ride. Like we used to."

"Why?" The look he sent her silently called her a lunatic.

"Because I can't just stand here and have you start accusing me of God only knows what! It used to work, you know. Whenever we were angry with each other, we'd ride—get rid of our aggressions. You do have horses around here, don't you? What about Sampson?" She didn't wait for a response, just stormed off toward the barn where she'd seen the ugly reddish horse earlier in the day.

He caught up with her in three long strides. "You're crazy, lady," he accused, as she flung open the barn door and stepped into the dark interior. She reached for a switch, found none and fumbled in the dark. "We have a son, a kid I didn't know about, a boy who needs a transplant, for God's sake, and you want to ride?"

"I just don't want to argue anymore!" She swung around and faced him. High in the rafters of the barn a bat's wings fluttered. "I'm scared, Turner. Scared out of my mind. And I don't want you or anyone else to start in on me about what I did or didn't do wrong. I only want to deal with the here and now!"

"You want me to forget about six years?" he asked, his voice low and angry.

"Yes. Because it doesn't matter. Nothing matters except Adam's health!" She found the latch to a stall and opened it, but the stall was empty.

"For God's sake, Heather, I have questions. A million of them."

"What you have is accusations!"

He grabbed her so quickly that her breath came out in a rush. Suddenly she was slammed against his chest, her back pressed into the rough boards of the barn walls. "I've spent the last six hours wondering how the hell this happened and why you didn't tell me about Adam."

"I explained that I—"

"I heard your story, Heather, but it doesn't wash. You didn't have to jump into marriage right off the bat. You could've waited."

"For how long, Turner?" she asked, tears clogging her throat. "Until you got back to the Lazy K? Until you were through with the circuit? Until you couldn't ride anymore because you'd suffered too many injuries? I had a baby to think about. I didn't have any time to waste."

His lips curled in disgust and his fingers dug into the soft flesh of her arms. "You weren't thinking about the kid. You were worried about your reputation. You'd told me often enough about your sister and what she'd suffered in Gold Creek—and then you turn up pregnant, with no husband. You couldn't face the thought of being a single mother. People would talk. Everyone in Gold Creek would know. You probably couldn't face your parents!"

"Oh, Lord," she whispered, shaking her head. How far apart they were and yet how close. She swallowed the hard lump in her throat and lifted her chin a fraction. "I thought I loved you, Turner. I had myself convinced that you were the man I wanted to spend the rest of my life with. And you walked out. It's that simple."

"Not quite. You were pregnant. I'd say things got a lot more complicated."

She felt the heat of his body, smelled the scent of soap on his skin and stared at the small cleft in his chin. Her breasts were flattened against his chest, her thighs imprisoned by his legs. She ignored the tingle that swept through her blood and told herself that he no longer attracted her. He was a broken-down cowboy, cynical and cold.

"Just what kind of a woman are you?" he asked, but his hard grip loosened a bit.

"I just want to start over," she said. "For Adam's sake."

"Like nothing between us ever happened." His hands moved down her arms to manacle her wrists, and a thrill shot through her—a thrill she refused to acknowledge.

"I...I can't forget what happened, Turner, and I don't expect you to. But if we could just start out without being enemies, it would be best for Adam."

His hands, warm as the breath of summer, tightened a little, and pulled her even closer. She noticed the thin line of his lips, and her stomach seemed to be pressing hard against her lungs, her blood heating despite her determination to ignore his sensuality.

"So what're you going to do, Turner?" she asked with surprising calm. "Are you planning to keep punishing me for the rest of my life—are you going to try and find ways to make me atone for my mistake?"

"Is that what I'm doing? Punishing you?"

His voice was so low, so sexy against her ear that she could hardly respond. But she forced the words past her lips. "I think you plan on making me pay for my mistake for the rest of my life."

He stiffened, and she knew that she'd finally gotten through to him. But he didn't move away, and his body molded over hers as closely as if they were making love. Hard contours pressed intimately to hers and she could hardly catch her breath. The smell of him, the heat of his body, his dark looks as he stared at her assailed her senses, and her mind wandered dangerously backward in time to when she and he had so innocently, so desperately made love. She licked her lips and wondered if he was thinking of kissing her again. Somewhere in the barn a horse snorted.

"My mistake wasn't sleeping with you, Turner. My mistake was loving you and thinking I could make you love me." Her voice was low and she forced her gaze to his. "I

was wrong. All you wanted from me was what I gave you—
a summer fling. A distraction from hard work at the ranch.''

His back teeth ground together and she saw the protests
forming on his tongue. "I cared about you—''

"Don't lie, Turner. It belittles us both and only makes
things wor—''

His mouth slanted over hers and his arms tightened
around her body. His hands pulled her tighter still and her
breath was lost between her throat and her lungs. Raw passion surged between them, racing hot as wildfire through her
blood, pounding in her brain, shutting down all her defenses. The taste and feel of him brought back memories
she'd tried for years to forget. Her body responded of its
own accord, knowing instinctively that this was the man, the
only man, who could arouse a desire so torrid, she lost all
reason and abandoned herself to him.

This can't be happening, she thought wildly, and yet she
was unable to stop the seductive assault of his tongue pressing hard against her teeth, gaining entrance to her mouth
and exploring her with exquisite little flicks that caused her
to tremble inside.

His hands caught in the silver-blond strands of her hair,
forcing her head back farther so that he could kiss her throat
and neck, as if he had every right to kiss her, to touch her,
to make love to her.

Stop him! Stop him now! This can only lead to trouble!
one side of her mind cried desperately, but another part of
her melted against him, thrilled by the sensations he aroused
in her, toying with the idea that making love would be a
good way to bury the pain of the past, to start a new relationship, to... to conceive a child.

She yanked herself away. "No!" she cried, and he jerked
back, lifting his head. What was she thinking? Conceiving
a child. Oh, God, no! She couldn't deceive him. He al-

ready thought she'd used him. She wouldn't do this…. She was shaking so badly, she had to touch the side of the barn for support.

"What the hell?" Turner took a step back and shoved his hands through his hair. He kicked at the stall in frustration. A frightened horse whinnied nervously. Outside a dog barked and in the barn bats took flight yet again.

"I'm sorry, Turner," she said, then hated the weak sound of her apology.

"Hell, Heather, I wasn't going to force you to—"

"Oh, I know that," she said, flustered. Her hands trembled as she finger-combed her loosened hair back to her ponytail and felt like an awkward teenager. "I—I—just don't know if this is such a good idea."

His lips twisted into a cold smile. "I understand," he said, and there was something in his words that forewarned her of dangers to come. "You still don't want a cowboy."

"That's not true—"

"Oh, so you do want a cowboy?"

"Of course not."

A trace of sadness touched his eyes. "There's the problem, Heather. Always has been. You have trouble admitting exactly what it is you do want. You claimed you loved me—yeah, I remember. And you probably believed it yourself. But all along I knew that you thought I wasn't good enough."

"Oh, Turner, that's not true—"

"Of course it is! I wasn't blind, damn it!"

"I loved you!"

"You convinced yourself you loved me so that you wouldn't feel so guilty about what we were doing. You confused love with lust—"

"I never—"

"Oh, yes, Heather," he hissed. "You did. We both did. What we shared, hell, it was the best sex I've ever had—the kind of passion that cut right to the bone and turned me inside out. And you felt it, too." He touched her neck, rubbed the tiny pulse at the base. "You still do. We both do."

She couldn't argue with his logic. Even now, when she burned with fury, his hand touched the hollow of her throat and she wanted to melt. Instead, breathing hard, she swiped his arm away and stepped back from him.

He held up both hands, as if in surrender. "I've never wanted a woman the way I wanted you, Heather. The way I still want you, but I knew, even then, that it wouldn't work between us. All we had was sex—great sex, but that's not enough."

His words stung as surely as if a dart had pierced her heart, draining it slowly of lifeblood. She ached, because he was telling the truth, at least as far as he knew it. Tears welled behind her eyes and she stumbled forward, her hands brushing against the rail of the stall. She had to get out, get away; coming here had been a vast mistake.

His voice jarred her. "The problem was, I didn't have this all figured out then, at least not clearly. I had a gut feeling that you weren't the right kind of woman for me, but I had trouble convincing myself." He leaned his back against the stall and closed his eyes, as if willing his passion to rest. "At least I didn't know until it was too late."

"And then?" she asked, her voice quavering.

"And then I decided I'd take a chance. Hell, why not? It wasn't as if I had this terrific life or anything. I came back home and you were gone. Married already."

"So I was just an alternative to a lonely existence."

"I wasn't sure what you were, Heather, but I couldn't stop myself from coming back." He threw a dark look to the ceiling as if condemning himself. "I draw the line with married women—always have. But with you, it was hard. I even thought about kidnapping you away from Leonetti, just to talk to you, but..." His jaw slid to the side at the irony of the situation. "I heard you were pregnant."

"Oh, God, you thought—"

"I didn't know what to think."

"Turner." She reached for him then, took his callused hand in her smaller fingers and squeezed. Torment wound through her soul. He'd thought she was pregnant with Dennis's child. And why wouldn't he? "I...I'm so sorry."

"So am I, Heather."

"If I'd known you'd come back..."

In the half-light, he stared at her with disbelieving eyes. "What would you have done, Heather? Waited for me?"

"I—I don't know," she admitted, realizing that she couldn't lie ever again. Tears glistened in her eyes and impulsively she threw her arms around the neck of her child's father. She held him close, refusing to sob for the years they hadn't shared together, forbidding the tears to drizzle from her eyes. Her lips moved of their own accord, gently kissing his cheek, and his arms wrapped around her—strong and warm and secure.

Without thought, she closed her eyes and tilted her face upward, molding her mouth to his. A tremor ripped through his body, and his kiss became harder, more insistent.

His arms held her possessively and her knees turned weak. Heat rushed through her veins and his mouth explored the hollows of her cheek and her ears. Desire spread through her veins like liquid fire. She trembled as his hands found the hem of her T-shirt and touched her skin. Sucking in her breath, she felt the tips of his fingers scale her ribs and move upward to cup her breast.

"Heather," he whispered into the shell of her ear, and her legs gave way. Together they tumbled onto the hay-strewn floor of the stall, legs and arms entwined. Dust motes swirled upward and the horse in the stall next door shifted, snorting loudly.

A thousand reasons for stopping him crowded in her mind, but as he lay over her, his rock-hard body fitting against hers, the reasons disappeared and desire, long banked, burst into flame.

As he lifted her shirt over her head, he stared down at her and a small groan escaped him. He pressed his face into the cleft between her breasts and he sighed against her skin. Her nipples grew taut as he removed the rest of her clothes and kissed her flesh, sending shock wave after shock wave of delicious hunger through her.

Her own fingers stripped him of his shirt and trailed in wonder over the hard, sinewy strength of his arms and chest.

Turner's mouth covered hers as he tore off her slacks and underwear and he kicked off his boots and jeans to lie beside her. She circled his chest with her arms and kissed the sworling mat of hair that hid his nipples. He groaned again and trembled.

"I've dreamed of this," he muttered into her hair as he poised himself above her. "I don't think I can...I can't stop."

"Don't stop," she whispered. "Please, don't ever stop."

His mouth slanted over hers and he parted her legs with his knees, hesitating just a second before entering her in one hard thrust.

"Turner, oh, Turner," she cried. The sounds of the night faded, and Heather, driven by a desire so hot she was certain she was melting inside, moved to meet the rhythm of his strokes. She clung to him, her fingers digging into his shoulders, his muscles contracting and flexing as she soared higher and higher, like a bird taking flight, rising to some unseen star until the night seemed to explode around them.

And Turner, his body drenched in sweat, fell against her, crushing her breasts and breathing as if he'd run a marathon.

"Oh, God, Heather, what're we doing?" he whispered, kissing her naked chest. Hay and straw stubble poked at her skin and she almost laughed.

"Making up for lost time." She held him close, kissing his crown, smiling sadly as she noticed the stubborn swirl of light hair at his crown—so like Adam's. Her throat grew thick and tears once again threatened her eyes as she realized that she was now, and forever would be, a part of his life. His lover. The mother of his child. The woman he alternately hated and made love to. But she would never be his wife, would never be the woman to whom he would turn when he needed compassion or empathy or comfort.

He rolled off her and cradled her head against his shoulder. Together they stared through the darkness up to the rafters. Turner's voice was still raspy when he said, "This was probably a mistake."

"Probably." Her heart felt bruised.

"But not our first."

"No."

"And certainly not our last." He sighed heavily. "You've always been a problem for me, Heather," he admitted. "I've never known exactly what to do with you."

Just love me, she silently cried, but knew her sentiment was foolish, the product of an emotion-wrenching day mixed with the slumberous feel of afterglow. "All I want from you is what you've already agreed to do," she said softly. "You don't have to worry about anything else."

"But I will want my time with him. You've had him a long time. Now it's my turn."

"I can't—"

"Shh." He said, kissing her again and stoking the long-dead fires to life once more. Heather couldn't stop herself, and saw no reason to. She'd leave a little later, resume her life in San Francisco and deal with the aftermath of making love to Turner then. But for now...she pressed her lips to his.

Chapter Eight

Turner threw a change of clothes into a battered old duffel bag and caught a glimpse of himself in the mirror. He didn't look any different than he had a week ago, and yet now he was a father... or at least it was beginning to look that way. And he was involved with Heather Tremont—make that Heather Leonetti—again. Even now, at the thought of her lying in his arms, his loins began to ache.

He forced his thoughts away from her lovemaking and concentrated on her tale about him fathering Adam. He couldn't see any reason Heather would lie, no angle she could play for her own purposes. He still didn't trust her, but he did believe that she was telling the truth about the boy—and that, yes, he was a father. He also didn't doubt that she loved the boy very much. He'd recognized the fire in her eyes when she'd talked of saving Adam's life, seen the fear tighten the corners of her mouth when she'd thought Turner might try to take the boy away.

He'd considered it, of course. For hours on end. His initial shock at having learned he was a father had given way to a quiet rage that swept through his bloodstream and controlled his mind. She'd had no right, *no friggin' right,* to keep Adam's existence from him.

And then to marry Leonetti and pass the kid off as his. He'd thought a lot of things about her in the past, but he hadn't really blamed her for their breakup. He'd been the one who had taken off, and though he'd been furious to find out that she'd gotten herself married before he returned to Northern California, he'd felt as if he'd asked for it.

He had felt a little like a fool, for he'd half believed her when she'd vowed she loved him six years ago. She'd seemed so sincere, and she'd given herself to him without any regrets, so he'd been confident that he'd been first in her heart.

Then she'd refused to answer his letters or return his calls and within weeks married the boy she'd sworn she didn't care a lick about. It had seemed, at the time, that she'd only been experimenting with sex, sowing some wild oats with a cowboy before she turned back to the man and the life-style she'd always wanted.

But he'd been wrong. Because she'd been pregnant with his kid. Her pregnancy didn't change the fact that she hadn't wanted anything more to do with him—hell, she admitted it herself that she would have kept Adam's parentage a secret for a long time if it hadn't been for this illness. This damned illness. He'd read up on leukemia and it scared him to his very soul.

It seemed too cruel to believe that he would be given only a short time with the boy and then have him snatched away.

Turner didn't believe in God. But he didn't disbelieve, either. He'd been raised a half-baked Protestant by his mother, but had developed his own reverence for the land

and nature after her death, blaming God as well as John Brooks for taking his mother from him. In the past few years he hadn't thought about religion much one way or the other, but now, when his son's life was nailed on the hope of a team of doctors in San Francisco, Turner wanted very much to believe in God.

Frowning at the turn of his dark thoughts, he grabbed his duffel from the bed and tossed it over his shoulder. He shot a glance to the sturdy oak frame of the double bed he'd slept in for as long as he could remember and tried to picture Heather lying with him on the sagging mattress, beneath the faded old patchwork quilt his grandmother had pieced. Heather with her calfskin shoes, diamond earrings and expensive suits. No, that mirage wouldn't come to life before his eyes. He was just being foolish.

He walked down a short hallway to the kitchen where Nadine was scrubbing an old kerosene lamp he used when the power went out. She'd tied her hair back into a ponytail and her cheeks were flushed from working on the floor and counters. Seeing his reflection in the brass works of the lamp, she smiled. "Thomas Fitzpatrick called while you were in the barn."

Turner's jaw tightened. "Some people just don't know when to give up."

She looked at him quickly, then her eyes fell on his duffel bag and her lips turned down a little at the corners. "Sometimes, when people want something desperately, they can't quit."

"Fitzpatrick never gives up."

"So they say. So... you're all packed?"

"I guess."

Turning, she attempted to hide a sliver of sadness in her eyes. "You're going to the city?"

"Hard to believe, isn't it?"

"There must be a reason."

Turner offered her his lazy grin. "Maybe it's time I got more sophisticated."

She swallowed a smile. "Well, be sure to tell me all about the opera and the ballet when you get back."

"I will."

She set the lamp on the windowsill and snipped off the extra leaves of three roses she'd left in the sink. "Why do I have the feeling that your trip has something to do with all those calls from Heather Leonetti?"

"I don't know. You tell me," he teased, then regretted the words when she pricked her finger on a thorn and avoided his eyes as she muttered something under her breath. She placed the roses in a vase and set them on the table—her last chore before she left each week.

"You don't really have to bother with those," he said, motioning to the heavy-blossomed flowers. "I'll be gone—"

"I like to," she cut in. "You could use more of a woman's touch around here."

"You think so?"

"I know it."

"Then why am I happy with the way things are?"

"'Cause you're a bullheaded fool, Turner Brooks, and if you think you're happy, I strongly suggest you take a good long look in the mirror." She grabbed her bucket and supplies and swung out the door.

Turner watched her leave. He should've told her the truth, explained about Heather and the boy. But how could he, when he barely understood it himself? It was his problem, keeping things bottled up, never sharing with anyone, but he didn't figure now was the time to tell Nadine his life story.

Right now, all he could worry about was the son he'd never met. And there was other, unfinished business he had to deal with. As he watched Nadine's dusty Chevy pull out of the yard, he picked up the phone and dialed the number of the Lazy K.

Mazie answered on the third ring. After a short discussion on the fact that she hadn't seen Turner for too long a period, she told him that Zeke was still in Montana, scouting up livestock, where he'd been for the past week and a half. If Turner would like, Mazie would give him a message.

"I'll call back," Turner replied, as he had the other two times he'd called. He didn't want Mazie or anyone else from the Lazy K involved. If Zeke had lied way back when, if he hadn't bothered to tell Turner that Heather had been looking for him six years ago, Turner wanted to hear it from the older man himself.

Heather wasn't lying about Adam. Turner had determined that she loved the boy and would never have sought Turner out unless she was desperate, which she was. No—he was certain now that the boy was his, but he still didn't trust her—not completely.

But if she only wanted Turner for his bloody bone marrow, then why make love to him—nearly seduce him? It didn't fit. He wanted to believe that she still cared for him, but he'd been fooled once before. No. Heather wanted something from him, something more.

He glanced at the acres of ranch land he owned free and clear. Thomas Fitzpatrick was more than interested in the land—the old man had called him just yesterday with another ridiculous offer, but Turner had held firm. A strange, uncomfortable thought crossed his mind and drew his brows into a knot of concentration. Jackson Moore, the man Heather's sister was planning to marry, was Thomas's son, his firstborn, the only decent male descendent left since Roy had been killed and Brian had bilked his father out of part of his fortune. Was it possible that Heather was trying to get close to Turner to get him to sell his land to Fitzpatrick? Maybe the old man had offered her a cut of the profits. Turner wouldn't be surprised. Fitzpatrick would stoop as low as a snake's belly to get what he wanted, and Heather— well, her track record proved how she felt about money and what it could buy. If Fitzpatrick had gotten to her... But that was too farfetched. Or was it?

Bile rose in the back of Turner's throat as he climbed into his pickup. First things first. He'd do what he had to do for his boy, and then he'd deal with Heather, find out just exactly what made her tick.

"He won't sell." Brian Fitzpatrick pulled at the knot of his tie as he flopped into one of the plush chairs near his father's desk on the third floor of the old hotel that now housed Fitzpatrick, Incorporated. "For some reason, Turner Brooks has decided to keep hold of that miserable scrap of land for the rest of his damned life."

Thomas studied his son carefully. Brian had never been his favorite; in fact he'd once, years ago, referred to the boy as a "backup" for his firstborn, golden boy, Roy. Although Roy hadn't really been his eldest. Thomas's firstborn had been a bastard, born out of wedlock to a woman Thomas had never been able to forget. Oh, he'd stopped his affair with Sandra Moore thirty years before, but he couldn't kid himself. Never once in all his years of marriage to June did he feel that same exquisite passion he'd had with Sandra.

And June had never let him forget it.

Oh, well, it was all water under the bridge, but it seemed ironic that of his only two living sons, one hated his guts, and the other was a weakling, a boy who'd never grown up, a man who had skimmed money from the logging company. Thomas was torn. By greed and the need to pull his family—all of his family—together. As much as he wanted the Brooks ranch, he wished he could make things right with Jackson. But what he'd put the boy through was unthinkable. He didn't blame Jackson for despising him.

It seemed as if his life had turned upside down ever since that Tremont girl—the reporter—had come back to town, wagging her cute little tail and luring Jackson back here.

Jackson. His insides shredded. Now there was a son of whom a man could be proud. But he couldn't think of pride right now. His mind was boggled with more important matters. Though few people knew it, Fitzpatrick, Incorporated was teetering on the brink of bankruptcy. Thomas had spent a lot of money greasing some palms in a senatorial bid that hadn't gotten off the ground. Now, with the truth about Roy's death, any political chances he'd had were gone. Besides which, logging was off and Brian had skimmed enough off the top to break a weaker company and the rest of his businesses were recession-weary. June was talking about an expensive divorce, and the cost of defending his son and daughter-in-law for their part in Roy's death was crippling.

And he'd made a decision about the house at the lake. He and his wife had never gone there, not since Roy was killed over twelve years before. It belonged to Jackson—if he'd take it—for all the pain he'd suffered at his father's hand. It wasn't much and Jackson would probably laugh in his face, but in Thomas's mind the land and house were the boy's.

But that didn't stop his need for dollars. Though the house and grounds at the lake cost him money in taxes and upkeep every year, they were valuable and June would hit the roof when she found out. Too bad. She was to blame as much as he.

And there were ways to make money. If Thomas knew nothing else, he knew how to turn a buck. He knew there was oil on Badlands Ranch. The geological tests he'd done on the surrounding acreage that he already owned had proved him out. If only he could find a way to make Turner Brooks budge. Money didn't seem to matter to Brooks—the damned cowboy was as stubborn as some of those sorry animals he tried to tame.

"So what have we got on Turner Brooks?" Thomas asked as Brian, restless, had shoved himself to his feet and walked to the bar. Brian poured them each a shot of Scotch.

"Not much. His old man was a drunk—killed his mother in that pickup wreck years ago."

"I remember," Thomas clipped out, irked that he'd sold the ranch for the pitiful amount of insurance money John had inherited at his wife's death. Brooks had mortgaged the rest of the debt and Thomas had been sure that John would drink himself into oblivion and default on the note. At which point Thomas had planned to step in and buy the place back for a song. That way, the Fitzpatricks would have collected the insurance money as well as ended up with the ranch. But Turner—damn that cowpoke—had always scraped together enough cash to keep the place afloat. How he'd done it, Thomas couldn't figure out.

"Well, when Turner sets his mind to do something, it would take an act of God to change it," Brian observed, handing his father the drink. "Brooks spent a lot of time taking care of his old man, getting him out of jams. Then John's liver gave up the ghost a few years back. I don't think there's more to his life than that."

"Everybody's got a past," Thomas said. He sipped the Scotch and enjoyed the burn that followed the liquor down his throat. "My guess is that there's something more important to Brooks than the ranch. All we have to do is figure out what it is."

Brian shrugged. "I'll look into it."

Not good enough. Brian was a bumbler. He'd cut corners. "Hire a detective."

"Do you really think—"

Thomas slammed his empty glass onto the desk. "Get the best P.I. that money can buy! Once we find out what skeletons Brooks has tucked away in his closet, then we can deal with him!"

Brian didn't need to be told twice. He finished his drink and was out the double doors of Thomas's office. But the old man wasn't satisfied. He walked to the window, where he could spy down on the parking lot. His white Mercedes hadn't moved and Brian's sleek green Jaguar was parked in the next spot. Within seconds Brian emerged from the back of the building. But he wasn't alone. Melanie Patton, Thomas's secretary, was with him. They shared a stolen kiss and Thomas's stomach turned to ice. No wonder the boy couldn't keep his mind on anything important.

Brian climbed into his Jaguar and roared off, but Thomas knew that he'd have to handle Turner Brooks himself.

Heather drove home from her gallery by rote, stopping automatically at the stop signs, slowing for corners, accelerating up the steep streets of San Francisco without even thinking. Pictures of Adam flashed through her mind. She remembered bringing him home from the hospital, giving him his first bath, watching anxiously as he tried to skateboard at four.... Oh, God, her life had been empty until he'd arrived. A lump settled in her throat. By the time she'd parked in the garage, on the lowest level of her home in Pacific Heights, the reality that Adam's life was in jeopardy nearly incapacitated her. What if she lost Adam? What if the boy died? Her own life would be over.

Her heart froze and she could barely breathe. A cold, damp sweat clung to her skin as she sat behind the wheel, unable to move. "You can't let it happen," she muttered, not knowing if she was talking to herself or to God.

She was in her mid-twenties and she suddenly felt ancient. Her legs barely carried her up the first flight, from the garage to the kitchen level, above which two more stories loomed in this prestigious part of the city.

"Mommy!" She heard Adam's squeal as she opened the door. Fifty-three pounds of energetic five-year-old came barrelling toward her, nearly throwing her off balance as Adam flung himself into her waiting arms.

Oh, precious, precious baby, she thought, squeezing her eyes against tears. Her throat worked over a huge lump. "How're ya, sport?" she said, managing a smile.

"Good!" he replied, though his skin was pale, and dark smudges beneath his eyes belied his insistence that he felt fine.

"And you were good for Aunt Rachelle?"

"Of course," he said, his impish eyes gleaming. He wrinkled a freckled nose. "She's crazy about me."

"Is she?" Heather couldn't help laughing, despite her fears about Adam's future. Adam was precocious and she overindulged him terribly, but she couldn't help herself.

"You bring me a treat?" Adam demanded.

"Did I ever," she replied, opening her purse and finding a minuscule little car, part of a set. She had the entire collection hidden in a closet upstairs, and when she left Adam, she always slipped a tiny car into her purse to surprise him when she returned. Today's gift, a candy-apple-red racing car, was unlike the taxi, ambulance and garbage truck he'd already placed in his toy box.

"Oh, wow!" Adam's eyes, gray and round, lit up. He scrambled out of her arms and began moving the tiny vehicle over the floor, the tables, the plants and everything else in his path as he made rumbling race-car noises deep in his throat.

The stairs squeaked. Heather glanced up as Rachelle descended from the upper living room level. Sunlight, refracting from the leaded windows over the landing turned her hair a reddish mahogany color for an instant. Tall and willowy, with intense hazel eyes, the "levelheaded one" of the two Tremont sisters, Rachelle was four years older than Heather and soon to be married to Jackson Moore, a New York lawyer who had once been the bad boy of Gold Creek. "I thought I heard you," Rachelle said, questions in her eyes. Though Heather had confided to her older sister about Adam's paternity, Rachelle was still a little hurt that her younger sister hadn't told her the truth long ago.

"Turner will be here a little later." Heather's nerves were strung tight. "He's already at the hospital, being typed." She thought about her conversations with Turner—short and to the point. All business. As if they'd never kissed, never touched, never made love in the hay...

"What happens then?"

Heather snapped herself back to the present and caught Rachelle observing her. Damn her sister's reporter instincts. Heather sometimes felt she couldn't do anything without Rachelle guessing her motives. "If the marrow's a match, we go through the procedure—when the doctor says it's the right time. Once Adam's given a clean bill of health, so to speak, we all go back to his ranch."

"And if the tissue doesn't match?"

"Don't even think that way," Heather said softly. "This has got to work." Her fists closed in silent determination. "It's got to!" There were no other alternatives.

Rachelle skated a glance down Heather's sleek dress and coordinated jewelry. "And then you're off to the ranch? Why is it I can't see you branding calves or hauling hay or whatever else it is they do at a place named Badlands?"

"You'd be surprised," Heather replied.

"I'd be flabbergasted."

Adam ran his racing car around a potted fern, and Rachelle hugged her sister. "We'll get through this. All of us," she insisted. She was always so positive and levelheaded, though now her hazel eyes were shadowed with worry.

"I will—"

"Hey, lookie, Auntie Rachelle!" Adam held up his new prize, the little red Porsche. He was beaming ear to ear.

"Boy, isn't that something?" Rachelle bent on one knee to examine the tiny car. "I bet you could win the Daytona 500 with that rig."

"I could even win the 'Tona five million!" Adam assured her confidently and snatched his small prize from her hand.

Rachelle glanced over her shoulder to Heather, still standing near the stairs. "You spoil him, you know."

"I know." Heather felt that infinite fear again, that she was tumbling through dark space to a cold, black hole where she would never see her son again. "But it won't hurt him."

"Don't worry, Heath. We'll work this out," Rachelle said firmly, as if she could read Heather's mind. "Come on, I'll buy you a cup of coffee."

"With a shot of brandy?"

"Whatever you want," Rachelle agreed, walking quickly into the kitchen. Heather followed behind, her own steps seeming to drag on the shiny mahogany floors. This house, once her pride and joy, seemed lifeless, as if it, too, had lost its vitality. The antiques and objets d'art were meaningless;

even her own work, paintings created with love and patience, seemed frivolous. All that mattered was Adam.

Rachelle was already pouring black coffee into heavy mugs as Adam careened into the room. "Hot chocolate for me," he ordered. "With marshmallows."

"You got it, kid." Rachelle winked at her nephew.

Heather slid into a chair and Adam crawled into her lap. He suddenly wrapped his arms around her neck. "Mommy, you sad?" he asked, wide eyes searching hers.

"No," she lied, her heart wrenching.

"Good. I don't like it when you're sad."

Rachelle turned to the cupboard, ostensibly to find the marshmallows, but not before Heather noticed the tears shining in her older sister's eyes. Even Rachelle, stalwart and sane in any crisis, was shaken this time.

Heather hugged her boy closer. *Just let him live,* she silently prayed, *and I'll be the best mother in the world.*

Chapter Nine

The doorbell chimed for the second time as Heather raced down the stairs. She checked the window and felt her heart take flight as she saw Turner, his arms crossed over his chest, his face shadowed by the brim of his Stetson. He was dressed in a clean pair of jeans and a blue cambric shirt, open at the throat. His eyes were dark and guarded but he didn't seem as threatening as he had when they'd first met in his barn. Neither were they glazed with passion as they'd been when she'd last seen him.

He'd had time to pull himself together, she realized, and they'd talked several times on the phone—short, one-sided conversations where she'd explained what he would have to do once he came to the city. He'd accepted her instructions with only quick questions and no arguments.

She opened the door. "Turner," she said, and hated the breathless quality in her voice. "Come in. Are you finished at the hospital?"

"For now. There was some sort of delay, then it took longer than they thought. The doctor will call us both when the results are in." He glanced at the exterior of the house. "Had a little trouble finding this place."

"Well, you made it." His gaze touched hers and her lungs seemed tight. She held the door open for him and he crossed the threshold slowly, his gaze moving up the polished walnut banister, over the gleaming wainscoting and wallpaper, resting for a second on one piece of art or another, before traveling to the Oriental carpets that covered the hardwood floors.

She'd never been self-conscious of her house before, but under his silent, seemingly condemning stare, the baskets filled with cut flowers and live plants seemed frivolous, the matching overstuffed furniture appeared impractical, the shining brass fixtures ostentatious.

"Adam's in his room."

"Asleep?"

"Not yet. I just put him down. I knew you were coming, but it was so late..." Her words trailed off and she licked her lips nervously. Lord, this was awkward. "Come on up." She led him up another flight of stairs and pushed open the door to Adam's room. The bedside lamp was still lit. Adam lay under a down comforter, his light brown hair sticking at odd angles. He was breathing loudly, nearly snoring, and Heather guessed he was pretending to be asleep. His red bedspread matched the curtains surrounding his bay window and contrasted to the border of wallpaper that rimmed the top of his walls. A built-in desk and bookcase housed toys, books, blocks and an ant farm. "Adam? Honey, are you awake?" He snored loudly as she crossed the room and touched his shoulder.

Two bright eyes flew open and he giggled. "I tricked you!"

"You sure did." As Heather sat on the edge of the bed, she caught a glimpse of Turner from the corner of her eye. Her heart felt as if it would break. Here they were, a family, at least in biological terms, together for the first time. "There's someone I want you to meet."

Adam shoved himself up from his covers and cocked his head up to see the big man standing behind his mother. "Who're you?" he asked, rubbing his eyes and yawning.

For once Turner didn't have a quick comment. He glanced at Heather, who shook her head ever so slightly, and he extended his hand to Adam's. "Turner Brooks. I...I knew your mother a long time ago." Slowly he released his son's hand.

Heather's throat swelled shut. She had to blink back unnecessary tears. "There's a chance Mr. Brooks—"

"Turner, for now," he cut in.

Heather stiffened. "There's a chance Turner might be able to help us when you go to the hospital."

"I *hate* the hospital!" Adam said firmly.

"You and me both." For the first time, Turner grinned. "They stuck a needle in me this long," he said, spreading his hands wide.

"Turner!"

"They did?" Adam was suitably impressed.

"Mr. Brooks tends to exaggerate," she said, though Adam's eyes gleamed.

"Only a little bit," Turner said. He sat on the edge of the bed and the mattress creaked a little. "When you get the okay from the doctor, your mama promised that you can come visit me at my ranch. Would you like that?"

"A ranch? You got a ranch? With horses and tractors and cows and Indians and—"

"No Indians," Turner said. "The rest comes with the place."

Adam's eyebrows drew together and he looked at his mother. "We goin' on a vacation?"

"Something like that."

"Is Daddy coming?"

Heather's heart nearly stopped. She noticed Turner stiffen and a muscle suddenly came to life, working reflexively in his jaw. "No, honey. This time it'll just be you and me."

Adam glanced warily at Turner, as if for the first time suspecting a threat to his mother's affection. "When?"

Heather stole a quick look at Turner. "As soon as Dr. Thurmon says it's okay."

"I *hate* the doctor."

Turner ruffled the boy's fine hair. "The doctor's a good guy. He's gonna help us all."

Adam yawned.

"You'd better go to sleep," Heather suggested. She didn't know just how much of this tender scene she could take. Turner wasn't her husband, he'd never met Adam before in his life, and she was beginning to feel maudlin, as if this were some great reunion.

"I'm not tired," Adam argued, though he tried vainly to swallow another yawn and his eyelids drooped. "Read me a story."

"Honey, it's late and—"

"Oh, pleeease!"

"I'll tell you a story," Turner offered, and Heather's throat turned to cotton. Turner's campaign to win his son was starting already.

"It's late. I don't think—"

"It'll be all right," Turner said with a quiet authority that caused fear to settle in her heart. He sat on the edge of the bed looking too tall, too ranch-tough, too damned cynical to be thinking of bedtime stories.

"Tell me about the Indians!"

"I already told you there aren't any Indians at the ranch, and besides, I think the term is Native American. So unless you want to get scalped—"

"Turner!" Heather cut in again.

"Just joking."

"He's only five, for crying out loud!"

Turner clucked his tongue and smiled at Adam. "What's wrong with your mom? No sense of humor?"

"I have—"

"Tell me! Tell me!" Adam demanded, bouncing on the bed.

This was going from bad to worse and quickly. Heather tried to intervene, but Turner grabbed hold of her hand and stared up into her eyes. "It's all right," he said calmly, though his voice sounded deeper than she remembered. Her pulse jumped where his fingertips brushed her wrist. "The boy and I need to talk."

Her heart tore a little. "But—"

"But nothing." The fingers around her hand tightened ever so slightly and she was reminded of the power he had over her. Turner's gaze slid back to his son. "How about if I told you about the wild horses I've ridden?"

Adam's eyes rounded. "Wild ones? Really?"

"Broncos, mustangs, you name it!" Heather heard the ring of pride in his voice.

"No way," Adam said, but his face was filled with silent adoration.

"Yes way." Turner smiled at his boy and Heather's insides shredded. When Turner glanced back at her, she received the unspoken message. "I remember one particularly wild bronco named Daredevil. Coal black. Eyes that were nearly red, he was so mean."

"Turner, please!" she cut in, shaking her head. "Horses aren't mean."

"You've never tried to tame Gargoyle," he replied with a lopsided grin, then shrugged. "Well, your mom's right. Most horses aren't mean, but old Daredevil, he had the worst reputation on the rodeo circuit. No one wanted to ride him. But I didn't have a choice, when they drew my number in Pendleton that year, I ended up on Daredevil."

"Tell me! Tell me!" Adam said, wiggling up to a sitting position, all thoughts of sleep driven from his mind.

Heather started to protest. "This wasn't the idea—"

"Sure it was," Turner replied, his face etched in stone. "This was all part of the bargain. Remember? I go through with the tests and you—"

"Scaring Adam wasn't part of the deal."

"I'm not scared!" Adam protested, his brow furrowing in disgust.

"Leave us alone, Heather. The boy wants a bedtime story."

The small of her back turned to ice at the warning hovering in the air. With a few simple words he could destroy her entire life. All he had to do was tell Adam he was his father. Everything she'd worked so hard for would crumble and she would be the bad guy—the creator of the big lie.

"Just remember, he's only five!" Her heart heavy, she walked out of the room with leaden footsteps. A thousand emotions knifed through her. This was only fair, one part of her screamed. Turner deserved to know his boy and Adam had the right to know his father. There was also Turner's sacrifice to consider. He'd agreed to leave his ranch, come to San Francisco and help her—perhaps save the life of a boy he'd never known existed.

And yet she was petrified. Afraid that Turner, with his ranch and horses and tales of wild West stories would seduce her son from her. Though Adam had been raised with anything money could buy, he wasn't always happy and

Heather knew she spoiled him rotten. Ever since Adam had been born and Dennis's reaction to his "son" hadn't been as enthusiastic as he'd promised, Heather had overcompensated, indulging the boy. And then the first signs of his illness and the horrid diagnosis. She'd been alone then. Dennis had lost his fascination with her.

"I'm sorry, Heather," Dennis had apologized, looking weak, his dark eyes frightened. "I just didn't figure on this.... I don't know what to do."

"He needs you now," Heather had told him, and Dennis had nodded, but never once picked up the boy he'd claimed to be his son. Almost as if he were afraid he'd catch the disease, Dennis had become more and more absent. They were separated soon after the diagnosis, divorced not long after. Dennis hadn't even fought her for custody. In fact, he'd given her the house, her car and the gallery just to end it quickly.

As anxious as he'd been to marry six years before, he'd been even more anxious to divorce. He'd found someone else, someone less complicated, someone without a sick child.

She heard the scrape of Turner's boot as he entered the room, and when she turned to face him, she found a new determination in his gaze. "This can't go on, you know."

"What can't?" she asked, hoping to sound naive, when she knew with a certain dread what was coming. Her hands trembled a little and she motioned him into the living room. Deciding that playing coy with Turner had never been a good idea, she admitted, "You don't have to explain—I know." She felt as cold as ice as she stared out the window to the winking lights of the city and the dark, reflective waters of the bay. Wrapping her arms around her middle, she told herself that it would be all right. That as long as Adam was healthy, nothing else mattered. That it was important for the boy to have a father—a man he could look up to, a man who would love him. But still she was frightened. "What do you want, Turner?" she asked again, in a voice that seemed detached from her body. A few cars passed on the street below the window, their headlights causing an uneven illumination in the room.

"After this is over, I want to be part of his life."

"How big a part?" She reached for a lamp switch, but Turner's hand stayed hers.

"I want to be his father."

"You are—"

"I mean day-to-day, Heather. Every day."

"But that's impossible," she said, her throat catching.

"Not if you move to Gold Creek."

She felt as if she'd stopped breathing. Move to Gold Creek? Oh, Lord. She couldn't speak for a minute, but finally found her tongue. "Are you out of your mind?" She whirled on him and saw that his eyes were dark and serious. "Are you really suggesting that..." Her voice failed her. He wasn't kidding. The look on his face was deadly serious, and Heather was suddenly very frightened. She'd known he'd demand partial custody, but she'd thought he'd only want a few weeks in the summer—maybe Christmas vacation and those would be hard enough to give up—but *this,* this insane plan for her to move back to the small town where she'd been raised... It was impossible. "I'd die in Gold Creek."

"Adam would be closer to me."

"Until a few days ago, you didn't even know you had a son and now—"

"Yes, and now I want him. And I'll do anything, got it? I mean *anything* to have him close."

"You can't be serious," she whispered.

"Oh, but I am, Heather," he said with a deadly calm that drove a stake of desperation into her heart.

The room was dark, and now the shadows seemed to envelop them. "You can't walk into this house and turn my life upside down just because—"

"—because I found out I have a son. Because for six years we've both been living a lie? Because I've discovered that my kid, *my* sick kid, is the most important thing in my life?" His hands were suddenly on her forearms, gripped in the fury that consumed him. "You walked into my barn and turned my life inside out, lady."

"You left me!"

"I never said I'd stay."

"Then don't start interfering now."

His eyes slitted and the hands upon her forearms clenched harder. "This isn't about sex. This isn't about love. This is about our child. And if you have some lame-brain notion that I'll do my part as a biological parent, donate whatever it is Adam needs and then just leave you alone until you have another crisis, guess again. I'm here for the duration, Heather, and you'd better get used to that idea."

"I—I know," she said, her throat catching. "But don't think you can start bossing me around, Turner. You're not my husband!"

As soon as she'd said the words, she wished she could call them back.

Turner's eyes flashed fire.

A knot formed in her throat, but she wasn't going to break down. She had shed her tears for Turner a long time ago and she was through. Wrenching free of his grasp, she turned on the switch to the gas starter in the fireplace and struck a match. Immediately the room was lighter, the gas flames flickering blue and yellow against an oak log. She felt him watching her. Nervous, she asked if he wanted a drink and when he declined, she reached into a liquor cabinet, found an old bottle of bourbon and poured them each a splash in the bottom of two glasses. "You may not need a drink, but I think I do," she said, handing him one of the glasses.

"No one *needs* a drink."

"Okay, so I want one." She sipped the hard liquor, and it burned the back of her throat, scorching all the way to her stomach. With a hiss and crackle, the moss on the oak log caught fire and sent out an orange glow throughout the room.

Turner sipped his drink, but his face muscles didn't relax and he looked out of place, a range-hard cowboy caught in a frivolous living room filled with women's art and furniture. "I think you'd better explain a few things," he said quietly.

"Like what?"

"How about starting at the beginning. Tell me why you married Leonetti. Why you didn't contact me."

She wanted to scream at him, to tell him to leave them both alone, that she didn't need this emotional torture, but she knew in her heart she was wrong. Adam needed him, and a deep, traitorous part of her needed him, too.

Unsteady at that realization, Heather sat on the wide windowseat, her knees tucked up beneath her chin, her drink forgotten. She began to tell him everything she could remember. Turner lowered himself to the floor, propped his back against the couch and stretched his legs toward the fire.

And for the next hour and a half, Heather explained about her realization that she was pregnant, of her calls to Mazie and Zeke at the Lazy K, of Dennis's anger, then acceptance. "Believe it or not, he wasn't a monster. He was obsessed with me back then, though I really don't know why, I guess because I was the only girl who'd ever said no to him and because I wasn't acceptable to his parents. They'd heard the gossip about my family, knew my sister's reputation was destroyed. Then there was the scandal with my dad when he married a woman younger than either of his daughters. We Tremonts weren't exactly blue bloods. So Dennis's folks were distraught to say the least. They were hoping he'd find some nice girl in college whose family was from 'old money.' " She laughed a little when she remembered the horror that the elder Leonettis had expressed at their son's choice of wife. "I wasn't even from 'new money.' Dennis's father offered to buy me out, but Dennis got wind of it and by the end of the week we'd eloped."

"How do they feel about Adam?" Turner asked, a possessive flame leaping in his eyes as he swirled his drink and watched the fire play in the amber liquor.

"Ambivalent, I guess. I would've thought they would have been all over the Leonetti heir, but, though they were never unkind to him, Adam just wasn't all that interesting to either of them. I expected some kind of custodial fight when we were getting divorced, but by then Dennis didn't want any part of Adam and his folks never once called him. My guess is that Dennis told them the truth—that Adam doesn't have a drop of Leonetti blood in him."

"So Dennis has given up all his parental rights?"

"He knew that sooner or later, with Adam's condition, the truth would bear out."

"So just because he didn't sire the kid, suddenly Adam's not good enough! Son of a bitch, what a great guy!" Turner's rage twisted his handsome features, making him seem fierce and dangerous. "You really know how to pick 'em, don't ya?"

"That I do," she replied, and the room grew quiet except for the soft hiss of the fire.

She twirled her drink in her hands, watched the reflections of the flames against the amber liquor. "We aren't here to discuss Dennis." She took another sip of bourbon and felt the first tingle of warmth run through her blood. "I'll tell you anything you want to know about Adam, but as far as my marriage is concerned, all you need to know is that it's over and Dennis doesn't have much interest in my son."

"*Our* son," he corrected quickly, and her throat tightened.

"Our son."

"Which brings us back to square one. What're we going to do about *our* son?"

"I guess that depends upon how he responds," she said, the darkness in her soul growing at the thought of Adam's illness. Turner's bone marrow had to match, it just had to. If not...oh, Lord, she couldn't think of the possibilities. Aching inside, she finished her drink in one swallow. "Until we know that he's well, I can't make any plans."

"I won't just walk out, Heather." Turner left his empty glass on the hearth and strode to the window. Outside, the summer wind stirred the leaves in the trees and a few pedestrians walked briskly up the hilly streets. Cars moved slowly. Street lamps pooled warm light on the sidewalk and cars parked along the curbs.

"And I can't move to Gold Creek."

"You'll have to let him visit me."

"He will—"

"Every other week."

"No way." Her head snapped up. "He can't be uprooted half the time just so you can play father! He'll be in school and—"

"I don't *play*, Heather."

"But he'll need the security of a home and—"

"He's my kid, damn it."

"A kid you didn't want!" The words tumbled out of their own accord, and she saw him wince, as if he'd been stung by the bite of a whip.

His face flexed and he sucked in his breath. With fingers of steel he grabbed her arms and lifted her off the seat with such force she gasped.

"A kid I didn't know about."

"Let go of me, Turner. It's easy for you. Just turn your back and walk away. You've done it before!"

"I've been trying to let go of you for years, Heather." His voice was as rough as scarred leather, his eyes as hot as a branding iron, and when his lips found hers, there was a force behind them as primeval as the range he rode.

She didn't want to kiss him, didn't expect to find his arms wrapped around her with a passion that sang from his body to hers. She told herself that she wouldn't kiss him, would fight him tooth and nail, but as she pushed against his shoulders, her body yielded, as if it had a mind of its own. Memories, like a warm western wind, blew through her mind, and the taste of Turner, as fresh as yesterday, triggered hotter thoughts of that long-ago summer.

She tried to protest, but couldn't, and the smell and feel of him drove out all thoughts of denial. For she knew they would make love. Again. As if destiny were charting its own preordained course, she felt her knees give way, her mouth yield, her sigh of contentment as his tongue teased her lips open.

This can't be happening, she thought wildly, yet her arms, rather than shove him away, wound enticingly around his neck, and her face lifted for more of his sweet caress. Her skin quivered where he touched her, and as he lowered both their bodies to the floor, she clung to him.

She wanted to blame the alcohol, or the desperate emotions that had ravaged her since she'd learned of Adam's illness and had known that Turner would try to take the boy from her. She wanted to accuse fate for tricking her into wanting Turner again, and yet, deep inside, she knew that the seeds of love she'd buried so long ago had never died, were planted shallowly enough to sprout again.

She closed her mind to the doubts that crowded in her brain and let herself go, kissing this man who smelled of rawhide and soap and tasted of bourbon. As he stripped her of her blouse, her fingers unfastened the buttons of his shirt and pushed the fabric over muscles as hard and lean as a Nevada winter.

His lips trailed across her skin, leaving a path prairie-fire hot and twice as deadly. She touched his abdomen and chest as he kissed her bare flesh. His fingers were callused and rough against her breasts as they traced the edge of her bra and quickly unfastened the clasp.

Unbound, nipples erect, her breasts spilled free and he kissed each mound with hungry lips that gave as much pleasure as they took. His arms surrounded her, his hands splayed upon the small of her back as he drew first one pink-tipped nipple into his mouth, then the other. She squirmed against him, her own hands tracing the line of corded muscles and a chest that was covered with downy brown hair that had turned dark and thick over the past six years.

One of his hands dipped beneath the band of her slacks and cupped her rump, pulling her hard against him. She felt his own desire against her abdomen and the bandage on his hip binding the wound where he'd given a part of himself for his child. As he gazed into her eyes, searching as if for the portal of her soul, she knew there was no turning back. He kissed her again, hard and long, and flung off their remaining clothes and there, on the thick handwoven carpet, with the crackle of flames and the hum of slow San Francisco traffic, Turner Brooks once again claimed the lady he'd never been able to forget.

Chapter Ten

Heather felt like a caged cat. All morning she glanced at the clock and paced from the living room to the kitchen and back again. Turner, too, was tense. His jaw was tight, his lips thinned. Today they would find out about the tests.

"It's gonna be all right," he told her, but she saw the doubts in his eyes.

"What if you don't match? What then?" she whispered, her voice cracking.

Turner's eyes darkened. He folded her into his arms and his breath whispered across her hair. "Let's not borrow trouble. Not just yet."

They were still embracing, still holding each other when the front door unlatched and Rachelle, hauling her brief-case, dashed up the stairs. "Hey, I'm here. Sorry I'm late— the crosstown traffic was murder—" she looked up at the last step, and her eyes landed on Turner, who, by this time had released Heather, but looked guilty as sin.

Heather sent up a silent prayer as she felt heat climb steadily up the back of her neck. Rachelle wasn't known for her tact or her ability to hold her tongue. Outspoken since she'd been a kid, she wasn't one to mince words, and the look she gave Turner in his faded jeans, worn suede jacket, cream-colored rough-spun shirt and Stetson was harsh enough to send a rattlesnake scurrying back under a rock.

Heather started introductions. "This is—"

"Turner Brooks," Rachelle guessed, her eyes flashing. "Adam's father. The cowboy."

Turner's jaw tightened just a fraction.

"Turner, my sister, Rachelle. She's going to watch Adam while we're at the hospital."

Immediately Rachelle's expression changed to concern and she crossed her fingers. "I'm praying that this will work."

"So am I."

"Mom's been lighting candles all week."

"She's not even Catholic—" Never had Heather heard of candlelighting in the Methodist church they'd attended in Gold Creek.

"I know, but some of her friends are and she figured it wouldn't hurt." Rachelle glanced around. "Where's Adam?"

"Napping—"

"Auntie Rachelle!" Adam squealed from the upper landing. Legs pounding, he flew down the stairs, arms outstretched so that Rachelle could scoop him up and fling him high in the air before catching him again and holding him close.

"Howdy, kiddo," she said, kissing his mussed hair. "How about a date with your favorite aunt? We could go to McDonald's and the video arcade and then get ice cream—"

"All the culture of the city," Turner drawled.

Rachelle cast him a superior glance. "Who needs culture? We're just gonna have fun, aren't we, sport?"

"Can we go to the toy store?"

"You bet. I'm gonna spoil you rotten today."

Turner's look darkened, but Heather touched his arm. "Don't blame the city. You could do everything Rachelle's talking about right in good old Gold Creek."

At the mention of their hometown, Rachelle's expression turned sober. "Gold Creek? What's this?"

Heather couldn't help herself. "Turner thinks Adam and I should move back."

"Heather, no!" Protectively, Rachelle clutched her nephew closer to her breast. "Not after...well, now that you know, with Dennis not being Adam's...and..." Her gaze flew to Turner. "Oh, Lord! The gossips in Gold Creek would have a field day!"

"So what?" Turner glanced at his watch, then tipped the brim of his hat slightly. "Nice meeting you," he said with more than a trace of sarcasm.

"My pleasure." Rachelle mimicked him without flinching. Then, as if deciding she'd been a little too harsh, she blew a strand of auburn hair from her eyes and balanced Adam on her hip. "Look, Turner, whatever's happened between you two—" she motioned toward Heather "—it's really none of my business. I'm just glad you're here and I want to thank you for helping Heather and Adam."

"No need for thanks."

"Yes, there is." Her intelligent hazel eyes held his for a second. Biting her lip, she shot out a hand and glanced at her sister. "Please, I didn't mean to come on so strong and I know...well, that this mess isn't all your fault."

Heather watched as Turner's big fingers surrounded her sister's tiny hand. "Thanks."

"And would you . . . I'm getting married in a few weeks. Jackson and I would love it if you came."

Heather held her breath. This might be too much of a commitment for Turner. Just because he was going to help Adam didn't mean he wanted to be entangled with Heather any further—at least not publicly. Their lovemaking was another matter—it had nothing to do with their future.

"The wedding will be held in Gold Creek, up at White-fire Lake," Rachelle said. "And we're inviting some old friends . . ." She glanced back at her sister. "Even Carlie's coming. From Alaska. She wrote me that she's moving back to Gold Creek. Can you believe that?"

Carlie had been Rachelle's best friend in high school, the one person in Gold Creek who had believed in Rachelle during the horrid period in Rachelle's life when Jackson had been accused of murder. After high school, Carlie, with her striking black hair and blue-green eyes had sought her fame and fortune modeling in New York. But something had happened, something no one in Carlie's family would discuss, and the last Heather had heard was that Carlie was in Alaska, working on the other side of the lens as a photographer.

"I'll be glad to see her again," Heather said, still waiting for Turner's response.

"So will I." Rachelle looked directly at Turner. "Please . . . we'd love to have you."

Turner rubbed the back of his neck. "All depends, I guess, on what we find out today." He looked at Heather and cocked his head to the stairs leading to the garage. "We'd better git."

Heather's stomach twisted. Her eyes locked with Rachelle's for just an instant and the fear they both felt congealed in their intermingled gaze. Turner placed an arm over

Heather's shoulders. "Don't worry," he advised, though his own expression was anxious.

Heather swallowed a lump in her throat, kissed Adam's cheek and with Turner's arm still securely around her, started for the stairs leading down to the garage. She closed her eyes and sent up a silent prayer—for the thousandth time that day.

Thomas Fitzpatrick was a fastidious man who took care of himself. His body was honed by exercise—tennis, golf and regular workouts at a health club. He prided himself on his patrician good looks, his thick head of hair and his practiced smile. Therefore, he wasn't impressed with the private investigator Brian had hired.

Mr. Robert "Bobby" Sands was seated in one of the living room chairs, his dusty boots propped on one of June's white ottomans, his thick fingers webbed over a belly that was paunchy for a man not yet forty. His hair was greasy black and pulled into a ponytail and an earring winked from his right ear.

"... That's right," he was saying, as if he felt right at home. Thomas poured them each a drink. "Turner's clean. A few barroom brawls when he was younger, but mainly those were caused by his old man. No major scrapes with the law. Kept his nose clean on the rodeo circuit—no booze or drugs or doped-up livestock."

Thomas, disgusted, glanced in the mirrored bar. At least June wasn't here to see their visitor. She'd decided to take Toni, their daughter, and spend some time in San Francisco with Thomas's sister, Sylvia Monroe. Hopefully Sylvia could talk some sense into her. When she came back, they'd discuss their marriage or their divorce.

He'd never really loved June, but, damn it, this house seemed cold without her. A few years ago, the house was teeming with life and now, without the kids and his wife . . . Quickly he snapped to attention and pulled himself together. He would not, *would not* show any signs of weakness to this scum bag of an investigator!

In the reflection he noticed Sands pick up a lighter from the glass-topped table, eye the gold piece, flick the flint and watch the flame snap up. Quickly he set the lighter back. For a second Thomas was sure the man was going to pocket it.

"You're telling me Turner Brooks has no secrets." He crossed the room and handed Sands a drink. His skin crawled as he noticed the man's chipped and dirty fingernails.

"Nope. I'm saying he looks clean. But he's had his problems and they all started surfacing just recently. He's started spending a lot of time with a woman. . . ." Sands's reptilian eyes slitted a fraction, as if he was enjoying stretching out this moment.

"What woman?"

"Heather Leonetti." Sands took a swallow from his bourbon and smiled as the liquor hit the back of his throat. "You know who I mean—Heather Tremont Leonetti, the girl who married that rich banker six years ago."

Tremont. The name sent a jolt through him. Jackson's fiancée was a Tremont. She had a younger sister . . . a pretty girl who had married well, above her station. . . .

"It seems as if Turner and Mrs. Leonetti knew each other a few years ago. Before she was married. Met up on a ranch owned by Turner's uncle, Zeke Kilkenny. Now, Kilkenny won't say much, won't even return my calls, and his housekeeper, Mazie, usually a gossip, wouldn't breathe a word about what went on between Brooks and Heather Tremont, who, by the way, was in an on-again, off-again engagement with Leonetti, but I did some digging. Came up with a few names. One of the ranch hands who used to work

for Kilkenny, Billy Adams—he said Heather and this cowboy were damned thick, and another girl who worked up
there during the summers—'' He set down his drink,
reached into the front pocket of his jacket—a shiny pin-
stripe—and pulled out a small notepad. Licking his fingers, he flipped through the pages. "Here it is. Yost. Sheryl
Yost. Seems she had a thing for our boy Turner, as well.
Anyway, she was more than happy to tell me anything I
wanted to know. According to her, Brooks and the Tremont girl had an affair, kind of a summer fling. Eventually
he rode off into the sunset and left her—this seems to have
been his M.O. at the time—and she ended up marrying
Leonetti."

Thomas, who had been interested, wasn't impressed.
"Lots of people have one last fling before they get married."

The fat man's lip curled outward and he moved his head
from side to side. "Maybe. The thing of it is Mrs. Leonetti
had a baby. Not eight months later. And the kid don't look
all that Italian, if you get my drift."

Thomas held his glass halfway to his lips. "Brooks's?"

"Again, your guess is as good as mine," Sands replied in
his oily voice. "But I found out that Dennis Leonetti had
some tests done a few years back and he can't father children. His sperm count is near zero." Sands picked up his
drink and finished it in one long swallow, then snapped
open his ratty leather briefcase and fumbled through some
papers. "Now, all of a sudden, Heather Leonetti, who's
managed to ditch Leonetti and strip him of some of his
money—she's shown up on Brooks's doorstep, at the very
ranch you want to buy, and he practically does back flips.
He's in San Francisco now—has a friend of his, Fred
McDonald, run the ranch while he's gone." Finding his report, he slid it across the glass expanse of the tabletop.

Thomas picked up the typewritten pages. "In San Francisco...to meet the child?" he asked, reaching into his pocket for his reading glasses.

Sands leaned closer. He grinned in pleasure. "He's there for tests. Been to a hospital. The staff is pretty mum, but my guess is it has something to do with the kid as the boy's got leukemia. Heather's kept it a secret, but she and Leonetti split up after the kid was diagnosed. My guess is Leonetti found out he wasn't the boy's dad and gave Heather the old heave-ho."

Thomas set his unfinished drink on the table. He didn't like this. Not when children, sick children, were involved. "The boy?"

"Is in remission, from what I get out of it. I don't know why she told Turner about the kid now, but she did...or at least it looks that way. Maybe she wants to take up with him again now that Leonetti's out of the picture. Again, your guess is as good as mine."

Thomas's voice was scratchy. Much as he wanted the Badlands Ranch, and the oil he suspected was pooled beneath the dried-out fields, a child complicated things. He'd always been a sucker for his own children, even Jackson, though he'd made too many mistakes where his firstborn, his bastard, had been concerned. He'd tried to atone, but Jackson hadn't heard of it. He sipped his drink, didn't taste the expensive blend. Hell, a kid. Brooks had a kid. A sick kid. This complicated things.

"You want me to keep digging?"

Thomas's head snapped up and he felt beads of sweat on his brow. "Yes. Please. Let's see if there's anything else." He folded the report neatly and stuffed it into the inner pocket of his jacket.

Sands grinned and plopped an ice cube into his broad mouth. "You're the boss."

* * *

Closed-in places made him restless, and this doctor's office, complete with diplomas on the wall and soft leather chairs, didn't ease the knot of tension between Turner's shoulder blades. He felt trapped and hot, barely able to breathe. His legs were too long to stretch between his chair and the desk, so he sat, ramrod straight while the doctor shifted the papers in a file marked: LEONETTI, ADAM.

That would have to change. Turner would rot in hell rather than have his son labeled with another man's name— a man who really didn't care one way or the other for the boy. As soon as possible, Adam's name would be Brooks. Heather would have to change it. There were no two ways about it; Turner intended to lay claim to his son.

Dr. Thurmon was a portly man with thin silver hair and a face right out of a Norman Rockwell poster. Behind wire-rimmed glasses, Thurmon had gentle eyes and Turner trusted him immediately. He'd always had a gut instinct about people, and usually his first impressions were right on target.

Thurmon took off his glasses. "Good news," he said, casting a smile at Heather, and Turner saw her shoulders slump in relief. "The marrow's a match and I didn't have a lot of hope that it would be. Siblings are the best source for transplants. But—" he lifted his hands and grinned "—we lucked out."

"Thank God," Heather whispered, tears filling her eyes. Without thinking, Turner wrapped a strong arm around her and they hugged. His own throat clogged, and he fought the urge to break down. His son was going to be well.

"While this is still very serious, Adam is in good shape," the doctor went on as he polished the lenses of his glasses with a clean white handkerchief. "We have his own marrow, taken while he's been in remission, and now Mr.

Brooks will be a donor. And as well as Adam's doing, there's no reason to anticipate that a transplant is necessary, at least not in the near future. But Adam will have to stay on his medication for a while."

Heather's voice was shaky. "And if he relapses?"

Dr. Thurmon's lips pressed together. "Then a transplant will be likely. We'll reevaluate at that time." He closed the file. "But let's not worry about it just yet. Right now, Mrs. Leonetti, your son is as healthy as can be expected."

"Thank you!" Heather cast a triumphant glance at Turner and smiled through the tears shimmering in her eyes.

"Does this mean that Adam can do anything he wants?" Turner asked.

The doctor nodded. "Within reason. I wouldn't want to have him become overly tired. And I'd keep him away from anyone you know who has a contagious disease."

Heather froze as Turner said, "Then there's no reason—no medical reason—why Adam couldn't visit me at my ranch."

"Absolutely not," the doctor replied, and Heather's smile fell from her face as Turner and Dr. Thurmon shook hands.

She walked on wooden legs along the soft carpet of the clinic, past open doors with children sitting in their underwear on tables and mothers fussing over their kids as they waited. She turned by rote at the corner to the exit and found herself in the elevator before she let out her breath.

"That wasn't necessary," she said as the elevator descended.

"What?"

"I told you I'd let Adam visit."

"Just making sure you didn't find a reason to weasel out of it."

"I wouldn't—" She gasped and nearly stumbled as Turner slapped the elevator button and the car jerked to a stop.

"You kept him from me for five years. You admitted that you probably wouldn't have told me about him until he was eighteen if he hadn't gotten sick! You probably would have kept him from me if your bone marrow had matched. When I think about that—" He slammed a fist into the wall and Heather jumped. Turner's face suffused with color. "Well, things have changed. He does know me and soon you're going to tell him that I'm his father and—"

"I can't just blurt it out! He's only five!"

"Then he'll have fewer questions."

"But—"

"Don't fight me on this, Heather," he warned, leaning over her, his face set in granite. "I've lived up to my part of the bargain. Now I expect you to come through."

"Why wouldn't I?"

Turner stared deep into her eyes and some of his hard edges faded a bit. "Oh, hell," he muttered, trying to control himself. He flexed his hands, then shoved them impatiently through his hair. "Look, the last few days, we've both been worried—on edge and we . . . well, we fell into a pattern of trusting each other and playing house."

Stung, his words cutting deep, she couldn't respond, just swallowed at the swelling in her throat.

"But now we know that Adam's safe. You don't need me anymore. Or at least not right away. It would be easy to step back into our old lives—you go your way, I go mine."

Oh, Turner, you're so wrong. So very wrong, she thought desperately. Perhaps he could forget her easily, but she'd never forget him. Never! She'd already spent six years with his memory; she was destined to love him, if just a little, for the rest of her life.

"But that's not going to happen. Now that I know about Adam, my way—my path—is wound with his. That can't change."

Fear took a stranglehold of her heart. "What're you saying, Turner, that you want custody?" Her knees threatened to crumple, and she leaned hard against the rail in her back.

He slapped the button again and, with a groan of old gears, the elevator continued on its descent. "Not yet. I'm not stupid enough to try to take him from you, but from this point onward, I'm going to have some influence over him." He sent her a look that cut clear to her bones.

"How much 'influence'?"

"That's up to you, Heather."

"Meaning?"

"As long as I see him often, and I'm not talking one weekend a month, I won't challenge you in court. But..." His eyes glittered ominously, with the same gleam she'd seen whenever he was trying to break a particularly stubborn colt. "...If you come up against me, or try any funny stuff, you'll be in for the fight of your life."

The elevator landed and the doors whispered open to a crowd of onlookers. One man was frantically pushing the call button; other people whispered about the wisdom of getting onto a temperamental car.

Turner cupped her elbow and guided her through the crowd.

"You really are a bastard," she whispered under her breath.

"Why thank you, darlin'. I'll take that as a compliment." With a smile as cold as a copperhead's skin, he shoved open the doors.

Outside, fog had settled over the city, bringing with its opaque presence the feel of nightfall. Heather, shivering, slid behind the wheel of her Mercedes. Turner hauled his long body into the passenger seat, propped his back against the door and stared at her.

"If you moved to Gold Creek, I wouldn't feel any need to demand partial custody," he said.

She shot him a look of pure venom and switched on the ignition. "Me move back to Gold Creek? I'd rather die first."

"Are you willing to take a chance on a custody hearing?"

Her hands tightened over the wheel. *Please, Turner, just leave it alone!* "This wasn't part of the deal. You asked me to bring Adam to your ranch for a week or two and I intend to, but I'm not moving. Just because you're Adam's father, doesn't give you the right to bully me." Muttering under her breath, she eased the car into the flow of traffic traveling through the city.

"Is that what I'm doing?"

"From the first time I stepped into your barn."

He turned his attention to the roadway. In the fog, brake lights glowed eerily and crowds of pedestrians crossed the streets at the stoplights.

"You've got a week," he said as the light changed. "I'll expect to see Adam then."

"But I have work—"

"So do I." He rubbed a big hand over the faded spot of denim covering his knee. "I've been gone long enough already. Fred can't watch my place forever. Work out whatever you have to, but bring Adam to the ranch."

She wanted to argue, to find a way out of the deal because she knew that if she took Adam to Badlands Ranch, it wouldn't be long before she lost her son as well as her heart to Turner Brooks.

Chapter Eleven

"I think you're making a big mistake." Rachelle eyed her sister in the mirror of her bedroom, grimaced, then adjusted one of the shoulder pads in Heather's gown. Layers of raspberry-colored chiffon and silk, the dress was to be worn at Rachelle's wedding. "You can't let him have the upper hand."

"What choice do I have?" Heather asked, holding her hair up and frowning at the sight she made. Modeling the elegant dress only reminded her of weddings and just how far apart she and Turner had grown. The city girl and the cowboy. An unlikely combination. An unlikely *explosive* combination. "He's holding all the cards."

Rachelle shook her head furiously. "I saw him with Adam. He wouldn't do anything to jeopardize his son's well-being. Hold still, will you? I think this should be taken in a little in the waist . . . what do you think?"

"That you're being overly concerned. You're the bride. No one will be looking at me."

Rachelle's brow puckered as she slid the zipper down her sister's back. "If it were up to me, Jackson and I would've taken off on his Harley, driven straight to Lake Tahoe and gotten married without all this fuss."

"So why didn't you?" Heather asked, stepping out of the dress.

"Because *His Majesty* wants to make a statement."

"I heard that," Jackson called from the living room of Rachelle's tiny apartment.

"Well, it's true." Rachelle's eyes lighted as she zipped a plastic cover over the gown. "You're tarnishing your rebel image, you know, by doing the traditional wedding and all."

"Good! Keeps the people in Gold Creek on their toes."

As Rachelle hung up the dress, Heather slipped on her jeans and cotton blouse, then slid her arms through a suede vest.

Rachelle arched an eyebrow at Heather's getup. "Well, aren't you the little cowgirl?"

"I figured I better look the part." Together they edged along the hall, past the stacked boxes and packing crates. Jackson was on the floor near the bay window, black hair tumbling over his forehead, his sleeves rolled up as he wrestled with a red-faced Adam.

"I got you, I got you!" Adam chortled triumphantly as he straddled Jackson's broad chest. "One, two, three, you lose!"

"You're just too tough for me," Jackson said with a laugh. His dark eyes gleamed as Rachelle approached. "I think we should have a dozen of these."

"A dozen?" she said, grinning. "I don't know. Sounds like a lot."

"Well, maybe just a half dozen. When do we start?"

"When I've got a legal contract, Counselor. One that spells out how many times you change the diapers and get up in the middle of the night and—"

"Okay, okay, I've heard this all before." With a quick movement, he lifted Adam off his chest and rolled quickly to his feet. Adam squealed with delight as he was tossed into the air and caught in Jackson's strong arms.

"Legally binding, mind you," Rachelle said. "And I plan to have a *real* attorney check all the fine print."

A devilish grin slid across Jackson's jaw and he motioned to his fiancée as he stage-whispered to Heather, "She just doesn't trust me. That's the reporter in her."

"Give it up, Counselor," she said, but he grabbed her, twirled her off her feet and left her suddenly breathless when she finally touched down again.

"Never," he mouthed, his lips only inches from hers.

Heather felt her heart twist when she saw them exchange a sensual glance, the same kind of glance she shared with Turner. Yet, while Rachelle and Jackson were head over heels in love, she and Turner were worlds apart and had no chance of planning a future together. He'd never once said he loved her, and as far as she knew, he still didn't believe that particular emotion existed. He'd told her as much six years before and Heather doubted he'd changed his mind. She cleared her throat, and the two lovers finally remembered there was someone else in the room. "Well, I guess we'd better get going. Adam can't wait to see Turner's ranch, can you?"

Adam let out a whoop. "I'm gonna learn how to break a . . ." He glanced to Heather for help.

"Break a bronco," she replied. "But I wouldn't hold my breath if I were you."

Adam's eyes were shining. "You can come visit," he told his aunt. "Turner will probably let you break one, too."

"I'll remember that," Rachelle said with a chuckle. "And while I'm at it, I'll rope me a steer, brand half a dozen calves and spit tobacco juice!"

"You're lyin'!" Adam accused, but curious doubts crowded his eyes, and Heather imagined he was trying to picture his trim aunt wrestling with livestock and shooting a stream of brown juice from the corner of her mouth.

"You might be surprised, sport," Rachelle teased, her eyes glinting mischievously. "Oh, Heather, would you mind dropping these in the mailbox?" She rifled through the papers on the desk and came up with a stack of wedding invitations, already addressed and stamped.

"No problem." Heather took the stack of cream-colored envelopes and headed down the stairs. A post office was on her way out of town and she was glad to do a favor for her sister. Rachelle and she had always been close, though Heather had kept more than her share of secrets from her sister. Not only had she hidden the fact that Turner was Adam's father, but she'd also kept quiet about Adam's illness for a long time, until the doctors had started talking about bone-marrow transplants.

Though Rachelle had known that Adam wasn't well, Heather had kept the extent of the illness to herself, always telling herself that she couldn't burden her sister or mother with her problems. They had both experienced enough of their own. Rachelle had been horrified, when six weeks ago Heather had told her the truth.

After strapping Adam into the passenger seat, she wove the Mercedes through the traffic until she reached the nearest post office and pulled into the lane near a series of mailboxes. As she stuffed the thick envelopes through the slot, she saw the names of people she'd known all her life, people who had lived in Gold Creek. Monroe and McDonald, Surrett, Nelson, Patton and... the last envelope surprised her. Addressed in Rachelle's bold hand, the invitation was addressed to Thomas Fitzpatrick, Jackson's father. The man who had never claimed him. The man who had almost let Jackson twist in the wind for the murder of his legitimate son, the man who all too late tried to make amends, the man Jackson still professed to despise.

Had he changed his mind? Heather doubted it. No, this had all the earmarks of Rachelle deciding it was time her husband-to-be put old skeletons to rest. And it spelled fireworks for the wedding.

"Oh, God, Rachelle, I hope you know what you're doing."

Heather turned the invitation over in her hand and a sharp beep from the car in line behind her startled her. This wasn't any of her business. Heather jammed the envelope into the slot and edged the car back into the flow of traffic. Certainly Rachelle wouldn't have been so silly as to send the invitation behind Jackson's back. Or would she?

Rachelle had a reputation for being stubborn and bullheaded. She'd stood on principle once before—for Jackson—and it had cost her the respect of her friends and family and soiled her reputation. But surely she'd learned her lesson....

This was Rachelle's wedding—if she wanted to make it her funeral, as well, it was her choice. Besides—Heather stole a glance at her son, his face eager, a small toy car clutched in his fingers—she had her own share of concerns.

"I already said I wasn't interested," Turner said, irritated beyond words. He'd made the mistake of picking up the phone as he'd walked through the house and ended up in a conversation with God himself: Thomas Fitzpatrick. Now the guy wasn't even working through his real estate agent.

"I'm willing to pay you top dollar," Fitzpatrick argued smoothly. "Why don't you think it over?"

"No reason to think." He could almost hear the gears grinding in Fitzpatrick's shrewd mind.

"Everyone has a price."

"Not everyone, Fitzpatrick," Turner drawled.

There was an impatient snort on the other end of the line. "Just consider my offer. Counter if you like."

"Look, Tom," Turner replied, his voice edged in sarcasm. "With all due respect, I'm busy. I've got a ranch to run. If you wanted this place so badly, you should never have sold it in the first place."

"I realize that now. At the time, I wasn't interested in diversifying. I had timber. Now I've changed my mind. There might be oil on the land and I'm willing to gamble. I'm offering you twice what the land is worth, Mr. Brooks. You couldn't get a better deal."

"Good. 'Cause I don't want one."

"But—"

"Listen, Fitzpatrick, you and I both know you never cut anyone a deal in your life."

"But—"

"The answer is 'no.' Well, maybe that doesn't quite say it all. Let's make it 'No way in hell!'" With that, Turner slammed the receiver into the cradle, turned off the answering machine and strode to the bathroom. He didn't want to think of Fitzpatrick with his starched white shirts, silk ties and thousand-dollar suits. The man couldn't be trusted and Turner wasn't interested in doing any kind of business with him.

Still bothered, he cleaned the dirt, grime and horsehair from his face and hands, then noticed the smell of oil that lingered on his skin from this morning, when he'd had to work on the fuel line of the tractor. Damned thing was always breaking down.

Scowling, he glanced at his watch. Three-thirty. She'd be here any minute. Calling himself every kind of fool, he stripped quickly, leaving his clothes in a pile on the floor, twisted on the shower and stepped under the cool spray. Within a minute or two the water warmed and he scrubbed his body from head to foot. Wrapping a towel around his waist, he headed down the hallway and nearly tripped over Nadine, who was walking through the front door.

"Oh—God—I... Oh, Turner... I knocked but no one answered." She flushed at the sight of his naked torso and legs. "I didn't mean to—"

He grinned. "Sure you did, Nadine," he teased, and saw her face turn several shades of red.

"Believe me, Turner, I'm not that hard up," she threw back, her chin angling defiantly, though her eyes caught his mischief. "I haven't reduced myself to bein' a Peeping Tom, and even if I had, *you* certainly wouldn't be on the top of my list." Her eyes shifted away from his, though, and he felt that same uncertainty he had in the past. He guessed that she was half in love with him. The poor woman. Beautiful and bright, she could do better than Sam Warne or himself.

Through the window, he saw Heather's Mercedes roll to a stop. "Look, Nadine, I've got to change." Without another word, he half ran into the bedroom, slammed the door, let the towel drop and changed into clean jeans and a work shirt. He ran his fingers through his hair and was opening the bedroom door as the rap of a small fist banged against the screen door.

"Turner?" Adam's voice rang through the ranch house as he pushed the door open. Quick little steps hesitated in the entry hall.

Turner felt a strange tightness in his chest as he turned the corner and saw his son standing in the hallway of his house, looking confused and worried. This wasn't how it was supposed to be. Any child of his should feel at home on the ranch, know every rock and crevice in the land, spend hours in the barn or astride a horse or exploring the wooded hillsides. Any child of his should live here, no matter what the sacrifice. Turner could barely find his voice, and when he finally spoke, his words sounded hushed, choked by emotions he'd never experienced before. "I wondered when you were gonna git here, cowboy," he said.

Adam's freckled nose crinkled and he giggled. "I'm not a cowboy!"

"You are now." Turner reached onto the scarred wooden coatrack, where on the highest spindle a small brown-and-white Stetson had been placed. "All you need is this hat—" he plopped it on Adam's head "—and a pair of boots."

"I got high-tops!" Adam proclaimed, proudly displaying white basketball shoes with a famous insignia.

"We'll fix that." With a grin that seemed to light his very soul, Turner picked the boy up and hugged him close. It felt right holding his boy—like nothing he'd ever experienced—and Turner knew that with each passing minute he'd want more until he had it all. There was no turning back, no way he could pretend Adam didn't exist.

But he wouldn't rip a son from his mother. He'd lost his own mom when he wasn't all that old and he'd missed her every day of his life since. No, somehow Turner would have to work out a compromise with Heather, find a way that they each could spend as much time with Adam as possible.

For a second, he thought of marrying her. There were certainly worse twists his life could take, but he didn't believe for a minute that she would agree. She'd be bored to death here on the farm, and he'd curl up and die in the city. And she would want love—not companionship, not sex, not even friendship. She wanted to be loved. And she deserved that much. Hell, what a mess! For a second he was furious with her again. If only she'd been honest with him way back when, bridging this abyss wouldn't be necessary.

He spied Heather walking across the porch, and again his heart leapt to his throat. God, she was beautiful—too beautiful. A graceful, intriguing creature who should have been modeling for some highbrow agency in New York. Without makeup, with the layers of sophistication peeled away, she was still the most sensual woman he'd ever met. Her blond hair was pulled into a ponytail and held by a leather thong. She was wearing an outfit befitting a country singer. Stylized cowgirl. Earthy with a touch of glitz.

The kind of woman that stayed with you long after she'd said goodbye. The kind of woman a man could get used to. The kind of woman he would marry. The idea sent a jolt through his brain. He'd never considered marriage—not seriously, though once before, when he'd found out that Heather had left the Lazy K, he'd contemplated tracking her down and proposing. The urge had passed when he'd realized that she'd married Leonetti.

But now...marriage didn't seem so unlikely, though he doubted she would give up her fast-paced life-style in the city to become a rancher's wife. He kicked the idea of marriage around and found it wasn't as distasteful as he'd originally thought.

"Momma's a cowboy, too!" Adam chirped as Turner held the door open for Heather.

"I'll get the rest of your things," he said.

Heather's blue gaze touched his for a second, before shifting to a point beyond him. Her smile faded, and the color seeped from her face. "Heather?" he asked, before glancing over his shoulder and spying Nadine, dust rag in one hand, mop in the other as she stood in the archway to the kitchen.

"Company?" Nadine asked, her smile frozen, her eyes dark with quiet emotions.

Turner couldn't stand the deception a second longer. He hated lies and wasn't about to let Heather's web of deceit tie him into knots—especially not where Nadine was concerned. He should have used his hard head and told her earlier. "Nadine, I'd like you to meet Heather Leonetti." Nadine's arched brows inched up a bit. "And this is Adam. My son."

Heather gasped.

Nadine's mouth dropped open and she quickly snapped it shut. "Excuse me?"

"Turner!" Heather cried, glancing in horror at her boy. Adam's little face was puckered a bit, but he didn't seem all that concerned about the fact that every grown-up in the room was nearly apoplectic.

"And this is Nadine Warne, my housekeeper."

Heather's throat closed in on itself. She wanted to strangle Turner right then and there. What right did he have to break the news to Adam this way? And Nadine, who from the knowing glance she cast Turner, cared more for him than she did for mopping his floors . . . what did she think?

After a second's hesitation, Nadine left her mop in the kitchen and stuffed her dust rag into a pocket. She managed what appeared to be a genuine smile as she walked toward Adam with her hand extended. "Well, how are you?"

"He's confused, that's what he is," Heather cut in, though she wasn't angry with Nadine. Obviously the woman was shocked and making the best out of a bad situation. But

Turner...he was another matter. She'd love to pummel him with her fists, and the look she shot him told him just that.

"Maybe I'd better come back another time," Nadine said, her sad gaze landing on Adam.

"It's all right," Turner replied. His strong tanned arms surrounded his son with such possession that Heather didn't know whether to laugh or cry. Adam needed a father, a man to care for him, but Heather couldn't find it in her heart to let go of her boy even a little. "I'll bring in Heather's things and we'll be out of your hair. Adam wants a tour of the ranch, don't you, kid?"

"I want to break a bronco!"

Turner smiled and winked. "Slow down, son. We have to save something for tomorrow."

"I won't let him—"

"Enough," Turner said sharply, then at Heather's gasp, added in a gentler tone to his son, "Come on, let's bring the rest of the bags inside." Hand in hand, father and son walked through the door, leaving Heather standing in the entry hall, trying to think of some kind of conversation she could drum up with Nadine.

"I would've known anyway," Nadine admitted to Heather. Through the window, she watched Turner as he stepped out of the shadow of the house, into the dry dust of the yard. He set Adam on his feet and the boy took off, pell-mell to the fence nearest the barn. "Adam's the spitting image of his pa."

"I think so, too."

Nadine nodded. "I grew up with Turner, you know. Seeing Adam...well, it takes me back about twenty-five years." She wiped her hands on the rag in her pocket. "I'm surprised he didn't tell me."

"He didn't know," Heather said, deciding it was time for the truth to be told. There was no reason to lie any longer.

Even if Nadine didn't turn out to be the biggest gossip in Gold Creek, the news was bound to get out. Turner would see to it. "It...it's complicated," she added.

"With Turner, it always is," Nadine replied. Then, as if shaking herself out of a great melancholy, she cocked her head toward the kitchen. "Come on inside. Look around. I don't know if he's got anything in the refrigerator but beer and milk two weeks beyond the pull date, but there might be a soda."

Heather followed Nadine into the kitchen, where a bucket, mop and basket of cleaning supplies had been set. She envied Nadine's familiarity with the house, with the routine, with Turner, and yet she knew that she had no one to blame for the distance between herself and the father of her child but herself. She could have told him the truth anytime in the past few years, but she hadn't. *Coward! Now, look at the mess you're in!*

"I met your sister when she was back in Gold Creek," Nadine said, opening the refrigerator and searching at the meager contents. "How about that? He knew you were coming. Pepsi all right?"

"Fine. You know Rachelle?"

"Mmm." Nadine popped the tabs on two cans of soda and handed one to Heather. "I have a lot of respect for her. Stood up for what she believed in and came back to prove it. I was there, you know, the night Roy was killed. God, it was awful." She shook her head and sighed. "And now things are really jumbled up. Who would've believed that Jackson was Thomas Fitzpatrick's son? Believe me, that little bit of news set the town on its ear. Those Gold Creek gossips couldn't talk of much else for three or four weeks." She managed an amused smile. "Not that Gold Creek didn't need to be set on its ear, mind you. But for years the Fitz-

patricks and the Monroes have owned and run everything in
this town. Aside from your husband's family—''

"My ex-husband," Heather clarified.

"Well, aside from the Leonettis, the Fitzpatricks and
Monroes own Gold Creek lock, stock, and barrel. I just find
it hard to believe that old Thomas Fitzpatrick let Jackson,
his own son, take the rap for Roy's death."

"I think Thomas believed it because of June," Heather
said, a little uncomfortable with the subject. Mention of the
Fitzpatricks always made her skin crawl.

Nadine shrugged and took a long swallow of her drink.
"Well, I'd better get to work so I'm not late for my own
boys." She reached for her mop and smiled wistfully. "I've
always thought that Turner could be the best father in the
county. He just didn't know it. Now, maybe, he'll really
settle down."

"Hey, Mom! Come on!" Adam yelled from the back
porch. He was waving furiously. "We're gonna go see the
life stock."

"Livestock," Turner corrected, holding the door open for
Heather. Adam was already leading the way, running
through the dappled sunlight, dust kicking up behind his
new shoes. Turner and Heather fell into step together.

"She's in love with you, you know," Heather finally said,
worried that Nadine had a place in Turner's heart and sens-
ing that down-to-earth Nadine, the woman who spent a lot
of her time here, would be a perfect mate for him.

"Who? Nadine?" He swatted at a wasp that flew near his
head.

"Don't pretend you haven't noticed."

Brackets tightened around the corners of his mouth. "She
deserves better."

"Maybe she doesn't think so."

Turner stopped and stared down at Heather. "Don't be playing matchmaker," he said, his voice steely with determination. "And don't try to get me interested in another woman or her kids. It's Adam I want."

She felt her face drain of color. What did he think? "I was only saying—"

"I know what you were doing, damn it, and it won't work. Now that I know about Adam, I'm not going to fill in with some substitute."

"I didn't..." But her words faded when he opened the barn door and the scents of dust and hay, horses and leather assailed her. She walked past the very stall where they'd made love and her throat caught at the vivid memory. Adam dashed deeper into the interior, sending dust motes into the air and mice scurrying. "I didn't suggest that you should be a father to just any child," she said indignantly. Several horses snorted, and Heather caught Turner staring at her, his eyes dark and serious.

"Good," he drawled in a low, emotion-packed voice, "because Nadine Warne isn't the woman for me."

The walls of the barn seemed to close in on them. Heather's breath was lost in her lungs at the words he hadn't spoken, the insinuation that hung, like a thin diaphanous cloud, between them.

Heather fought the thrill of hope in her heart that she might just be that woman. Angry with that thought, she shoved it out of her mind. Would she be happy here, in a run-down ranch house, living less than five miles from Gold Creek, with a life-style made up of horses, leather, bacon grease and P.T.A. meetings? Where would she paint? She'd have to have a studio.... She glanced back, through the still-open barn door to the weathered sheds and barns and rambling ranch house. Where would the best natural light filter in? She'd need water and light and privacy and... She caught herself up short.

What was she thinking? That Turner would ask her to marry him? Gritting her teeth, she changed the course of her thoughts and watched Adam scamper along the stalls, petting one velvet-soft nose of a horse before hurrying on to the next. His cheeks were rosy, his eyes alight with anticipation. He looked happier and healthier than he had in weeks, and Heather's heart twisted.

As she walked to the first stall, she noticed the horse within, a stocky sorrel mare, was saddled. The mare shook her head and the bridle jangled. "What's going on?"

"Seems to me the last time you came here, you wanted to ride."

She flushed at the memory.

"Least I could do is accommodate you."

"Adam doesn't know how to stay astride a horse," she protested.

"He'll be with me." Turner didn't wait for another argument. He opened the stall gate, grabbed the reins of the mare's bridle and stuffed them into a surprised Heather's fingers. "This is Blitzen." His lips twitched a bit. "I didn't name her. She came that way."

"But—"

He walked to the next stall, and a tall buckskin nickered softly. Heather smiled as she recognized Sampson. Turner patted the big horse fondly on the shoulder.

"I didn't think you still had him," she said.

Turner's eyes flashed. "He's the best horse I ever owned. I'd never sell him." One corner of his mouth lifted. "Don't you know by now that I'm true-blue, Heather?"

A basket of butterflies seemed to erupt in her stomach, but he didn't miss a beat and swung Adam up into the saddle.

"Hold on, honey," Heather said automatically, her eyes riveted to her son's precarious position.

"Oh, Mom!" Adam actually rolled his eyes.

"He'll do fine." Turner tugged gently on the reins and the horse's hooves rang on the concrete as they headed back to the door. Outside, the daylight seemed bright, and Turner spent a few minutes explaining to Adam about the horse and how he could be controlled by simple tugs on the reins.

"Just don't whistle," Heather added, and was rewarded with a sharp look from her son's father. They were both reminded of the first time they met and Heather's misguided attempt to steal Turner's horse from him.

With Adam propped in the saddle, Turner tied Sampson to a rail of the fence. "I'll be right back. Don't go anywhere."

"Where would we go?" she called after him as he dashed along a well-worn path to the back porch and disappeared around the corner.

"What's he doin'?" Adam asked, frowning slightly as the screen door creaked and banged shut. His little fingers held on tight to the saddle horn and a perplexed look crossed his freckled features. "And why'd he say he was Daddy?"

Oh, Adam, what have I done to you? she wondered silently. "I don't know," she said, unable to tell her son the truth of his parentage while they sat astride two separate horses. When it came time for telling the truth, she wanted to be able to hold him and kiss him and tell Adam that he was the most loved child on this earth.

Damn Turner. Why did he think he had the right to blurt out that—

Because he's Adam's father.

Still that didn't give him the right to go spouting off—not until the time was right.

And when would that be? When would the time ever be right?

Before she could answer her own question, Turner strode back with sacks he'd stuffed into the saddlebags that were strapped to his horse. He swung into the saddle behind Adam, and led the way, through the sprawling acres of the ranch.

Despite her worries, Heather felt herself relax. The day was warm, sunlight heated the crown of her head. Bees floated over the few wildflowers caught in the dry stubble of the fields, and a bothersome horsefly buzzed near Blitzen's head, causing the little mare's ears to flick in irritation.

The ranch, in its rustic way, was beautiful. The buildings were time-worn and sun-bleached, but sturdy and practical. Rimming the dry fields, thin stands of oak and pine offered shade while the sun sent rippling images across the dry acres. Turner stopped often, pointing out a corral where he trained rodeo horses, a field that was occupied by brood mares and their spindly legged colts, and a pasture that held a few head of cattle. Adam's eyes fairly glowed as he watched the foals frolic and play or the calves hide behind their mothers' red flanks. His small hands twisted in Sampson's black mane and he chattered, nearly nonstop, asking questions of Turner or laughing in delight when a flock of pheasants rose before the horse, their wings flapping wildly as they flew upward.

"Like in the park!" he exclaimed, obviously delighted.

"Yeah, but those are doves. These are pheasants. Ring-necked Chinese," Turner told him.

When Turner released the reins and kneed Sampson into a slow lope, Heather panicked, sure that Adam would fall. She started to cry out, but held her tongue when she saw the strong grip of Turner's arm around his son's chest. If she was sure of nothing else in this world, she was certain Turner wouldn't let Adam fall. The thought was comforting and unsettling alike. Things were going to change. Her life with Adam would never be the same.

She urged her mare into an easy lope and the wind tugged at her hair and brought tears to her eyes. She felt eighteen again and couldn't keep the smile from her lips. "Come on, girl, you can keep up with them," she told her little mount, and the game little mare didn't lose much ground.

Turner pulled up at the crest of a small hill. A crop of trees shaded the grass, and a creek, dry now, wound jaggedly along the rise. From the hilltop, they could see most of the ranch. As he tethered the horses, Turner glanced at her over his shoulder. His eyes were thoughtful and guarded as he looked at Heather. "My mom and dad rented this place for years," he said, frowning slightly as he revealed more of himself than he ever had. "From Thomas Fitzpatrick. Dad bought it from him with the proceeds of the life insurance he had on Mom. Now Fitzpatrick wants it back."

"Why?"

"Don't you know?"

Heather lifted a shoulder. "How would I?"

"The man who's going to be your brother-in-law is Fitzpatrick's son."

"A trick of fate," Heather replied, surprised at the train of Turner's thoughts. He seemed to be asking deeper questions, questions she didn't understand. "Jackson and Thomas Fitzpatrick are related by blood only. There's no love lost between those two."

Turner opened the saddlebags and pulled out brown sacks filled with sandwiches, fruit and sodas. Adam wandered through the tall, dry grass, trying to catch grasshoppers before they flew away from his eager fingers.

Stretching out in the shade of an oak tree, Turner patted the ground beside him, and Heather, feeling the need for a truce between them, sat next to him, her back propped by the rough bark of the tree.

"Fitzpatrick says he's interested in the mining rights to the place, thinks there might be oil. My guess is he already knows as much, though how he goofed and sold the place back to my old man beats me. Either John Brooks was sharper than we all thought, or Fitzpatrick made a mistake that's been eating at him for years. Old Tom never likes to lose, especially when money's involved. He made a bad decision years ago—concentrating on timber. Now he realizes with all the environmental concerns and restrictions, he'd better find new means to keep that Fitzpatrick wealth." He plucked a piece of grass from the ground and twirled the bleached blade between his thumb and forefinger. "What do you think?"

"I wouldn't even hazard a guess." She drew her knees up and stared after Adam, though she was all too aware of Turner and that he was watching her reaction, as if he expected her to start telling him everything she knew about Thomas Fitzpatrick. Which she had. What she knew of the man was common knowledge to the citizens of Gold Creek. "Ever think about selling?"

"Nope." He leaned back against the tree, his arm brushing hers as he squinted into the lowering sun. Smiling slightly, watching Adam squeal and run, he seemed more content and relaxed than she'd ever known him.

"What about joining the circuit again? Ever consider it?"

He shook his head. "Busted my knee too many times already. And my shoulder's not in the best of shape."

"So you're going to live out the rest of your days here?" It all seemed too pastoral, too quiet for the Turner she knew.

"That's the plan."

It didn't seem so horrible, she thought, staring at the rolling hills and fields. The sounds of birds in the trees and the relaxing view of horses and cattle grazing brought a sense of peace she hadn't felt in years. Deep down, she knew she could lose a little bit of the frenetic pace of the city and enjoy the leisure that she'd somehow lost.

But to live in Gold Creek? Seeing Turner day in and day out and knowing that their relationship would go nowhere?

"This place is special to you."

"It's all I've got," he said simply, then frowned. "Or it was. Now there's Adam."

Heather's heart twisted. "Yes, now there's Adam."

He glanced at her from the corner of his eye. "I've thought a lot about this, Heather. Ever since you showed up here. I told myself it would be best to leave it all alone. To see the boy occasionally. To pretend to be like a . . . well, a favorite uncle or something. But that won't work. And I told myself to stay away. Let you and Adam live your lives without me interfering." He glanced to the distant hills, and the breeze teased at the golden-brown strands of his hair, lifting them from his forehead. "But it won't work. It can't. I can't let it. It's not the way I'm made. Even if I'd convinced myself that staying away from him would be best, I couldn't do it once I'd laid eyes on him. It's...well, it's like nothing else in the world. I never planned on having kids—hell, I didn't think I'd be much of a father—but now that he's here and he's mine, I'm going to be the best damn dad this side of Texas."

Heather's throat closed in on itself. "That's what I've said about being a mother."

Turner's eyes narrowed on the horizon, as if he were wrestling with an inner decision. "I grew up without a mom, leastwise for the last half of my growing-up years. I wouldn't do that to a kid. And my old man..." He shook his head, his eyes troubled. "That son of a bitch was a piece of work. But he was my dad, and like it or not that's the way it was.'' He leaned back again, resting on an elbow and staring up at her, his gray eyes frank and serious. "You may as well know it right now. Nadine was just a start. From this point on, I'm claiming my boy to everyone I meet. And you can rant and rave and raise holy Cain, but I'm not backing down on this one.'' He stared at her for a long minute. "In fact, I think we'd better straighten out this whole mess with the person it means the most to.''

"Turner, don't—''

But he didn't listen. "Hey, Adam, come on over and have some supper. We've got a lot to talk about.''

"Turner, I'm warning you,'' she said, her motherly defenses springing into position.

"Warn to your heart's content, darlin'. This little man is gonna find out he's got a real pa!'' Waving, he flagged his boy over, and Adam raced back to him, face red, legs flying wildly. The look of pure joy on the boy's face almost broke Heather's heart. She wanted to think that this visit to the ranch was just a lark, a diversion no more interesting than their trips to Candlestick Park or Fisherman's Wharf, but she had the deep, unsettling fear that what Adam was feeling was more—a deeper bond to the land that ran through his veins as naturally as his father's blood.

And in her heart, she knew that some of Turner's arguments were valid. She did spoil Adam. She did overprotect him. Because of Dennis's ambivalence toward the boy and then the horrid fear brought on by his disease, she had overreacted and coddled her sick son, praying that a mother's love could conquer all.

But maybe her love had overshadowed the fact that what he needed was freedom to explore, a chance to see the world away from the high rises of the city. Maybe what he needed was his father.

Adam, dust smearing his face and the brown "tobacco juice" of grasshoppers staining his fingers, landed under the tree with a loud thump. Automatically, Heather wiped his hands, but the brown dye didn't come off easily.

"Won't hurt him," Turner said. He'd unwrapped a sandwich and handed half to Adam, who promptly turned his nose up at it. "Don't like lettuce," he said.

"Adam..." Heather tried to step in, but Turner waved off her arguments, stripped the lettuce from the sandwich and tossed the green leaf over his shoulder.

"That's littering."

"Not out here," he said, stretching out in the shade of the tree. "Some rabbit or cow or crow or field mouse will find it." He handed Adam a can of soda and the boy grinned widely. "Now look, there's something your mom and I want to tell you."

While her guts wrenched, Heather shot Turner a look that spoke volumes.

Adam sat cross-legged and held his sandwich in two hands. "What?"

"From now on you can call me Dad."

"Why?"

"'Cause I'm your father."

Adam's brow beetled, and he sent Heather a glance that said he thought Turner had lost his marbles. "Already got a dad."

"And you don't want another one."

"Can only have one," he said, in simple five-year-old terms. Having set the older man straight, he took a big bite from his sandwich.

"Well, that's not necessarily true. Lots of people get married and divorced these days."

"My mom and dad are divorced."

"Right. But they may remarry, and when they do, you'll have a stepfather and a stepmother."

Adam chewed his ham sandwich thoughtfully. "So you're gonna marry Mom. Right?"

Turner's jaw slid to the side and Heather hardly dared breathe. "I don't think she'd have me," he said, and cast Heather a look that melted her insides.

"So how can you be my dad?"

"Your mom and I knew each other a long time ago," Turner said carefully, his voice oddly distant. "And...well, we fell in love, I guess, and she ended up pregnant with you, but I was far away. So she married the man you call your father."

"He *is* my father," Adam insisted, and Turner's muscles tightened a bit.

We fell in love? Heather wished she could believe the fairy tale he was spinning. Talk about lies! Turner was staring at his son, and Adam, arms crossed importantly over his chest, wasn't listening to any more of this craziness. He knew who his father was.

"I'm your pa, too," Turner told his boy.

Adam snorted. "Can't have more than one."

Don't argue with him, Heather silently pleaded, and for once Turner used his head.

"Sometimes things aren't so cut-and-dried. I know it'll take a little getting used to and you might still want to call me Turner, and that's okay." Turner's voice had thickened, and he looked down at the boy with an expression of concern and tenderness. "But I want you to know that I really am your pa."

Adam just shook his head and swallowed a drink of grape soda. When he set down the can, his lips were a pale shade of purple. He eyed Turner and Heather with unhidden suspicion. Obviously, he thought the grown-ups around him had lost any lick of common sense they'd been born with.

Heather ruffled her son's hair, letting the silky strands tickle her fingers. She forced words past her lips she hadn't planned on uttering for years. "He's telling you the truth, Adam. Turner is your dad." Looking at Turner, Heather smiled. Somehow this felt right.

"And what about Daddy?" Adam asked belligerently. His entire world had been turned upside down.

"He's your daddy, too. Your stepdaddy."

"I don't get it," he complained.

Heather offered him a tender smile. "Don't worry about it. Turner just wanted you to understand when he tells people you're his son why he's saying it."

"Sounds crazy to me," Adam said, but didn't seem much concerned one way or the other. There was just too much to do here, too much to explore to worry about grown-up things. He left his sandwich half-eaten and ignored three quarters of his soda.

Turner, radiating pride, stared at the boy who was his son, and Heather felt the urge to kiss him, not with passion, but just to let him know that she appreciated the fact that he cared, actually cared, for his son. After so many years of Dennis's apathy, Turner's concern, though irritating sometimes, was a breath of fresh air. At least now, if anything happened to her, Adam would be with a parent who loved him. What more could she ask?

They ate in companionable silence, eating and watching their boy play in the tall grass while the sun lowered and a breeze laden with clover and honeysuckle danced through the dry leaves of the oak tree. Sunlight dappled the ground, shifting as the leaves rustled in the wind. The silence grew between them, and Turner rubbed his chin thoughtfully, as if wrestling with an inner dilemma.

Well, God knew, they had their share.

"Adam brought up an interesting point," Turner said quietly.

"Which is?" she hardly dared ask.

"That, in a perfect world, you and I would be married."

Her heart missed a beat and she looked up sharply to find flinty eyes regarding her without a trace of humor. He wasn't teasing her, but she had the feeling he was testing her. "It's not a perfect world," she said, meeting his gaze boldly.

"Growing up with only one parent isn't easy."

"Lots of kids do it."

His nostrils flared. "Not mine."

"If you're still trying to talk me into moving back to Gold Creek—"

"I think it's gone further than that, Heather. We both know it. Neither of us will be satisfied playing part-time parents, now, will we?"

Her throat was as dry as the last leaves of autumn. "What're you getting at?" she asked, her heart hammering wildly, her fingers nervously working the hem of her vest.

He eyed her long and hard, assessing her as he would a wild mustang he was about to break. "Well, Heather," he said, his gaze traveling up from the cleft at her breasts to settle on her eyes, "I guess I'm asking you to marry me."

Chapter Twelve

Heather almost laughed. Except for the dead-serious glint in his eyes, she would've thought he was joking. But marriage? She bit her lip. How long had she waited for a proposal from this lonesome cowboy? She would've done anything to hear him beg her to marry him six years ago. Now, however, she understood his reasons, the motives for making a commitment he would otherwise have avoided. "You don't have to do this," she said quietly, as she picked a flower from the dried grass and twirled it between her fingers. "I won't keep Adam from you."

His expression tensed. "You mean he can stay with me?" Unleashed anger sparked in his eyes.

"Part of the time, yes. When he's not in school." She swallowed back the impulsive urge to throw caution to the wind and tell him she'd gladly become his wife. However, she wouldn't allow his nobility, if that's what it was, or his love for his child, to interfere with his happiness.

"All summer long?"

"I—I can't promise—"

"Every weekend?"

"Well, no, but—"

Turner's expression turned as thunderous as a summer storm. "But nothing! The only way I'm going to see him as much as I want is for you to live with me."

"Here?"

"Is it so bad, Heather?" His voice was deeper than usual, and she saw the pride in his eyes when he looked over the acres that he'd sweated and bled for.

Hot tears filled her eyes. "No, Turner, it's good here. It's good for you. Maybe even good for Adam. I can feel it. But I don't know if I can fit in. I'd die if I had to spend my days making jam, or tending garden, or...or cleaning out stalls." She stared up at the sky, watching as a hawk circled near the mountains. "It's not a matter of not liking to make jam," she added. "Or even tending the garden. I... I'd enjoy it, some of the time. Even mucking out the stables. But... I need more. I'd go crazy if I couldn't paint, if I couldn't ever sculpt again, if I didn't have time to sit down with a sketch pad and draw." If only he could understand. "It's the same feeling you'd have if you knew you'd never climb on the back of a horse again."

He tipped back his hat and studied the horizon, his eyes narrowed against the sun. "Can't you do those things here?"

"I...yes."

"But you don't want to."

Close to tears, she offered him a tender smile. She'd never loved him more in her life, but she didn't want him to throw away his own life-style. His own needs. "This is no time to sacrifice yourself, Turner. You never wanted to marry. You as much as told me so."

"Maybe I changed my mind."

"Then maybe you'll change it again," she said, her throat closing upon itself as she stared into the intensity of his gaze. "And I'd hate to be the woman you were married to when you realized you wanted out."

"I won't."

"Oh, Turner—"

"Think about it," he suggested, bristling. He dusted his hands on his jeans as he stood.

She doubted she'd think of little else.

That evening, Turner drove them into town. Heather's fingers tightened over the edge of the pickup seat as they passed familiar landmarks, the park with the gazebo built in memory of Roy Fitzpatrick's death, the yellow-brick building that had once been the Gold Creek Hotel and now housed Fitzpatrick, Incorporated, the post office on Main Street and the old Rexall Drugstore still standing on the corner of Main and Pine.

"I thought Adam would like one of the best burgers this side of the Rocky Mountains!" Turner said as he eased his pickup close to the curb.

They walked into the drugstore and a bell tinkled. The ceilings were high, with lights and fans, never renovated in the seventy years that the building had stood in the center of town. Shelves were neatly stacked; row upon row of cosmetics, medications, jewelry, paper items and toys stood just as they had most of the decade. The items had changed, turned over for new and improved stock, following the trends of small-town tastes, but the shelves were the same metal inlays that Heather remembered from high school.

The soda fountain in the back hadn't changed much, either, and Thelma Surrett, Carlie's mother, her hair grayer, her waist a bit thicker, was still making milk shakes. She glanced over her shoulder and offered Heather a surprised grin. "Well, well, well...look who's back in town," she said, turning on the milk shake mixer and snapping up her notepad as the blender whirred as loudly as a dentist's drill. "First Rachelle and now you. Don't tell me this town has changed its name to Mecca."

Heather grinned. "Rachelle said Carlie will be back for the wedding."

Thelma's eyes shifted a little, and her mouth tightened slightly but she nodded. "In a couple of weeks. Guess she got tired of those long nights up in Alaska. Uh-oh. Who's this?" she asked as Adam climbed up on a stool.

"This is my son, Adam," Heather said, unable to keep the pride from her voice.

"Well, howdy, partner," Thelma replied. She tapped the brim of Adam's hat. "Should I rustle you up some grub?"

"Three burgers, onion, fries, the works," Turner ordered, as Thelma turned off the blender and poured a thick strawberry milk shake into a tall glass.

"I want one of those!" Adam demanded, and Thelma, handing the drink to another customer, winked at the boy.

"You got it."

"Take off your hat while you eat, Adam."

"No!"

"Your ma's right," Turner added. "It's just plain good manners." He lifted the hat from his son's head.

Adam clapped his hands over hair that raised with static electricity. "I *hate* manners."

"Me, too," Turner said with a chuckle.

Heather felt as if she'd been transported back to high school and the days she'd walked to the pharmacy after school, tagging along with Rachelle and Carlie. Eventually Laura Chandler had joined the group and Laura had flagrantly ignored Rachelle's younger sister. "She's such a drag," she'd told Rachelle. "Can't we ditch her?"

Rachelle, none-too-thrilled to be stuck with Heather, had, nonetheless stood up for her. "It's okay," she'd argued, and Laura had pouted, though Carlie had never minded. Well, things had changed—turned around in the past twelve years. Laura had ended up married to Brian Fitzpatrick. Years later she'd been accused of killing Roy, the boy who, had he lived, would have become her brother-in-law.

Thelma started burgers sizzling on the grill, and soon they were eating again, laughing and talking, listening to Thelma go on and on about Rachelle's upcoming wedding and how she hoped Carlie would find a nice boy to settle down with and marry.

After finishing their meal, they wandered through the drugstore for a while, and as they were leaving, nearly ran into Scott McDonald. Turner's face stretched into a grin, but Heather had trouble finding a smile. Scott had been one of Roy Fitzpatrick's friends who had been with Rachelle the night Roy had been killed. After Roy's death, Scott had been vocal in pointing out Jackson's guilt, and had given Rachelle a rough time thereafter.

"I want you to meet someone, Scott," Turner said, and Heather thought she might drop through the yellowed linoleum of the drugstore's floor.

Turner introduced Scott to his son, and Heather managed a thin smile. Scott's eyes flickered with interest, but he congratulated Turner on such a "fine-looking boy." He and his wife, Karen, were expecting their first in February.

"I don't know if that was such a good idea," Heather said, as they wandered along the streets, window shopping at the bakery, jeweler's and travel agency.

"He would've found out anyway. He's Fred's brother and Fred works for me." Turner slid a comforting arm around her shoulders. "Sooner or later it's all gonna come out."

"I vote for later."

"But it's easier now. Less to explain."

Her chest felt tight and worry crowded her brow as they strolled down the sidewalks. Adam found a pair of cowboy boots in the window of the shoe store, and Turner eyed a stove on display at the local Sears catalog store.

The town had a lazy summer feel. A few birds twittered and traffic rolled by at a snail's pace. The city lamps began to glow as dusk crept over the land and they walked unhurried to the park and past the gazebo erected in Roy's memory.

While Adam scrambled all over the playground equipment, Turner chased him, and Heather sat alone on a park bench. In the evening, with the wind soughing through the trees, Gold Creek didn't seem so horrible. She had fond memories of the town where as a child she'd drawn hopscotch on the cracked sidewalks, jumped rope and ridden her bike along the flat tree-lined streets. Her family hadn't had much money, but they'd made up for it in love.

And then her father had started drinking and his wandering eye had ripped apart that cozy blanket of security. Their mother had been devastated, the girls stunned. Tears and anger, pity and anguish had been followed by deep embarrassment. Gossiping tongues had wagged. Her father had filed for divorce and married a younger woman. The rumors had exploded. Later, Roy Fitzpatrick had been killed and Rachelle, alone, had stood up for Jackson Moore, the bad boy, telling the world that she'd spent the night with him, ruining her reputation.

Scandal had swept like a tornado through Gold Creek and the Tremonts were at its vortex. The friends and neighbors

Heather had known all her life seemed to look at her differently, some with compassion, some with worry, others with out-and-out disgust. Life had never been the same. Heather had learned what it felt like to be an object of speculation while her sister became an object of ridicule. And Heather had begun to hate the small town she'd once felt was the center of the universe.

But now... if she faced the past, stood proudly with Turner by her side, maybe she could learn to feel comfortable in Gold Creek again. Not all the citizens were gossips. Not all were cruel. Not all had long memories. Not all cared. The people, and the town, had grown up, and Rachelle had been vindicated.

However, when the truth about Adam's parentage came out, she feared her innocent little boy would become grist for a long-dry gossip mill. But now she was stronger. She and Turner would protect their son.

For Heather, what people thought was no longer as important as it once had been. She'd survive, with her head held high. As for changing her life-style, there were drawbacks to living in the city where oftentimes she'd felt isolated. In San Francisco there were so many people, but so few good friends. Knowing people from the time they were children created a bond that was like no other in life.

Rachelle, though she hadn't seen Carlie in years, would never find a friend she understood better.

Wrapping her arms around herself, Heather watched as Turner pushed Adam on a swing. Adam shrieked in delight and Turner laughed, a deep, rumbling sound of pure happiness. In her heart, Heather knew she could never separate father and son. Now that they'd come to know each other, she wouldn't stand between them.

Stars winked in the heavens and other children played a game of tag on the baseball diamond near the equipment.

Mothers and fathers pushed strollers down the cement walkways. Teenagers cruised by in cars, searching for their friends.

There was a charm to this town, and whether she liked it or not, it was, and always would be, home. Tears touched the back of her eyes. She could return. Her mother was here. Her father was in a town nearby. Jackson had told Rachelle he thought they should buy some property here eventually, though that might have been a joke. But if he was serious, there was a chance he and Rachelle would visit occasionally.

And Turner, bless and curse him, Turner belonged here.

The course of the rest of her life depended upon Turner. As it had since the first time she'd made love to him six years before.

It was after nine by the time they returned to the ranch. Nadine had made the spare room up for Adam, and after a quick bath, he was asleep as soon as his head hit the pillow.

Turner and Heather were alone. They sat on the porch swing, hearing the chorus of crickets and watching thousands of diamondlike stars glitter in the dark heavens. The old swing rocked slowly back and forth, creaking on rusty hinges. Roses, gone to seed, scented the air. Turner placed his arm over the back of the swing, gently holding Heather closer. "I wasn't kidding this afternoon," he said, his voice surprisingly rough. "I want you to consider marrying me."

She was touched, and her heart screamed "yes." "You wouldn't be happy," she said, her head resting against his shoulder.

"*You* wouldn't be happy."

Right now she was more content than she'd ever been. She couldn't imagine spending another day alone, without

Turner. "I could be happy, Turner," she heard herself say, "with you. With Adam."

"But...?"

"But I'm not sure if I could live in the town."

"We're miles from the town, and there's a fairly substantial lake between the ranch and Gold Creek. It wouldn't be like before, when you were smack-dab in the middle of the city limits. And if you want to paint and draw, we'll find you a place. You could still keep the gallery in the city and go there anytime you got the urge."

Was it worth it? She gazed into Turner's steel-gray eyes and her heart swelled with love. She knew there was only one answer. "Of course I'll marry you, Turner," she said, as his strong arms surrounded her. His lips touched hers, gently at first, softly exploring, until he brazenly covered her mouth with his own.

Four days later, Heather had settled herself into the ranch routine. Though she did cook breakfast and dinner for Adam and Turner, she drew the line at lunch for the hands. She figured they'd gotten along without her all these years and they could get along without her now. Besides, she planned to spend a lot of her time sketching or painting.

She and Adam had scouted through all the old buildings and finally, though it needed a lot of work, she'd settled on an attic over the stables for her studio. Every evening, Turner had helped her haul out the junk—books, magazines, old bikes, broken saddles, trunks of clothes and everything else under the sun. She was ready to start work refurbishing the room and she eyed it critically.

The attic was unique with its windows, pitched ceiling and inoperable ceiling fan. Though the room was smaller than her studio in the city, and it would require a lot of elbow grease to clean it up, the attic definitely had potential. With a couple of skylights, new paint and refinished floors, the room just might convert into an attractive workplace.

"I think you're right," agreed her mother, who had come out to the ranch for a visit. "But you might check for mice," she added, her practiced gaze sweeping the baseboards.

"I'll get a cat," Heather replied with a grin.

Ellen swiped at a cobweb dangling from the ceiling. "You know, I don't approve of you living here," she said, chewing nervously on her lip.

"Mom—"

"In my book you live with a man *after* you marry him, not before—and I don't care how much you're involved with him. It just doesn't look right!"

It was on the tip of Heather's tongue to tell her mother that she planned to marry Turner, but she didn't. She didn't want to steal any of her sister's thunder. Rachelle had waited too many years for the moment when she would become Jackson Moore's bride, so Heather and Turner had agreed to wait until after Rachelle's wedding to make an announcement about their own wedding plans. There wasn't any hurry. Despite what her mother thought.

"Living in sin is against everything I ever taught you."

"It's not sin, Mom."

Together they walked down the outside staircase and crossed the yard. Nearby, Turner was breaking a mule-headed colt and Adam was watching in rapt awe.

"Well, I will admit, Dennis didn't seem like much of a father," Ellen said as they walked onto the back porch. She glanced at her grandson. "I always wondered about that, you know. And I do believe that Adam deserves better."

Heather smiled.

"Maybe Turner isn't so bad, after all."

"He's not," Heather assured her mother as they entered the kitchen. "Here. Sit down. I've got ice tea. You drink and

I'll start dinner." She poured them each a glass of tea, and while her mother lit a cigarette, Heather began slicing scallions and mushrooms. She nearly cut off her finger when Ellen announced that she was starting work as a clerk at Fitzpatrick Logging.

Heather dropped her knife and stared at her mother in disbelief. "But—"

"Look, I need any job I can get," Ellen said emphatically as she sat at the table in Turner's kitchen and ignored the glass of ice tea that Heather had set before her. The ice cubes were melting and her lower lip quivered. "That stepfather of yours is trying to make sure I'll have to work until I'm seventy," she said, trying to fight back tears of self-pity.

"I know, but I just find it strange. You applied at the logging company—what—six or eight weeks ago and you were told there were no positions, right? Fitzpatrick Logging was going to be laying off men, not hiring clerks."

"Well, things must've changed," Ellen said, a little miffed. "Anyway, I can't afford to be picky, and when Thomas called—"

"Wait. Time out. Hold the phone." Heather pointed the fingers of one hand into the palm of her other in an effort to cut her mother off, and her stomach began to knot. "Thomas Fitzpatrick called you himself?" Her suspicions rose to the surface. "Isn't that a little odd?"

"It is, but I thought, well, now that we're practically family..." Ellen let her voice drift off, and Heather decided not to argue with her mother, who had taken more than her share of heartaches in life.

"When do you start?"

"Tomorrow. Can you believe it? I was so worried that I'd have to get a job in Jefferson City or even farther away. This will be so close and handy." She stared up at her daughter. "It really is a godsend."

"Then I'm glad for you," Heather replied, though she felt uneasy. Thomas Fitzpatrick wasn't a man to be trusted, and her mother had always been susceptible to the rich— believing their stories, hoping some of their wealth and fame might rub off on her. Dennis Leonetti was a case in point. And the Fitzpatrick wealth was rumored to be much more than the Leonettis'.

Heather glanced out the open window to the corral where Adam was hanging on the fence and watching his father as Turner trained a feisty gray colt. Shirt off, muscles gleaming with sweat in the afternoon sun, Turner held the lead rope, coaxing the nervous animal to trot around him in a circle. In another pen, one of the men who worked for Turner, Fred McDonald, was separating cows from their calves. The fragrance of roses mingled with the ever-present smell of dust and filtered into the warm room. The cattle bawled, Adam yelled at his dad and Turner spoke in soft tones to the headstrong colt.

"He almost ran for state senator," Ellen said, still defending Thomas Fitzpatrick. Heather managed to change the subject as she heated a pot of water for the pasta and stirred the sauce. They talked about the wedding, less than a week away, and Ellen's face brightened at the thought that one of her daughters might find matrimonial happiness, an intangible thing that had eluded her in two trips to the altar. Ellen's opinion of Jackson Moore had turned around and she was beginning to trust Turner. A good sign. Now, if she'd just reform her opinion of Thomas Fitzpatrick...

"So how's my grandson been?" Ellen said, finally sipping her tea while Heather worked at the stove, trying, with Turner's limited cookware, to fix dinner. She'd invited her mother over for shrimp fettuccine, but cooking on the old range had been a trial. There were definitely some things about San Francisco that she would miss. In lieu of a whisk, she used a beat-up wooden spoon to stir the sauce.

"Adam?" she asked as the creamy sauce simmered. "He's been fine."

"And the surgery?"

"So far it's been postponed. As long as Adam's in remission, there's no reason . . ." She glanced out the window and smiled. Adam's new boots already were covered with a thin layer of dust, and his cowboy hat was, these days, a permanent fixture on his head.

Fred finished with the cows and waved to Turner as he climbed into his old Dodge pickup. Turner let Adam help him cool down the horse.

"Boots off," Heather ordered as the two men in her life approached the back door. "And hands washed."

"Mine are clean," Adam replied holding up grimy palms for inspection as he tried to nudge one boot off with the toe of another.

"Not good enough," she said. "March, kiddo . . ." She pointed toward the bathroom with her wooden spoon.

"Drillmaster," Turner grumbled.

"You, too—oh!" He grabbed her by surprise and silenced her with a kiss that stole her breath.

"*I* don't take orders from no woman," he said, in a gritty voice. With a wink, he let her go, leaving her breathless as he headed for the bathroom.

"My goodness," her mother whispered. "I wondered what you saw in that man, but now, I guess I know."

Preparations for the wedding started to pick up. Rachelle and Jackson had moved into Heather's cottage in town—the small house where she and Rachelle had grown up—and the old, forgotten summer camp on the edge of Whitefire Lake was being overhauled. Rachelle, usually calm under any condition, was a mess, and their mother, too, was a nervous wreck.

Heather imagined she might be a little more nervous, but she had her own problems to contend with. Doing a quick calculation with the calendar, she realized that she had missed the last menstrual period of her cycle.

She couldn't believe the cold hard facts of the calendar, so she counted off the weeks. No doubt about it. There was no disputing the fact that she was nearly two weeks late. And her periods had always come like clockwork. Except when she'd been pregnant with Adam.

Mentally kicking herself for not being more careful, she checked the calendar one more time. She'd just been too busy with her worries for Adam and her relationship with Turner to consider the fact that she might be pregnant. It had been stupid—as often as she and Turner made love. This was bound to happen...and deep down, she knew, she'd hoped it would occur. But not just yet. Not until things were settled.

A part of her thrilled at the prospect of pregnancy, but the saner side of her nature was scared to death. She wasn't married, for crying out loud. What would Turner do? What would he think? Just when everything was going so well...

She thought about confiding in him, but decided to wait until she was more certain. He had enough on his mind and shouldn't have to worry about another baby until Heather was positive of her condition, until she'd checked with a gynecologist or done a home pregnancy test.

While Turner was working with the cattle, she and Adam drove into town, and after a frantic meeting with Rachelle, who was dead certain the florist and band were going to foul up everything, Heather stopped by the pharmacy. She bought Adam a butterscotch soda, and while he was slurping up the gooey concoction, she purchased a few supplies—tissues, candles, wrapping paper and a pregnancy test. A young girl she didn't recognize helped her, and all her items were packed carefully in a brown sack before she returned to the soda fountain.

Glancing nervously over her shoulder to the pharmaceutical counter where Scott McDonald worked, she saw him at his elevated station, busy filling prescriptions. Though he had a bird's-eye view of the counters, fountain and shelves, she doubted he had paid much attention to her purchase.

As Adam finished his soda, she sipped a diet soda and chatted with Thelma about Carlie's arrival, which was scheduled for the very next day. Thelma and her husband, Weldon, could hardly wait to see their daughter again.

Hours later, when she returned home, Heather kept the pregnancy test in her large shoulder bag. She had to wait until morning to administer the test, so she planned to pick a morning when Turner got up early to feed the stock. A deceptive whisper touched her heart, but she told herself she was doing the right thing. No need to worry him without cause.

So why did she feel like a criminal?

Positive.

The test results were boldly positive.

Heather, hand trembling, touched her abdomen where deep within, Turner's child was growing. She leaned against the wall for support and didn't know whether to laugh or cry. A new baby! Ever since Adam had turned one year old, she'd hoped to conceive another child. But Turner's child? A full-blooded sister or brother to Adam—who would've ever thought? Certainly not Heather Tremont Leonetti.

Tears of happiness formed in her eyes. This unborn baby, this miracle baby, was a dream come true.

"Oh, God, thank you," she whispered. She'd bought the test three days before but had to wait until this morning. Turner hadn't woken her when he'd gotten up, and though she'd been awake, she'd feigned sleep until she'd heard the kitchen door close shut behind him.

He hadn't come back in yet, and Heather had enough time to perform the simple test and wait for the results. Without a doubt, the test told her she was pregnant, and with that knowledge came a contentment. Having her children growing up here on the ranch, where the air was fresh, the water clear, the work hard but satisfying, wasn't such a bad idea. They weren't that far from the city and could take weekend excursions to San Francisco or anywhere else they wanted to.

She could paint and sculpt and more importantly be a mother to her children and a wife to Turner Brooks.

Yes, life was going to change, but only for the better. Humming to herself, she threw on her robe and walked to the kitchen. Through the back window, past the heavily blossomed clematis that sprawled over the back porch and across a yard parched from the dry summer, she spied Turner deep in conversation with Fred McDonald. Fred had his own spread to run, but he spent his extra time here, with Turner, helping out and making a few extra bucks. Turner's ranch wasn't as large or as busy as the Lazy K, but it was paid for and, along with her own income, could provide well enough for a small family.

Smiling to herself with the knowledge of her secret, she plugged in the coffeemaker and added coffee and water. After checking on Adam, who was still sleeping soundly, she quickly showered and slipped into a sundress and planned what she would say to Turner and when. Maybe tonight. After Adam was asleep. She'd make a dinner, light candles, and in the warm candle glow, reach across the table for Turner's hand and tell him of the child...

Pregnant! The word whirled through her mind. She thought of her maternity clothes, sophisticated expensive outfits tucked away in her house in San Francisco. The silks, wool blends and velours would hardly do on the ranch. She didn't even own a pair of maternity jeans. That would have to change.

She combed her wet hair and decided to let it dry in the sun. With only a quick touch of lipstick and blush, she padded back to the kitchen, set out three empty cups and arranged the sugar and creamer and three spoons beside a vase she'd filled with roses the day before.

Feeling unusually domestic, she decided to bake biscuits. She was busy with her work, her mind already moving ahead to planning a nursery here on the ranch, as she rolled out the dough on an old breadboard.

She heard the grind of a pickup's engine. Looking out the window, she spied Fred's old truck lumbering out of the drive, which was strange, considering he'd just arrived. But maybe he was running into town for parts or supplies.... Turner's tractor was acting up again and he'd ordered a part from the farm machine store in Gold Creek. She'd convinced herself that she'd figured out the reasons for Fred's abrupt departure when she spied Turner walking toward the back porch. Smiling, she lifted her hand to wave to him when she noticed his expression—hard and grim, his skin stretched tight across his nose and the blades of his cheekbones. His mouth was a thin white line and his nostrils were flared in rage, not unlike those of an angry stallion.

Heather's heart plummeted. She barely noticed the dog romping at his heels, a half-grown puppy, part German shepherd from the looks of him, bounding playfully in the dust that Turner's furious strides stirred. Every once in a while the pup would stop, snap at the air to capture a fly, then romp forward again.

"What's going on?" she asked, as Turner shoved open the door and the dog followed him into the kitchen.

"You tell me."

"Fred left . . . and this dog . . . ?"

"For Adam." He glared at her then, and her throat closed in upon itself, for the hatred that glittered in his gunmetal eyes was unmistakable. "Every kid needs a dog."

"Something's wrong . . ." The temperature in the cozy kitchen had seemed to plummet and Heather's stomach turned sour. She dropped her rolling pin and wiped her flour-dusted hands on a towel. "What is it, Turner?" she asked, her mind racing before landing upon the answer. There could only be one reason for the anger seething from him.

He knew. Somehow he knew about the baby. And rather than the happiness she'd expected he would feel, his emotions had turned the other direction until he was in a black rage.

"What, Heather?" he said, striding over to her and glaring down at her with condemning eyes. "What's wrong?"

"I . . . I . . ."

"Spit it out, woman. You're pregnant."

She felt like a Judas. All the happiness she'd felt just moments before melted away. "Yes, but I just found out—"

"Like hell! How come half the town already knows?"

"It couldn't . . . I mean I just took the test this morning . . ." she said, as her words faded, for she understood what had happened. This town. This bloody small town! When she'd bought the pregnancy detection kit, someone at the drugstore had put two and two together, and though most clerks weren't supposed to discuss their customer's purchases, someone had. The clerk at the drugstore, or

Scott McDonald, or even Thelma Surrett, must have seen her and started speculating.

Heather's insides churned. Her hands shook.

"The whole damned town knows I'm gonna be a father before I do," he spat out, kicking the wall. The puppy, nervous already, slithered to a hiding spot beneath the table and cowered against the wall, whining pitifully. "Hell, Heather, didn't you think I might want to know?"

"I was going to tell you—"

He grabbed her then, his grip on her arms punishing, the fierce fire in his eyes reminding her of the very devil himself. "When?"

"As soon as I—"

"When we were married? Or before? You know, I've heard of a lot of low-down, despicable things to do, but to get pregnant, plan it all out, just to make sure you had a donor—"

"What are you talking about?"

His voice was as cold as a bottomless well. "Don't pretend, Heather. It belittles us both."

"What the devil are you talking about?" she demanded, but back in the darkest corner of her mind, she knew, and, God help her, some of those very thoughts had been with her. Hadn't she once considered making love to him just to create a child so like Adam that the baby might be able to eventually become a bone-marrow donor? But that would never have been the sole reason. No. She'd wanted another child for years. Her thoughts must've reflected in her eyes, because he let go of her then and his lips curled in disgust. "I don't like being used, Heather. Not for any reason."

"I didn't use you," she protested.

"Like hell! I was a stud. Nothing more."

She felt as if he'd hit her hard in the stomach. "Oh, Turner, you can't believe—"

"Do you deny that you thought about this? That you hoped we could start a new child? A sibling for Adam? A damned *donor?*"

"Oh, God," she whispered, as the color drained from her body and she had to hold on to the counter for support.

"I just find it hard to believe that I fell for it."

"You didn't fall for anything—"

"Don't lie to me, woman!"

Something inside her snapped, and her temper exploded. "I'm not lying, Turner, and I shouldn't have to remind you that this baby wasn't created by me alone! You were there and, I might add, enjoyed doing your part!"

His breath came out in a hiss. "I don't object to a child! What's the difference between one or two? But it's the reasons for creating this child I hate. Cold and calculating. You didn't even consult me—"

"Why would I do it?" she nearly screamed. "Your bone marrow is a match!"

"Maybe you didn't want to be saddled with me. Maybe you didn't trust me."

"No, Turner, it's you who never trusted me," she said, wretchedness whirling deep in her soul. "You never loved me. And that was my mistake, because I loved you, Turner. For six years I didn't do right by Dennis, because it was you I loved, you I'd always loved. But you never have believed me." She was visibly shaking by this time, and she blinked hard against tears that burned her eyes. "With Adam or without, with this baby or without, I loved you. Stupidly, blindly, with no reason behind it, I loved you."

She noticed the muscle ticking near his eye, saw the contempt in his expression and knew all her plans for happiness had been shattered. She glanced away from him, unable to stare him down, and noticed the biscuit dough beginning to rise, smelled the warm scent of coffee she'd never drink, noticed the pathetic grouping of cups and spoons near a vase of freshly cut flowers that she would no longer enjoy. She felt more miserable than she had in her entire life.

"Mommy?" Adam's sleepy voice stopped her short, and she quickly cleared the lump of self-pity from her throat. She couldn't break down in front of her child. He needed to know that everything was all right, that he was secure. He'd already lost Dennis as a father; it wasn't going to happen again! Her fingers curled into fists of determination and she blinked back any remnants of her tears.

Turning, she managed a thin smile and thought her heart would break. He was getting well. Heather noticed the color in his cheeks and the dark circles beneath his eyes had disappeared. Living here, with Turner, had helped Adam. "Good morning, pumpkin," she whispered over a clogged throat.

"You sad?" He looked from Turner to Heather with worry etched in his small features, and Heather swept him into her arms.

"I'm fine, sweetheart. Look what Turner got for you—"

Adam's eyes rounded as he spied the puppy, still cowering under the table. Slowly the gawky pup inched forward one big paw at a time. Adam pushed his way back to the floor. "He's mine?" Adam whispered, his adoring gaze flying to Turner's hard face. For just a second, Turner's harsh visage cracked and he offered his son a smile as warm as a Western sunset. Heather's heart shredded.

"All yours."

"What's his name?"

"You get to name him."

"Can I really?" Adam looked to his mother as if he expected her to refuse.

"Of course you can."

Adam's freckled face squinched into a thoughtful frown. "Then I'll call him Daytona—that's where they have car races!'' He reached out to pet the dog's broad head and was rewarded with a long tongue that swiped his skin. Adam shrieked in happiness and within minutes he and the dog were outside, running along the fence line, kicking up dust and trampling dry grass and wildflowers.

''I won't let him go, you know,'' Turner said in a low voice edged in steel.

She bit her lip to keep from crying. ''I know.''

Turner stormed out of the house and she didn't think twice, just turned on her heel, marched to the bedroom she'd shared with him and stripped her clothes from the closet and bureau drawers. He didn't love her, never had, never would—and she'd be damned if she'd spend the rest of her life with a man who couldn't return her feelings.

Call her a hopeless romantic, call her a fool, but call her a woman who knew her own mind. She packed her things quickly and did the same with Adam's. In short order she was ready to leave. She'd take Adam, she'd take her unborn child, she'd even take the dog, but she knew she'd be leaving behind a part of her heart.

Chapter Thirteen

"You could do worse." Thomas Fitzpatrick tented his hands beneath his chin and waited as Turner read through the offer. "That's two and a half times what the place is worth—four times what your dad paid for it when he bought it from me. Quite a profit."

Turner clicked his pen a few times. The papers looked straightforward enough, and he wanted to sell. Hell, ever since the fight with Heather three days ago, he'd thought of nothing but running.

But he hadn't. Because things weren't settled. Not only was there Heather and Adam, but now a new baby to consider. He and Heather hadn't talked; she'd packed up the boy and said something about visiting her mother until the wedding, and Turner, because of his stubborn streak, hadn't bothered to call. But he hadn't slept a wink, either.

Then, out of the blue, Thomas Fitzpatrick showed up on his front porch offering money, bigger money than before.

His ticket out. Almost like destiny. Trouble was, Turner didn't believe in destiny.

"I thought I told you I wasn't interested," Turner said, slapping the contracts and deeds and all the rest of the legal mumbo jumbo onto the table.

"But that was before."

"Before? Before what?"

Thomas pulled at his silk tie. His silver hair, as always, was cut just above his collar. He smoothed one side of his trim white moustache, then spread his hands in a supplicating gesture. "Gold Creek is a small town. There are no secrets in small towns."

"Meaning what?" Turner didn't like the feel of a noose around his neck, and he definitely was feeling that he was about to be strung up—by one of the best.

"I've heard about you and the Tremont girl."

"What have you heard?" Turner demanded, the noose tightening and his rage turning black.

"Just that she left you. With your boy. Well, I know the cost of lawyers and I figure if you're planning a lawsuit—for custody, you could use some quick cash. And if you do end up with the kid, you'll have medical bills—more bills than you can imagine—"

Turner was on his feet in an instant. He kicked back his chair and grabbed Fitzpatrick by his fancy silk tie. It was his turn to pull the rope and he'd strangle the old man if he had to. "Where'd you hear all this—"

"Doesn't matter."

"Like hell it doesn't! Now, if you don't want to tangle with me any further, you'd better spill it, Fitzpatrick."

Beads of sweat dotted Thomas's brow and trickled down his temples. "You can't—"

"Tell me!"

"You have no right—"

Turner's cold smile moved from one side of his face to the other. "You're on my property, now, Fitzpatrick. Leastwise it's still mine until I sign your damned papers. So, while you're here, you're going to play by my rules. Who told you?" To add emphasis to his question, he jerked on the tie. Thomas came forward, falling onto the scarred table, sending documents scattering to the floor.

"Ellen Little," he finally said. "Ellen Tremont Little."

Deceit seemed to run in the family. Turner dropped the tie and Fitzpatrick fell back into his chair. "Heather's mother," he snarled. So Heather had run to Mama and told her everything and Ellen had seen fit to give Thomas the information he wanted. Turner's guts twisted into hard little knots and he could barely see beyond his fury.

Recovering somewhat, Thomas offered Turner a grin as icy as his own. "Ellen works for me now. Seems to think she owes me something for giving her a pathetic little job."

"You bastard!" Turner lunged for the man, but Fitzpatrick was out of his chair in an instant. He moved as quick as a sidewinder to the back door.

"Think about the offer. Believe me, it's the best one you're gonna get." He was gone as quickly as he'd come, and Turner looked at the scattered papers on the floor. Unfortunately some of what Fitzpatrick had said made sense. Heather had plenty of money from her divorce from Leonetti and she would use every dime she had to keep her child—his child—their child. His lungs felt tight and he could barely breathe. There was the chance that Adam would need more extremely expensive medical care—Turner's insurance company wouldn't touch a child already diagnosed with leukemia.

All he had was this ranch, and Fitzpatrick was offering him a fortune for it.

Bile rising in his throat, he grabbed up all the papers and without thinking too hard, started signing the documents wherever they were marked. With Fitzpatrick's dirty money, he could fight for custody of his boy and his unborn child; then he'd figure out how he'd spend the rest of his life.

"You're a fool!" Nadine scrubbed the stove as if her very life depended on it. "You let that woman go? Couldn't you see that she loved you, that she wanted to have your children, that she would've done anything... Oh, for crying out loud, why am I talking to you?" Still polishing the damned stainless steel, she hazarded a quick glare in his direction. "Men!"

Turner wasn't going to let Nadine rattle him. He wouldn't have confided in her at all except she already knew half the story and when she'd come here and found Heather gone, she'd guessed the rest. He grabbed a bottle of beer from the refrigerator, plopped himself down at the table and twisted open the cap.

"What about your son?" Nadine asked. "What're you going to do about him?"

"Probably sue for custody."

"Oh, great! Just wonderful!" Nadine didn't even attempt to hide her scorn. "Really confuse the kid." She threw her dirty rag into a pail and put her rubber-glove-encased hands on her slim hips. "First the man he thought was his father rejected him, and now the guy claiming to be his real dad is getting into a bloody legal battle with his mom. And he's the prize. 'Course he'll be pushed and pulled and put through a damned emotional wringer before it's all settled! Think, Turner! Use that brain of yours if you can find it! What's going to happen to Adam and, as far as that goes, not that it really matters, mind you, think what's going to happen to you!"

"I'm—"

"Miserable." Nadine yanked off her gloves, and her anger was suddenly replaced with a deeper emotion. She took in a long breath and said in a voice that was surprisingly even given the state of her emotions, "Look, Turner, believe me, I, of all people, wouldn't steer you into a relationship you didn't want. But for the past week or two, you've been different—a changed man. Whether you know it or not, Heather Leonetti got under your skin so deep, you'll never be able to shed yourself of her. So you'd better stop being a coward and face up to the fact." She made a quick motion to the bottle of beer he cradled, untouched, between his hands. "And that's not going to help. Your father was proof enough of that."

To gall her as much as anything, he took a long swallow. The beer tasted sour, and he hated to admit it but she was right, damn it. He missed Heather. He missed waking up with her; he missed hearing her sing; he missed the scent of her perfume on his pillow and the lilt of her laughter. He missed making love to her at night.

And that didn't even begin to compare to how empty he felt without Adam. Since the boy had been gone, Turner felt as if a hole had been torn from his heart.

"Don't let your pride be your downfall," Nadine said as she reached for the pile of papers he was about to throw out. "You know where you can find her." With a flip of her wrist, she sailed the wedding invitation for Rachelle Tremont and Jackson Moore onto the table. "That's all I've got to say."

Thank God she didn't know he planned to sell the ranch to Fitzpatrick.

He watched as she strode out the door in a cloud of self-righteous fury. She was right, damn it, Turner thought, picking up the invitation. Heather would be there. At the wedding.

Oh, to hell with it! He crushed the engraved sheet of paper in his fist and finished his beer. Then he picked up the phone and placed a long-distance call to the Lazy K Ranch. If Zeke wasn't there, he'd track him down all across the damned country, and Mazie was going to help him. He needed answers. Answers he should have had six years before!

"Something's wrong. I feel it," Rachelle said as she eyed her reflection in a free-standing full-length mirror in the back room of the tiny chapel by the lake.

"You worry too much. Everything's perfect." Heather adjusted her sister's veil and sighed. Rachelle looked beautiful. Her long auburn hair, trained into loose curls that fell to the middle of her back, shimmered beneath the beaded veil and her dress, off-white with a nipped waist, lace and pearl bodice and billowing skirt, fit her exquisitely.

"Heather's right. You're always borrowing trouble," Carlie agreed. With sleek black hair and blue-green eyes, she smiled at her friend. What a fiasco Carlie's arrival had caused just a few days before the wedding. Rachelle had insisted Carlie become part of the wedding party. Somehow the seamstress had made the gown, another usher, a cousin of Jackson's, was fitted with a tuxedo and here she was, an encouraging smile in place.

"I don't know." Rachelle's forehead was lined as she looked from her best friend to her sister. "I did something I shouldn't have."

"You invited Thomas Fitzpatrick," Heather said.

"You knew?" Rachelle asked.

"It doesn't take an investigative reporter, Rachelle. You gave me the invitations to mail."

"Didn't you tell Jackson?" Carlie asked.

"Not until last night."

"And?"

"Let's just say he didn't jump for joy," Rachelle said, though she laughed.

"That takes a lot of nerve." Carlie tugged at her zipper, then smoothed her skirts.

"Or no brains," Rachelle joked.

"Or both." Heather tried to join in the fun. She wasn't going to ruin Rachelle's big day. She wasn't! And yet she had trouble thinking of anything other than Turner.

"Okay, so I've bared my soul," her sister said, eyes narrowing on Heather. "Now out with it. Something's bothering you."

"Nothing—really."

"Adam's okay?"

Heather managed a smile. "Adam's great! Now he thinks he's a cowboy."

"Because of Turner." Rachelle fiddled with the fasteners at her back. "Something's not right. Can you get that—?" She held her hair and veil out of the way.

"Here. No problem." Quickly Carlie took charge, hooking the fastener at Rachelle's nape into place. "These are always a pain," she said.

"You know about wedding dresses? Come on, Carlie. Were you married?"

For a second Carlie blanched but she recovered. "While I was modeling, I did a lot of bridal stuff."

"I'll just be glad when this is over." Rachelle let her hair fall down her back again. She sent her sister a sidelong glance. "So tell me about Turner."

"I don't know if he'll show up," Heather hedged.

"Don't tell me you broke up." The dismay on Rachelle's face cut Heather to the bone. Carlie, who'd caught up with the Tremont girls' lives in the past three days knew most of the story.

"Don't worry about Turner. We just had a little argument," Heather lied, and hated the fact that, once again, because of Turner Brooks, she was stretching the truth. Her mother, bless her soul, had been right: one lie did beget another. She shrugged. "Really, that's all."

"It had better be," Rachelle said, her lips tightening a bit.

With a sharp rap, the door flew open and Ellen stormed inside. "I can't believe it! What was he thinking! That father of yours brought—"

"I know, Mom, I invited her," Rachelle admitted, wincing a little at the hurt in her mother's eyes. "She's his wife, whether you like it or not."

For a second, Heather thought their mother might break down and cry, but Ellen, made of stronger stuff, squared her shoulders. Her hair was freshly done and she was wearing a gold suit. "You look great, Mom," Heather told her, and kissed her cheek.

"Thanks, honey." Ellen's eyes glistened with pride as she looked at her two daughters.

"Places, everyone," the minister's wife called through the partially opened door.

Impulsively Rachelle hugged her younger sister. "You and Turner will work things out, I just know it." The sound of music drifted into the little room, and Rachelle took a deep breath. "I guess this is it."

"Good luck!" Heather said. She squeezed Rachelle's hand.

They emerged from the small room near the back of the crowded little chapel. Near the altar, backdropped by long white candles, Jackson Moore fidgeted in his black tuxedo as he waited for his bride. His hair was shiny and black, his eyes anxious, and if he saw Thomas Fitzpatrick sitting in the fifth row, he didn't show any sign of emotion other than love for the woman who planned to spend the rest of her life with him.

Heather's throat was in knots. Taking the arm of Boothe Reece, Jackson's partner in his New York law firm, she began her hesitation step to the music. Soon Rachelle would be starting her new life with Jackson, and Heather would have to begin again, as well—a life without Turner, a life with a new baby, a life of sharing her children with an absent father. Heather forced a smile, and the tears that shimmered in her eyes were tears of happiness for her sister. Nothing more. Or so she tried to convince herself.

Strains of romantic music drifted on the air, and the breeze, smelling of the fresh water of the lake, was cool against Heather's face. The sun had dropped beneath the ridge of westerly mountains and the sky was ribboned with brilliant splashes of magenta and pink.

Twilight was coming. That time of night—dusk really—when her thoughts would always stray to Turner. Stars were beginning to wink, and the ghost of a crescent moon was rising. She wrapped her arms around herself and began walking along the sparsely graveled path toward the lake, the very same lake she'd sipped from only a few weeks earlier. Drat that darned legend! She'd been a fool to think there was any hint of truth in the Indian lore.

With a rustle, the wind picked up and the chilly breath of autumn touched her bare neck. Still wearing her raspberry-hued gown, she picked her way along the ferns and stones.

She'd stayed at the wedding and reception as long as she could, watched Jackson and Rachelle exchange vows, witnessed them place rings upon each other's fingers, smiled as they toasted their new life together and laughed when they'd

cut the cake and force-fed each other. All the old traditions.
New again.

She'd even watched as Rachelle had tossed her bouquet
into the crowd and a surprised Carlie Surrett had caught the
nosegay of white ribbons, carnations and baby pink roses
only to drop the bouquet as if it was as hot and searing as a
branding iron. Rachelle, good-naturedly, had laughed and
tossed the bouquet over her shoulder again and to everyone's joy their mother, Ellen, had ended up with the flowers.

"Can you believe this?" she'd said. "Well, maybe the
third time's the charm!"

The big moment, when Thomas Fitzpatrick had shaken
his bastard son's hand and wished him well, had come afterward. Thomas had seemed sincere, and Jackson, his face
stony, hadn't made a scene. He'd even accepted the envelope Thomas had given him and had said a curt "thanks."
It hadn't been a joyous father-son reunion, but it hadn't
turned into the worst disaster since the Titanic, either.

Now, as she glanced back over her shoulder, Heather noticed that a crowd had joined Rachelle and Jackson on the
portable dance floor they'd had constructed for the cere-
mony. Tucked in the tall pine trees, with torches and color-
ful lanterns adding illumination, the old camp was a cozy
site for a wedding. A great way to start their lives together.

Heather had her own set of plans. Tomorrow she'd return to San Francisco, the city she loved, and start her life
over. Without Turner. Her heart wrenched and her throat
thickened. Tears burned behind her eyes. Why couldn't she
find any comfort in the thought that she was going home?
Why couldn't she find any consolation that she wouldn't
have to move back to Gold Creek? Why wasn't she happy?
The answer was simple: Turner Brooks.

Gathering her skirts, she followed the path until the trees gave way to a stretch of rocky beach. The wedding was far behind her now, the music fading, the laughter no louder than the sound of crickets singing in the dusk.

Twilight had descended, and the stars reflected in the purple depths of the lake. "Oh, Turner," she whispered, kicking a stone toward the water and watching as it rolled lazily into the ebb and flow of the lake.

Again she felt a tickle of a breeze lifting the hairs at her nape. She looked to the west and her breath caught in her throat, for there, just as he'd been six years earlier, was the lone rider, a tall cowboy on horseback, his rangy stallion sauntering slowly in her direction.

Her heart turned over and she wanted to hate him, to tell him to stay out of her life, but she couldn't. Staring up at his rugged features, her heart tumbled and she knew she was destined to love him for the rest of her life.

She waited, unmoving, the wind billowing her skirts until he was close enough that she could see the features of his face. Strong and proud, he'd never change. Her throat closed in on itself, and it was all she could do not to let out a strangled sob.

She thought for a moment that he was coming for her, but she knew differently. He'd known where she would be and was probably here to tell her that he'd talked with a lawyer and was going to sue her for custody of their children. Oh, Lord, how had it come to this? Her fingers twisted in the fabric of her skirt and she wished she could hate him, could fight him tooth and nail for her children, but a stubborn part of her wouldn't give up on the silly, irrational fact that she loved him. As much as she had six years ago.

His jaw was set and hard, but his eyes were dark with an inner torment. Heather braced herself, refused to break down. He slid from the saddle and without a word, wrapped strong arms around her. Pressing his face into the crook of her neck, he held her, and the smells of leather and horse, sweat and musk, brought back each glorious memory she'd ever shared with him.

She clung to him because she had no choice, and tears filled her eyes to run down her cheeks and streak the rough suede of his jacket. Her heart ached, and she wondered if she would ever get over him.

As the night whispered over the lake, Turner's voice was low and thick with emotion. "I love you," he said simply.

Heather's heart shredded. "Y-you don't have to—"

"Shh, darlin'. Don't you know I've always loved you? I was just too much a fool to admit it."

"Please, Turner, don't—" she cried, unable to stand the pain.

He pulled back and placed a finger to her lips. Staring straight into her eyes, with the ghosts of Whitefire Lake as his witnesses, Turner repeated, "I love you. Believe me."

"But—"

"Don't fight it."

Tears slid down her cheeks. Could it be true? She hardly dared believe him, and yet the gaze touching hers—caressing hers—claimed that she was and always had been his whole life. "Oh, God," she whispered, and threw her arms around him. "I love you, too, Turner. I always have."

"Then marry me," he said simply. "Let's not wait. It's time we gave our son a family and time we built a life for our new little one."

"But—"

"Now, marry me."

Things were going so fast. Heather's mind was spinning. "Now?" she repeated as he kissed away her tears.

"Isn't there a preacher over there?" He cocked his head toward the old summer camp and the lights flickering through the trees.

"I don't know.... Yes, I suppose, but do you think—?" Without another word, he lifted her onto his horse, then swung into the saddle behind her. Wrapping one solid arm around her middle, he urged the horse forward toward the bobbing colored lights and the music. "Where's Adam?"

"With my mother—"

He grimaced at that. "Well, as soon as we find him and a preacher we're getting married."

"But Rachelle . . . Jackson . . ."

Turner laughed low in his throat. "Somehow, I don't think they'll mind. They seem to like to cause a stir."

"But why—why now?" she asked.

"You're as bad as Mazie with all your questions," he said, but chuckled. "I finally got hold of Zeke, and the next time I see that old coot, I intend to fill his backside with buckshot."

"Why?"

"He admitted you called, that you were frantic to reach me, but by the time I returned, you'd already married. As for the letters I sent you, I mailed them to the Lazy K with instructions to forward them 'cause I didn't have your address. Zeke, thinking he was doing us a big favor, burned every last one."

"Oh, no—"

"As I said, 'buckshot.'" But he smiled and kissed her temple.

Then, as if he'd truly lost his mind, he reached into the inner pocket of his suede jacket, withdrew a crisp white envelope, and while Sampson broke into a lope, started shredding the neatly-typed pages.

"What—?"

"Confetti, for the bride and groom. Compliments of Thomas Fitzpatrick."

"I don't understand—"

He let the torn pages disperse on the wind, the ragged pieces drifting to the lake. "All you have to understand, lady, is that I love you." With a kiss to her rounded lips, he spurred the horse forward. The wind tore at her hair, and the waters of Whitefire Lake lapped at the tree-studded shore. Turner's arm tightened around her, his lips buried against her neck, and they galloped toward their future as husband and wife.

Together forever, she thought, as the lake flashed by in a blur, and she thought she heard laughter in the trees. Hers? Turner's? Or the ghosts of the past who knew the powers of Whitefire Lake?

*   *   *   *   *

Author's Note

The Native American legend of the Whitefire Lake was whispered to the white men who came from the east in search of gold in the mountains. Even in the missions, there was talk of the legend, though men of the Christian God professed to disbelieve any pagan myths.

None was less believing than Kelvin Fitzpatrick, a brawny Irishman who was rumored to have killed a man before he first thrust his pickax into the hills surrounding the lake. No body was ever found, and the claim jumper vanished, so a murder couldn't be proved. But rumors around Fitzpatrick didn't disappear.

He found the first gold in the hills on a morning when the lake was still shrouded in the white mist that was as beautiful as it was deceptive. Fitzpatrick staked his claim and drank lustily from the water. He'd found his home and his fortune in these hills.

He named the creek near his claim Gold Creek and decided to become the first founding father of a town by the same name. He took his pebbles southwest to the city of San Francisco, where he transformed gold to money and a scrubby forty-niner into what appeared to be a wealthy gentleman. With his money and looks, Kelvin wooed and married a socialite from the city, Marian Dubois.

News of Fitzpatrick's gold strike traveled fast, and soon Gold Creek had grown into a small shantytown. With the prospectors came the merchants, the gamblers, the saloon keepers, the clergy and the whores. The Silver Horseshoe Saloon stood on the west end of town and the Presbyterian church was built on the east, and Gold Creek soon earned a reputation for fistfights, barroom brawls and hangings.

Kelvin's wealth increased and he fathered four children—all girls. Two were from Marian, the third from a town whore and the fourth by a Native American woman. All children were disappointments as Kelvin Fitzpatrick needed an heir for his empire.

The community was growing from a boisterous mining camp to a full-fledged town, with Kelvin Fitzpatrick as Gold Creek's first mayor and most prominent citizen. The persecuted Native Americans with their legends and pagan ways were soon forced into servitude or thrown from their land. They made their way into the hills, away from the white man's troubles.

In 1860, when Kelvin was forty-three, his wife finally bore him a son, Rodwell Kelvin Fitzpatrick. Roddy, handsome and precocious, became the apple of his father's eye. Though considered a "bad seed" and a hellion by most of the churchgoing citizens of Gold Creek, Roddy Fitzpatrick was the crown prince to the Fitzpatrick fortune, and when his father could no longer mine gold from the earth's crust, he discovered a new mode of wealth and, perhaps, more sacred: the forest.

Roddy Fitzpatrick started the first logging operation and opened the first sawmill. All competitors were quickly bought or forced out of business. But other men, bankers and smiths, carpenters and doctors, settled down to stay and hopefully smooth out the rough edges of the town. Men with names of Kendrick, Monroe and Powell made Gold Creek their home and brought their wives in homespun and woolens, women who baked pies, planned fairs and corralled their wayward Saturday night drinking men into church each Sunday morning.

Roddy Fitzpatrick, who grew into a handsome but cruel man, ran the family business when the older Fitzpatrick retired. In a few short years, Roddy had gambled or squandered most of the family fortune. Competitors had finally gotten a toehold in the lumber-rich mountains surrounding Gold Creek and new businesses were sprouting along the muddy streets of the town.

The railroad arrived, bringing with its coal-spewing engines much wealth and commerce. The railway station was situated on the west end of town, not too far from the Silver Horseshoe Saloon and a skeletal trestle bridged the gorge of the creek. Ranchers and farmers brought their produce into town for the market and more people stayed on, settling in the growing community, though Gold Creek was still known for the bullet holes above the bar in the saloon.

And still there was the rumor of some Indian curse that occasionally was whispered by the older people of the town.

Roddy, always a hothead and frustrated at his shrinking empire, was involved in more than his share of brawls. Knives flashed, guns smoked and threats and curses were spit around a wad of tobacco and a shot of whiskey.

When a man tried to cheat him at cards, Roddy plunged a knife into the blackguard's heart and killed him before a packed house of gamblers, drinkers, barkeeps and whores. After a night in jail, Roddy was set free with no charges leveled against him by the sheriff, who was a fast friend of the elder Fitzpatrick.

But Roddy's life was not to be the same. One night he didn't return home to his wife. She located Kelvin and they formed a search party. Two days later, Roddy's body washed up on the shores of Whitefire Lake. There was a bullet hole in his chest, and his wallet was empty.

Some people thought he was killed by a thief; still others decided Roddy had been shot by a jealous husband, but some, those who still believed in the legend, knew that the God of the Sun had taken Roddy's life to punish Kelvin Fitzpatrick by not only taking away his wealth but the only thing Kelvin had loved: his son.

The older Fitzpatrick, hovering on the brink of bankruptcy, took his own life after learning that his son was dead. Kelvin's daughters, those legitimate, and those who were born out of wedlock, each began their own lives.

The town survived the dwindling empire of the Fitzpatricks and new people arrived at the turn of the century. New names were aded to the town records. Industry and commerce brought the flagging community into the twentieth century, though the great earthquake of 1906 did much damage. Many buildings toppled, but the Silver Horseshoe Saloon and the Presbyterian church and the railroad trestle survived.

Monroe Sawmill, a new company owned and operated by Hayden Garreth Monroe, bought some of the dwindling Fitzpatrick forests and mills, and during the twenties, thirties and forties, Gold Creek became a company town. The people were spared destitution during the depression as the company kept the workers employed, even when they were forced to pay in company cash that could only be spent on goods at the company store. But no family employed by Monroe Sawmill went hungry; therefore, the community, which had hated Fitzpatrick's empire, paid homage to Hayden Garreth Monroe, even when the forests dwindled, logging prices dropped and the mills were shut down.

In the early 1960s, the largest sawmill burned to the ground. The police suspected arson. As the night sky turned orange by the flames licking toward the black heavens, and the volunteer firemen fought the blaze, the townspeople stood and watched. Some thought the fire was a random act of violence, others believed that Hayden Garreth Monroe III, grandson of the well-loved man, had lost favor and developed more than his share of enemies when the company cash became worthless and the townspeople, other than those who were already wealthy, began to go bankrupt. They thought the fire was personal revenge. Names of those he'd harmed were murmured. Fitzpatrick came to mind, though by now, the families had been bonded by marriage and the timber empire of the Fitzpatricks had experienced another boom.

Some of the townspeople, the very old with long memories, thought of the legend that had nearly been forgotten. Hayden Garreth Monroe III had drunk like a glutton from the Whitefire Lake and he, too, would lose all that he held dear—first his wealth and eventually his wife.

As time passed, other firms found toeholds in Gold Creek and in the seventies and eighties, technology crept over the hills. From the ashes of Kelvin Fitzpatrick's gold and timber empire rose the new wealth of other families.

The Fitzpatricks still rule the town, and Thomas Fitzpatrick, patriarch of the family, intends one day to turn to state politics. However, scandal has tarnished his name and as his political aspiration turns to ashes and his once-envied life has crumbled, he will have to give way to new rulers—young men who are willing to fight for what they want. Men like Jackson Moore and Turner Brooks and Hayden Garreth Monroe IV.

Old names mingle and marry with new, but the town and its legend continue to exist. To this day, the people of Gold Creek cannot shake the gold dust of those California hills from their feet. Though they walk many paths away from the shores of the lake, the men and women of Gold Creek—the boys and girls—can never forget their hometown. Nor can they forget the legend and curse of Whitefire Lake.

Silhouette

SPECIAL EDITION

Continuing in March
be on the lookout for

MAVERICKS

LISA JACKSON'S
MAVERICK MEN

They're wild...they're woolly...and they're as rugged as the great outdoors. They've never needed a woman before, but they're about to meet their matches....

HE'S A BAD BOY (#787)—January
HE'S JUST A COWBOY (#799)—March
HE'S THE RICH BOY (#811)—May

All men who just won't be tamed!
From Silhouette Special Edition.

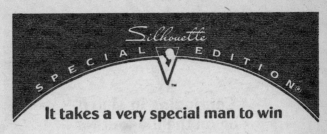

Silhouette
SPECIAL EDITION ™®

It takes a very special man to win

That SPECIAL Woman!

She's friend, wife, mother—she's you! And beside each Special Woman stands a wonderfully *special* man. It's a celebration of our heroines—and the men who become part of their lives.

Look for these exciting titles from Silhouette Special Edition:

January   BUILDING DREAMS by Ginna Gray

February   HASTY WEDDING by Debbie Macomber

March   THE AWAKENING by Patricia Coughlin

April   FALLING FOR RACHEL by Nora Roberts

Don't miss THAT SPECIAL WOMAN! each month—from some of your special authors! Only from Silhouette Special Edition! And for the most special woman of all—you, our loyal reader— we have a wonderful gift: a beautiful journal to record all of your special moments. Look for details in this month's THAT SPECIAL WOMAN! title, available at your favorite retail outlet.

Take 4 bestselling love stories FREE

Plus get a FREE surprise gift!

COMING NEXT MONTH

#805 TRUE BLUE HEARTS—Curtiss Ann Matlock

Rough-and-tumble cowboy Rory Breen and mother of two
Zoe Yarberry knew that getting together was unwise. But
though their heads were telling them no, their hearts...

#806 HARDWORKING MAN—Gina Ferris

Family Found

The first time private investigator Cassie Browning met
Jared Walker, he was in jail. Cassie soon discovered that
clearing Jared's name and reuniting him with his family
were easier tasks than fighting her feelings for him!

#807 YOUR CHILD, MY CHILD—Jennifer Mikels

When confirmed bachelor Pete Hogan opened his door to
Anne LeClare and her child, he thought he was saving them
from a snowstorm. But the forecast quickly changed to sunny
skies when they offered him the chance for love.

#808 LIVE, LAUGH, LOVE—Ada Steward

Jesse Carder had traveled far to rekindle the flames of an old
love—until she met sexy Dillon Ruiz. Dillon brought Jesse's
thoughts back to the present, but was their future possible?

#809 MAN OF THE FAMILY—Andrea Edwards

Tough cop Mike Minelli had seen Angie Hartman on the screen as
a former horror movie queen! Now he sensed vulnerable Angie
was hiding more than bad acting in her past!

#810 FALLING FOR RACHEL—Nora Roberts

That Special Woman!

Career-minded Rachel Stanislaski had little time for matters of the
heart. But when handsome Zackary Muldoon entered her life,
Rachel's pulse went into overtime!